# REDESIGNED

An Off the Subject Novel

# Other books by Denise Grover Swank

## *Rose Gardner Mysteries*

(Humorous Southern mysteries)
TWENTY-EIGHT AND A HALF WISHES
TWENTY-NINE AND A HALF REASONS
THRITY AND A HALF EXCUSES (July, 2013)

## *Chosen Series*

(Paranormal thriller/Urban fantasy)
CHOSEN
HUNTED
SACRIFICE
REDEMPTION
A CHANGE IN THE WIND short story collection
(Fall 2013)

## *On the Otherside Series*

(Young adult science fiction/romance)
HER
THERE

## *The Curse Keepers*

(Adult urban fantasy)
THE CURSE KEEPERS (November 19, 2013)

## *New Adult Contemporary Romance*

AFTER MATH
REDESIGNED
BUSINESS AS USUAL (FALL 2013)

# REDESIGNED

An Off the Subject Novel

Denise Grover Swank

This book is a work of fiction. References to real people, events, establishments, organizations, or locations are intended only to provide a sense of authenticity, and are used factiously. All other characters, and all incidents and dialogue, are drawn from the author's imagination and are not to be construed as real.

To Dr. Donald Knuth, who made me think math is cool

# Chapter One

I push damp hair off my forehead, irritated with the heat. It's too hot for late September, even in Tennessee. Still, if I'm honest, my irritation is partially due to the man drinking a beer six feet away from me.

He's exceptionally good-looking—blond hair, blue eyes, a tan that doesn't end at his biceps. I've seen him without a shirt, and it's easy to see why many of the girls on campus have nicknamed him Adonis. But more importantly, Dylan Humphrey is pre-law, and he comes from a family of lawyers. Not ambulance chasers, but a prestigious firm in Memphis. I should be happy I've finally gotten this close to him, but right now he's not paying the least bit of attention to me. His attention is focused on my roommate Tina.

"Caroline." My best friend Scarlett calls my name and pulls me into a hug. I'm a good three inches taller than her in my brown suede stiletto boots. I heard Dylan would be here, and I came dressed to impress with my boots and a jersey dress even though it's an outdoor party. Scarlett squeezes my arm. "I miss you."

A lump burns in my throat, but I swallow and force my lips into a smile. "I find that hard to believe with Tucker Price in your bed."

She swats my arm. "You've been hanging around Tina too much."

"Whose fault is that? I needed a roommate after you moved out." I try to keep the bite from my words, but a hint of it is there nonetheless.

Tina is the world's biggest flirt and some would call her a slut, which is probably why Dylan is paying more attention to her right now instead of me. But everyone knows that good southern boys don't bring bad girls home to their mommas. They bring home well-behaved ladies. I may not have been born a cultured Southern girl, but I play the part well now. I just need to bide my time.

Scarlett rolls her top lip between her teeth and studies me. I recognize this look after living with her for three years—our freshman and sophomore years in a dorm room and our junior year in an apartment. But Scarlett moved out the end of May and into an apartment with her boyfriend, Tucker.

Who would have ever thought that math major/introvert Scarlett Goodwin would end up with a perfect devoted boyfriend—an ex-man-whore before settling down with her—while I'd been single for eleven months? A year ago, I'd felt sorry for her. Funny how things change.

Scarlett finally breaks her silence, her face expressionless. "I'm sorry to hear about the dress store closing. Are you going to be okay?"

I'm trying not to freak out that I'm currently without a part-time job. "I'm fine. I saved a bunch of money working overtime there this summer." I force a smile. "But I've had to talk to Tina about being more prompt with her share of the rent and utilities."

"I'm sorry I deserted you."

I shrug. "At least my night life is livelier with Tina."

Scarlett rolls her eyes. She's been out with Tina a few times. She knows how wild Tina is. "Well, I'm glad you came to our party, even if you didn't find a date. Although why you think you need one is beyond me."

Of course, it's beyond her. Scarlett wasn't looking for love when she found Tucker. The boy practically fell in her lap. "Time is short, Scarlett. I'm a senior and have less than a year to find the future Mr. Caroline Hunter."

"You don't need a man to make your life fulfilling." Scarlett sighs. This has to be Round Twenty-Eight of some variation of this discussion. "You need to make yourself happy first."

"Says the woman with the sexy soccer player for a boyfriend."

"You forget he left me for two months before he came back. I found my own happiness without him. He only makes my life so much better."

As if hearing his name, Tucker sneaks up behind Scarlett, wrapping his arms around her stomach and pulling her back to his chest. She looks up at him and smiles. Her face is so full of joy, I nearly gag with envy. I'm not jealous of my friend. I'm happy Tucker came into her life. Scarlett deserves every bit of happiness he brings her and much, much more. I'm jealous of what she has, of what remains so elusive for me. I've never had what she has, not even with my two-year relationship with my ex-boyfriend.

"Great turnout, Tucker," I finally say with a smile. "I'm glad you gave Scarlett a party for her near-perfect GRE score. She'd never celebrate it on her own."

She turns around to face me, lowering her voice. "You know I hate parties."

I shake my head. "Talk about an understatement. But you deserve a celebration. Besides, Tucker's invited mostly people you know, with only a few soccer players sprinkled here and there for my and Tina's amusement."

Tucker laughs. "You have to admit I'm a great host."

I lift my eyebrows in a smirk and take a sip of the wine in my red plastic cup. "That you are. Now if you can just get Dylan Humphrey to pay more attention to me than Tina, I'd be a happy girl. Getting him to go out with me would be icing on the cake."

An ornery look spreads across Tucker's face. "Done."

I groan, but I'm secretly happy. Tucker's not one to back down from a challenge, and I'm positive he'll follow through without embarrassing me.

For a guy who was narcissistically self-centered less than a year ago, he's remarkably attentive to Scarlett and her needs, always mindful that social situations tend to make her anxious. And concern for her friends, specifically me, seems to fall under Tucker's attentiveness. He hardly seems like the guy he was before Scarlett. The guy I'd repeatedly warned her to stay away from. I'm glad he proved me wrong.

"Congratulations, Scarlett." A male voice interrupts my thoughts.

Scarlett turns around and her face lights up. "Reed! I'm glad you came."

A guy at least a half-head taller than me stops next to Scarlett. An awkward grin tugs at the corner of his mouth as he hands her a small wrapped box. "I wasn't sure what type of gift one was supposed to give for passing your GRE with such a remarkable score." The wrapping is crisp white and the bow is gauzy and perfectly tied. It's obvious he didn't wrap it unless he's gay. I look him over. Even though he's impeccably dressed in pants, shirt and tie, his shoes are scuffed. Not gay.

A rosy color spreads across Scarlett's cheeks. She hates getting gifts. "I'm sure it's perfect. Thank you." Scarlett turns to me in an attempt to take attention from herself. "Caroline, this is Reed. He's just moved here from Boston and started his first year as a grad student in the mathematics department."

A math man. That explains the professorly attire. He's cute in a geeky kind of way. His dark, brown hair is a bit shaggy and in need of a trim. His dark chocolate-colored eyes are framed by long lashes. His face is pale, which tells me he spends a lot of time inside. He's wearing a long-sleeve light blue shirt and a navy tie, but he doesn't seem to break a sweat even though it has to be at least eighty-five outside.

One of Scarlett's math department friends wanders into the courtyard, and she goes over to greet him.

"Mathematics graduate student?" I know most of the people in the math department are conservative, but Reed has run past conservative headlong into the middle of the last century. "Do you plan to go into analytics like Scarlett?"

He studies me for a moment. "No, my focus is the analysis of algorithms."

"And what will you do with that? Something with the CIA or Department of Defense?"

His eyebrow rises in surprise and a hint of appreciation. "No, I hope to find a university position and teach."

I strike him off as potential date material. For one, he's in the math department so we would have nothing in common, but most importantly, I can't imagine a college professor makes much money. I've seen the cars parked in the faculty parking lot. "Boston? Where did you go to school before coming to Southern?"

He looks wary of my question. "Out east."

Totally vague answer, but I decide it's not worth pursuing. "So how do you like Tennessee?"

"It's hot." He tugs at his sleeve. "Are you from Tennessee?"

It's a simple question, common conversation, but it always makes me edgy. "Yes, born and raised."

"I thought so. You have a southern drawl."

I can't tell if it's a compliment or an insult. "Most everyone around here does."

"Not everyone," he murmurs, and I realize he's really looking at me now.

My skin flushes from his examination, and to my surprise, it's not from embarrassment.

"As Scarlett mentioned, I'm new here this semester and my courses and teaching schedule keep me busy. I don't know many people." He clears his throat. "Would you be free to go to dinner next weekend?"

I stare up into his dark brown eyes, and I'm so very tempted. They're pulling me closer to him. Literally. There's something about him I can't pinpoint, like a physical awareness arcing between us. But a relationship needs more than physical attraction, and I've wasted the past six months going out with good-looking guys. It's my senior year, and it's time to think of my future. Even if some inexplicable part of me wants to kiss him right here and now.

All the more reason to say no.

The question is, what should I tell him? He's a bit abrasive, but I tack that up to his left-brain tendencies. Scarlett does the same thing and needs to be reminded from time to time that the rest of us aren't robots. Still, I don't want to be rude and flat-out decline. I decide to pick up on his busy theme. That's believable. "Thanks for the invitation, Reed, but I'm a fashion design major, and I have a fashion show coming up that could possibly determine my future." My excuse sounds lame, even to me. "I'm hoping to make it on the committee so I have to give every spare moment proving I'm capable."

I expect him to get irritated, but he smiles with approval. "I respect hard work. Maybe I can get a rain check for next semester."

I certainly hope I'm not still single next semester, so I nod. "Sure."

Tucker drags Dylan toward us, his arm around Dylan's shoulder, and I resist the urge to cringe. Talk about terrible timing.

"Caroline, there you are. I was telling Dylan all about you."

I smile, but it's not natural as I cast a worried glance to Reed. "I hope you didn't spill *all* my secrets," I joke.

"Don't worry. I saved a few for you to share." Tucker winks, then notices Reed. "Reed, have you met Dylan Humphrey?"

Reed extends his hand, but his face hardens as Dylan shakes it. "I haven't, but I've heard a lot about you." He doesn't look happy about what he's heard.

Tucker misses Reed's glower. "Say, Caroline, I was telling Dylan about my friend's band playing at the Voodoo Lounge next Friday night. Dylan's interested in coming to check them out, you still in?"

I finally get the full meaning of being caught between a rock and a hard place. It would be rude of me to accept after I just told Reed no, but this might be my only opportunity to go out with Dylan. I've had my eye on him since the beginning of the semester. The reality is that I really don't have a choice. "Sure," I say, but I purposely avoid looking at Reed. "I'd love to."

Dylan's eyes move down over my body, hesitating on my breasts. "It was nice meeting you." His gaze rises to my face.

I'm suddenly unsure this is a good idea.

Reed releases a hard cough.

Tucker whacks Reed on the arm. "You all right, dude?"

"Surprisingly, great" is his terse reply.

Tucker remains clueless as he winks at me again, then follows Dylan to a huddle of his old soccer teammates. Tucker came through for me, so why do I feel so miserable?

"Is it my major that throws you off or the fact you can't do your laundry on my abs?" Reed's voice is unyielding.

The truth is that I feel much more drawn to Reed than Dylan, apparent lack of abs and all. I feel a connection to Reed I've never felt before and the tension between us only feeds my libido. "Reed, let me explain."

"Caroline, that really isn't necessary. Perhaps I'm just not your *type*."

I want to lie to him and say he's right, I'm not attracted to him at all, but that would be a flat-out lie. For some reason I can't make myself say it. Maybe because it's so far from the truth. "What type would that be?" I finally say. Because for some inexplicable reason, I can't walk away from him.

"Rich, good-looking, *powerful*." Ugliness drips from his words, snapping me out of my lustful stupor.

I lift my chin. "There's nothing wrong with any of those attributes."

He shakes his head in disgust. "I've seen *your* type before, and I can usually spot them a mile away. Somehow you slipped past my radar."

Anger boils the blood in my veins. "My type? And what exactly would that be?"

"Isn't it obvious? You're a fortune hunter. An opportunist. A gold-digger."

My mouth drops open in shock, partially that he's pegged me, even if he makes it sound so vile. What's so wrong with wanting to be assured that I'll never be poor again? But even so, what gives him the right to speak to me like this? Ugly words slip over my tongue before I can stop them.

"There's no way you'll make much money as a professor. Nothing that could compete with a respected attorney. Besides, Dylan looks like a Greek god and his family has money. Why wouldn't I want to go out with him?"

The moment I finish, I want to take back every word.

His face reddens, and I'm about to apologize when a perky blonde literally bounces up to him. She wraps her arm around his and pulls him to her in such a familiar way that it's apparent they aren't casual friends.

Reed Pendergraft just asked me out with his girlfriend on the other side of the courtyard. And he has the nerve to condemn *me*? Nausea rolls in my stomach. And here I was about to convince myself I should blow off Dylan and accept Reed's date instead. I'm grateful his girlfriend has saved me from myself.

"Reed, are you going to introduce me to your friend?" She looks up at Reed's face, her big blue eyes shining with happiness. I wonder if I should tell her what just happened, but I won't be the one to destroy her. I'm sure Reed will take care that himself.

Reed pauses, long enough for me to jump in. "I'm no one." Then I turn and walk away.

.

# Chapter Two

I sigh as I pin fabric to a mannequin. Our required design lab time is almost over, but I plan to stay longer. I've spent far too much time thinking about my love life and not enough on this class.

"If everyone could listen up," our instructor's voice interrupts my thoughts. "I have important news about this season's show."

Southern University is known for its strong business school—one of the many reasons I chose it—and the administration typically gives the most funding to the business department and athletics. The fall fashion show has always been a fundraiser for the apparel department. While seniors and juniors provide designs for the fashion show, seniors are in charge of the production. The announcement of this year's theme should have been announced last week, and many of us are nervous that we'll run out of time to complete our projects.

Ms. Carter waits until all eyes are on her. "As you all know, there's been a delay releasing the details of this season's show. I hope when I tell you the reason why, you'll be as excited as the instructors and I are and think the delay is worth the wait."

I glance at my friend Megan, and she casts me a nervous glance.

"This year the prestigious Monroe Foundation has approached the department about sponsoring this fall's show."

Gasps fill the room. While I'm familiar with Monroe Industries—well known for its pharmaceutical companies and many scientific advancements, my brain scrambles to recall anything about the company's foundation.

"As many of you might know, the Monroe Foundation is an enthusiastic supporter of enriching the lives of children in need. They've agreed to match, dollar for dollar, the funds that the fashion show raises and donate their portion to Middle Tennessee Children's Charity, a local nonprofit for underprivileged children. They have also generously offered to provide funds to pay all expenses for the program itself."

The class breaks into shouts and applause. The show's proceeds have always covered the expenses in the past. This means more money will go to the department.

Ms. Carter's smile fades. "However, there are certain stipulations."

The class quiets and an undercurrent of worry fills the room.

She pats her hands in the air. "Not to worry, nothing terrible. The foundation wants us to incorporate clothing for children—they must be in twenty percent of the show."

Tension slides off my shoulders. I can live with that, even if it means we'll have to find child models.

"One more thing," she says, and her smile loses some of its brightness. "The foundation has requested to be part of the student committee that oversees the program." She pauses and takes a breath. "The committee will still consist of six members, but this year three of the members will be design students and the other three will be from non-apparel degrees."

"What?" someone asks and a chorus of dismay spreads throughout the room.

"Now, I know this goes against tradition, and the instructors had a difficult time deciding whether to accept their offer. But the foundation is providing resources to make the show bigger and better than it's ever been, which in turn will hopefully earn more money for the department. And not only that, but we'll be raising money to help local children. While the Monroe Foundation is providing the donation, our name is attached. This is wonderful for the university's community outreach."

I raise my hand.

Ms. Carter nods. "Yes, Caroline?"

"Who picks the committee members?"

Her smile remains but turns grim. "The instructors have picked the fashion degree members and the foundation, along with the guidance of the chancellor, has picked the non-department students."

The chancellor? I wonder how many students the chancellor actually knows on a first-name basis. The only time I've known of the chancellor becoming personally involved in something like this was when he convinced Scarlett to tutor Tucker by dangling funding for the mathematics department.

"Which fashion students did the instructors pick?" Megan asks. I know she's as anxious as I am to be on the committee.

"We wish to speak to our three choices before we make the announcement. We want to make sure they accept the position with the new criteria, then we'll post the nominees."

Some of my classmates grumble. Everyone wants a coveted position on the committee and our chances have just been halved with the inclusion of non-design students. With my recent work effort, or more importantly, my lack of it, I expect my own chances are slim to none.

"What's the theme?" one of my classmates asks.

"Oh." Ms. Carter shifts her weight. "How could I forget? The theme is *Everyday Living*."

"*Everyday Living*?" Megan mutters, scrunching her nose.

Ms. Carter pauses and the slightest bit of irritation creases her forehead. "This year's theme was picked by the foundation."

So we completely sold out to the Monroe Foundation? This is the lamest theme any show has had in the history of the show. But I keep the thought to myself. My biggest worry at the moment is the likelihood that I won't be part of the committee.

Megan turns to me and lowers her voice. "*Everyday Living*? What are we supposed to do with that?"

I turn my attention back to the fabric pinned to the mannequin. I had turned the fabric on the bias, hoping it would help the hang of the dress, but now I'm not so sure it works. I can't afford to waste these three yards of silk. Literally. "We'll figure something out." I'm referring to the designs for the show as well as the dress for my recent project.

"Are you going to stay much longer, working?" Megan asks, shifting her glance out the window.

"Yeah." This dress is for our current project, which is due the next class period. Megan finished her design only moments ago. I study the pinned dress and sigh again. For the last few weeks, I've been creatively stifled. I was hoping the theme for the show would help inspire me. Now I'm not so certain.

Most of the students clear out and only three of us remain. I have no idea what's wrong with me. I can usually whip an idea out of my head and onto paper or the design computer program, then construct the garment while the rest of my classmates are still gathering their thoughts. But the last two projects have been like dragging the dress out of my head, thread by thread.

"Caroline, can I steal a few minutes of your time?" Ms. Carter murmurs behind me, and I jump.

"Of course."

But Ms. Carter continues to stare at my design, and I squirm under her scrutiny. "It's still not right, and I know I've usually completed my project by now—"

She shakes her head, placing her glasses on her nose as she leans closer. "No, don't apologize. I'm impressed."

My mouth hangs open before I quickly close it. "But—"

"It still needs work, I won't deny it. But for once you're not playing it safe. You're taking a risk. Finally."

"What?"

She slides her glasses off and looks at me, crossing her arms. "I've always thought you had great potential, Caroline, but you've always taken the safe route. We've discussed this before."

It's true, we have. Ms. Carter has been my advisor since I started my first design class in my sophomore year.

"There are designers who simply regurgitate what they see around them and put a slightly different spin on it. Then there are designers who think outside the box. Their designs stand out. I've always seen a hint of different in your designs, but you play it safe. Go for broke this time, Caroline. Give me different."

My ideas all seem stale and boring lately. I've decided to take a risk on the dress hanging on my form, even if subconsciously, but the result is disastrous so far. I shake my head. "It's not working. It's a failure."

"There's no such thing as failure as long as you learn from your mistakes."

I'm not sure what I've learned at this point.

She points to the bodice. "Try a tiny dart here. I think it will help give a hint of definition. But I like that you've hung it on the bias. A very flattering silhouette, especially for real women."

I pin a dart on either side directly beneath the bust line and the dress is already improved.

"Sometimes it doesn't take much. Just a little tweak to vastly alter something." She winks. "It's like that in life too."

My life needs more than a tiny tweak, but there's no sense telling her that.

She pauses. "I wanted to talk to you about the committee."

I steel my back. Ms. Carter knows how badly I want to be on it. We've also discussed how tight the competition is.

"After a heated discussion with the other instructors, we've picked our three members." She smiles. "I'm pleased to say you were one of the three chosen."

I stare at her in disbelief. "But I don't understand ... a few weeks ago you told me it would be close with six members. How could I make it with only three?"

She leans her hip into the table next to me. "The involvement of the Monroe Foundation is a blessing and a curse. The increased operational and marketing budget could bring outside attention to our department, but their involvement also brings constraints. Like the theme." She rolls her eyes. "And that was the best of all the suggestions."

I shudder, wondering what could have been worse.

"You were chosen for two reasons. The first is because you're well-known for being level-headed in disagreements. In group projects, you're often the peacemaker. You're diplomatic and on more than one occasion have brought opposing sides together into a compromise. I'm worried the addition of members outside the design department will make the committee a battleground. The design department needs an ambassador. Someone who is capable of knowing when to stand her ground and when to compromise. I'm positive that person is you, Caroline."

I blink, letting her words sink in. "Thank you. I'm honored." I take a deep breath. "You said there were two reasons. What's the second?"

She smiles and points to the disaster hanging on the dressmaker form. "That. You're taking risks and your design— even in its unfinished state—is one of the most exciting things I've seen you create in the two years I've known you. Take that excitement with you into the committee."

I want to tell her that there's no excitement in this design, only fear, but I don't want to risk my newly gained position. "Thank you. I don't know what to say."

Ms. Carter moves behind the mannequin. "You don't have to say anything. Just don't let me down."

I nod. "I'll try my best."

"In the end, that's all I can ask, although I'm not sure it's fair of us to throw you into this potential mess. I suspect not only will this be a hornet's nest, but it will be an even larger time commitment than previously anticipated. Will this be a problem?"

"The timing couldn't be more perfect." With no boyfriend and no job, I've got nothing but time.

Ms. Carter starts to walk away then stops, looking over her shoulder. "And even if the theme is lame, put your own unique spin on it. Think outside the box."

Think outside the box with *Everyday Living*? That seems impossible.

Just add it to my list of impossible tasks to hurdle.

# Chapter Three

The Voodoo Lounge is packed. It's Friday night and a large population of the Southern University campus has assembled to hear Blue Tiger, the band that's set to take the stage soon. Dylan drapes his arm around my back, his fingers slightly stroking my side, just below the band of my bra. The placement of his fingers is disheartening. They're high enough to be a hint of a threat yet not high enough to make him stop without looking like a frigid bitch.

I cast a glance at Scarlett on the other side of the table. Her face is guarded, and it's obvious she's only here because of Tucker. And me. She swings her gaze to check on me and I give her a smile. Even if I don't feel like smiling.

My date with Dylan is rushing headlong into failure.

For some reason, Reed pops into my mind, and I imagine how a date with him would be going if I'd said yes. I'm pretty sure he wouldn't be trying to cop a feel.

Why am I thinking about Reed?

In fairness, everything else in the world has triggered thoughts of him since last Saturday night. His reaction when I so thoroughly insulted him still haunts me. I don't behave this way. Not since high school. Back in Shelbyville, I was Carol Ann Hunter from Pine View Trailer Park. I fought stares, whispers, sneers and outright taunts, and unlike Scarlett, who grew up in the same raggedy trailer park, I stood up for myself. Not that it did me much good. I can't help wondering if

Scarlett had it right all along, burrowing deep within and cocooning until she felt safe to emerge.

Carol Ann Hunter didn't burrow. Oh, hell no. She didn't understand the concept of backing down. She accepted every challenge, every fight. She was hardened and jaded when I came to Southern three years ago. I knew I couldn't be her and achieve my goals, so I changed, a metamorphosis of my own. Carol Ann is the old me and I thought she was gone until last Saturday night, when somehow, Reed set her loose. And that scares the shit out of me.

My only consolation is that I'll probably never see the man again. But instead of easing my prickled conscience, it stirs an ache deep inside. I find myself surprised that I want to see him again.

Apparently, I've become a masochist now.

I pick up my drink, a cosmopolitan, and take a larger sip than I intended. Dylan's fingers brush the flesh underneath my breast. I shift in my seat, forcing his hand to drop, but he shoots me a cocky grin. This guy thinks he's getting lucky tonight. Obviously, he's never heard about my five-date rule.

I can't help thinking that Reed wouldn't treat me this way. *No, Caroline, he wouldn't because he'd be with his girlfriend.*

What the hell is wrong with me? I'm obsessing over some man I hardly know. *Get over it.*

The band goes on stage, and Tucker whistles to his friend. The guitarist straps his instrument over his shoulder and waves to Tucker.

Dylan's hand slides on my hip, trailing down to my thigh.

I stand abruptly. "I'm going to the restroom."

My sudden behavior draws the blank looks of the three people with me. Dylan's face darkens, but Scarlett kisses Tucker's cheek and stands. "I'll go with you."

Scarlett doesn't say anything until we get into the ladies' room, not that I could have heard her if she tried. The band has begun to play, deafening my ears.

"What's going on?" she asks the minute the bathroom door closes behind us.

"Dylan's handsy. More so than I'd like." I'm used to guys like him. I know how to handle them, a skill learned long ago when teenaged boys expected poor white trash trailer park girls to be easy. The problem isn't how to get him stop. The problem is my bitter disappointment.

Scarlett leans her back against the wall and releases a heavy sigh. "What do you want to do?"

I shake my head. "Nothing. I just needed a moment to regroup, is all."

"We can leave." I think she secretly wants to leave. She hates this kind of thing and only tolerates it because Tucker wants to come. That's the beauty of their relationship. They respect each other's needs and try to make it work. They've definitely learned the art of compromise.

"No." Although I want to leave, I have to save face. I'll look like a fool if we leave now. "But I don't want to stay out too late. I still need to figure out my designs for the fashion show."

Scarlett grins. "Look at my Caroline, all grown up. Thinking about work on a Friday night."

I stick out my tongue.

She laughs. "Okay, maybe not so mature."

The bathroom door opens and Reed's girlfriend walks in and heads straight for a stall. I cast a glance toward Scarlett, but she doesn't seem to notice. I'm suddenly very interested in the girl Reed is dating. I decide to hang around until she gets out of the stall and try to learn more about her.

I think this might technically be called stalking, but I have just enough alcohol in me to convince myself otherwise.

"I want to freshen up my lipstick." I tell Scarlett. "If you want to get back to Tucker, I'll be there in a minute."

Scarlett's eyes narrow slightly, then shift to the stall Reed's girlfriend disappeared in. So her entrance didn't escape Scarlett's notice. To my surprise, Scarlett agrees. "I'll see you at the table." Then she walks out, a grin lifting the corners of her mouth.

I move to the sink and run my fingers through my hair, fluffing it a little before I pull a tube of lipstick out of my purse. Reed's girlfriend's door opens, and she walks to the sink to wash her hands.

I know I shouldn't call attention to myself, but the only thing I'm learning about her is that she's an extra-thorough hand washer. That's obviously not enough to satisfy my curiosity.

I force a smile and twist to face her. "Didn't we meet at Scarlett's party last week? You were with Reed."

Her wary gaze brightens. "Yes, you're Caroline, right?"

It's my turn to hesitate. I never introduced myself. "Yeah...."

"After you left, I insisted that Reed tell me your name." She smiles. It seems genuine and not the smile of a jealous lover. She must not have figured out that he asked me out.

"Are you with Reed tonight?" I ask before I can stop myself.

She sighs, the first sign of disgust crossing her face. "He's here but we're not here *together*." The way she stresses the word makes me think she wants me to be aware that he's unattached. If they broke up, what ex-girlfriend would encourage the woman her boyfriend had been interested in? "You should come out and say hi."

I shake my head, my eyes widening. "That would be a *very* bad idea."

Her grin turns playful. "Oh, come on. It will only take a second."

Before I realize what's happening, she's looped her arm through mine like I saw her do with Reed last week, and she's practically dragging me into the bar.

Reed sits at a table in a dark corner, wearing a scowl as he surveys the dance floor, which has begun to fill up with people. His discomfort isn't surprising, since he and Scarlett seem to be cut from the same antisocial cloth.

She stops in front of the table and shouts to be heard. "Look who I found in the restroom."

His scowl deepens. "I didn't know you were now trolling public restrooms for friends."

To my surprise, she belly-laughs. "Reed, you're a really funny guy when you let yourself have a little bit of fun."

I wonder if I've walked into the middle of a disagreement between them. If so, I have no intention of being used as a weapon. Or a shield. "I need to get back to my friends."

Reed's eyebrows rise conveying his distaste. "You mean your date?"

I stare at him for a moment. Is that why he's here? Because he heard Tucker say we were coming here tonight? I'm about to become outraged when I remember my own recent stalking experience only moments ago. "Yeah, *my date.*" I cast a glance to our table. Tucker and Dylan are clueless about what's going on in this corner, but I have Scarlett's full attention.

I head back to our table, and I can feel Reed's eyes on me as I leave. Instead of irritating me, I revel in it.

I really am a masochist.

Dylan's arm and fingers return to their previous positions when I take my seat. Scarlett's eyes question if I'm okay or if

I'm ready to call it quits. It's barely after ten o'clock, and I now have Reed's attention. He'll know my date isn't going well if I leave now.

Dylan ordered another cosmo while I was gone and I down it before I've realized what I've done. But holding a glass keeps me busy. Anything to make me look like I'm having fun. I soon find myself on my third drink in only an hour, more than I usually consume, but I need the alcohol to steady my nerves. Dylan might have my nerves on edge, but Reed has the rest of me on alert.

The band switches to a ballad. Dylan leans his mouth in to my ear, his lips brushing my earlobe. "Do you want to dance?"

Not really, but I can't sit here much longer or I'll drink myself senseless. I'm now trying to pace myself as it is. "Sure."

My response is less than enthusiastic, but Dylan doesn't seem to notice as he pulls me to the dance floor, then settles my chest against his. His arms encircle my waist, his hands resting on the rise of my ass.

Maybe this wasn't such a good idea after all.

Dylan presses his body flush to mine and leans into my ear. "I've wanted you all night."

I can honestly say I don't feel the same. If someone had told me a week ago this would be my response, I would have called them crazy. The only thing I feel at the moment is disgust. Disgust with Dylan but also with myself. I let Dylan's family money and status fool me. I try not to let my body stiffen as Dylan's hand begins to slide up the curve of my waist, inching higher. I reach for his hand and pull it down. I just need to make it through this dance and then I'm going home. Who the hell cares what Reed Pendergraft thinks?

But Dylan doesn't like my redirection and pins my hand between his chest and mine. When I try to pull back, his grip around my back tightens and he looks down at me with a smile that doesn't reach his eyes. "Where're you goin', Caroline? I thought you wanted to be with me. Isn't that why you had Tucker set us up?"

I'm livid with Tucker, but then I realize Tucker would never tell Dylan what he'd done. He might tease me, but he respects me too much to betray my trust. Not to mention that he'd never risk Scarlett's wrath.

Dylan must have read my mind. "Fuck no, Tucker didn't tell me. I overheard you, baby. But not to worry. You've got me now. I'm all yours." He grinds his pelvis into mine to show me how much of him I get.

His hold on me tightens enough that I'll have to make a scene to get away from him. It's not ideal, but I'll do it before I let this shithead get away with molesting me any more than he already has. I'm about to forcefully insist he release me when someone interrupts.

"I'd like to have this dance." Reed stands to my right and it's not a question. It's an order.

Dylan stops swaying. "Can't you see we're busy?"

Reed stares at Dylan, and I'm surprised Dylan hasn't curled up into the fetal position under his scrutiny. "I spoke to Caroline, not you." His gaze turns to me. His eyes are deadly cold, but I know his anger isn't directed at me. Well, most of it. "Caroline, would you like to dance?"

I nod, shocked into silence.

Reed pushes Dylan's hand off my waist and takes me into his arms. Dylan stares, probably wondering what in the hell happened.

I'm wondering the same thing.

The raw power rolling off Reed's body makes my knees weak and I stumble, but Reed's arm tightens around my waist until I'm steady on my feet.

Reed lowers his face next to mine. "Did he hurt you?"

I shake my head. "No, of course not."

"Are you saying he didn't have you trapped against him when I showed up?"

"Well, yes," I say in annoyance. "But the only thing hurt is my pride. I'm embarrassed, although I'm not sure why. I didn't do anything wrong."

He leans his head back to look at my face and relief mixes with something that looks like respect. "You're right. I've never understood a misogynistic society that shames the woman for a man's boorish behavior."

His speech is the first sign I've seen tonight to remind me that he's really a nerd at heart. Moments ago, he was anything but. My pulse pounds in my temple, and my skin tingles where we touch. I've never wanted a man to touch me as much as I want to be in Reed's arms right now. I look into his face and wonder why I'm wasting time fighting this reaction to him.

And then he speaks.

"Although, I'm not sure you're one hundred percent inculpable here. You seem experienced enough to recognize an asshole like Dylan."

I'm not sure what to be most outraged about: that he finds me partially responsible for what happened or his slam against my reputation. "*Excuse me?*"

"When you play with fire, you're liable to get burned. Even children know this platitude."

Just when I think he can't get worse, he proves me wrong.

I try to break free of his hold but his arm keeps me in place.

"Aren't you doing the same thing you just called Dylan out for?" I seethe.

His eyes darken. "The difference is you want to be here with me."

I want to call him a liar, but I'm too busy staring at his lips and wishing they'd do something else other than talk.

His arm falls from my waist and he lifts his hand to my face, tilting my head back so he has full access to my mouth. He stares into my eyes, his own a blaze of desire.

My breath comes in short pants as my stomach tightens and other parts of me throb. I want him to kiss me, more than I've ever wanted anything. Ever.

He leans down, his lips inches from mine, and his hands drop so that the only thing holding us together is pure want.

"I think I've proved my point," he murmurs into my ear.

It takes me a full two seconds to figure out what point he just made.

Reed Pendergraft has just made a fool out of me.

I take a step back, horror crashing through me. I thought he was different, but it turns out he's just as manipulative as Dylan. Their goals were different—Dylan wanted sex, while Reed wants revenge—but at least Dylan was up front about it.

I take a step back. "Congratulations, Reed. Bravo. Point made."

Confusion flickers in his eyes before I spin around to find Scarlett. She's dancing with Tucker and her eyes widen in alarm when she sees me. It takes me seconds to get through the crowd to her, but she's already out of Tucker's embrace, reaching for me.

"Caroline, are you all right?"

"I have to get out of here."

Reed is close behind, but Tucker has picked up that he's the person I'm escaping from. He blocks Reed's path, holding him back. Their shouts are lost in the noise of the crowd as Scarlett grabs my purse from our table and leads me through the crowd and out the doors to my car. "Do you want me to come home with you? You've been drinking."

I keep my face down, digging my keys out of my purse. "No. I've sobered up." This would be easier to take if I *was* drunk. "Go back inside to Tucker."

"I saw what happened with Dylan. Tucker was about to go beat the shit out of him before Reed stepped in. What happened after that?"

I find my keys and unlock my door with shaky hands. "Reed's an ass, just like every other guy on the face of the planet."

"Not every guy," Scarlett says quietly. "Tucker's not an ass."

I look into her face. "Well, congratulations, Scarlett." My tone is snottier than I intend, but I'm too broken right now to care. "You got the last good man alive." I open my car door and slide into the driver's seat.

"Caroline…." she pleads.

I see Reed push past Tucker out of the club. I can't face him right now. "I'm sorry. I didn't mean that. You know I love you, but I just want to go home."

She nods and backs away as I shut my door. I hold in my tears until I'm turning onto the street and then break into a sob. This is my first good cry since I broke up with Justin last year and I'm pissed as hell that I'm wasting perfectly good tears on Reed Pendergraft.

I'm the world's biggest idiot and Reed has just driven that point home. Again.

# Chapter Four

On Sunday afternoon, I'm in the same place that I've spent most of the weekend. I'm bundled under an afghan on the sofa with my two favorite guys—Ben and Jerry—watching marathon sessions of *Gossip Girl*. Watching rich kids with mundane problems turned glamorous usually makes me feel better. But not this time. Maybe it's because in the past, whenever I watched, I always presumed that I would live that life someday.

For the first time, I consider the idea that I might not.

The idea is terrifying. It's not because I want that life. Having money has never been about having things, although that would be nice. Having money has been about having security. I recognize my need for money is unhealthy. I'm smart enough to know this, but my irrational fear of living without it still exists. It's like people who hoard food. It's not about eating the food. It's about knowing the food is there if you need it.

Tina had never been subjected to my wallowing last winter, but she must have been warned because she's been scarce most of the weekend. I suspect she's complained to Scarlett, because Scarlett shows up with two containers of ice cream and a plastic container of macaroni and cheese.

She sets the ice cream and mac and cheese on the coffee table, then picks up my empty ice cream carton and the empty pot that I'd cooked macaroni and cheese in the day before. I hadn't wasted time putting it into a bowl. Scarlett disappears into the kitchen and returns with fresh spoons, handing me one before she plops down next to me, crosses her legs and tucks the afghan around her.

"Chuck has his French girlfriend," she murmurs, taking the lid off the macaroni and handing it to me. "You're already on season three."

I scoop a spoonful of noodles and shove them in my mouth, then shrug.

"What happened?"

"Dylan was a fucktard and so was Reed."

Scarlett pops a lid off the container of Phish Food. "Dylan's no surprise so I guess I'm really asking what happened with Reed." She digs ice cream out of the carton. "Caroline, it was obvious he's interested in you. Even to me. How about I tell you what I saw, and you tell me when I get it wrong?"

I eat another bite and nod.

"Dylan was a jerk who tried to feel you up on the dance floor. Am I right so far?"

"Yeah."

"Then Reed intervened."

"Yeah."

"Then you danced with him."

"Yeah."

"Caroline, *what happened?*"

I sigh and set the noodles on the table. "At your party last week, Reed asked me out and I told him no, that I was too busy. Then Tucker brought Dylan over and Reed was still there."

Scarlett groans. "Then Dylan asked you out."

With a grimace, I lift my shoulder. "Well, it was more Tucker matchmaking, but I said yes." My heart aches when I think about what happened next. "Reed got pissed, obviously, and wanted to know if I said no because of his major or because I couldn't do laundry on his abs."

"Ouch."

"I don't know what it is with him, but he gets me hot in zero to point-six seconds, and I said something I regret."

"I take it the hot you're referring to isn't sexual."

"Well that too, but in this instance, angry. It's like he knows exactly which button to push to piss me off." I pause, shame washing over me. "I told him it was because he didn't have enough money."

"Oh, Caroline. You didn't."

I cringe and grab for the other Ben & Jerry's carton. I can take anything but Scarlett's disappointment in me. "I was instantly sorry, Scarlett. I felt terrible and was about to apologize when his girlfriend showed up." The reminder makes my own bad behavior more acceptable. "*Who does that?* Asks a girl out on a date while they're on a date already?"

Scarlett releases a heavy exhale. "I don't know. So then why did Reed's girlfriend take you to his table Friday night?"

"She recognized me in the bathroom. She acted disgusted when I asked if they were at the club together, but she dragged me out to see Reed. He didn't seem happy to see me. So I went back to our table."

"And then he saved you from Dylan."

"I could have taken care of it." I say. "I thought he was saving me from embarrassing myself. Turns out he wanted to be the one to embarrass me." I pause. "He told Dylan he wanted to dance with me, and he looked so pissed that Dylan just backed down. But then Reed held me just as tight, and I asked him what the difference between him and Dylan was. Reed told me that the difference was that I wanted to be there."

Scarlett cocks her head, her eyebrows rising. "And…?"

"And then he acted like he was going to kiss me, and dropped his hold on me. I stood there waiting for him to kiss me, like a fucking idiot, and then said he'd just proved his point."

Scarlett shakes her head. "Wait. You wanted him to kiss you?"

"I told you he gets me hot in both ways." I press my head back into the seat and squeeze my eyes shut. "God, I'm an idiot."

"No, you're not an idiot."

I open my eyes. "I am, but the worst part is that I deserve what he did."

Scarlett's mouth presses tight in anger. "No, Caroline. I don't care what you did to him, it didn't warrant what he did to you. Especially after asking you out while he was already on a date."

I won't argue with her because she's loyal to fault, and she'd take my side even if I killed Reed in cold blood and stuffed his heart under the floorboards. "I should thank him."

"What?" She practically jumps off the sofa. "How can you say that?"

"Two men, two disasters, less than five minutes apart. I've had a wakeup call, Scarlett. I'm focusing on the wrong thing." I've given this a lot of thought as I've watched all the failed relationships on *Gossip Girl*. I've put too much stock into finding a guy and not enough into trying to shape my own future. Men are jerks you can't count on. My last boyfriend was proof of that. I found out two months ago that he's now engaged to the girl he cheated on me with.

"I'm going to focus on my career," I continue. "The upcoming fashion show is the perfect way to work on it. My advisor's friend from New York is coming to the show to pick one of us to work in her design house after graduation. I'm going to focus on that."

Scarlett looks thoughtful as she takes a bite of her ice cream. "New York?"

"*That's* what you focus on after my speech?"

"But it's so far away...."

I roll my eyes in exasperation. "What are you talking about? You're moving to Washington D.C."

"Not next year. I'm going to start graduate school while Tucker finishes his last year of college."

"So you *are* staying."

"It looks like it."

My lip begins to tremble, and I bite it to keep from crying. "We knew this day was coming."

"But not so soon."

"We're seniors, Scarlett. Of course, it's happening *so soon.*" I give her a halfhearted smile. "It's time."

"I don't like it."

"Neither do I, but we don't have a choice."

Her eyes are shiny with tears but she grins. "So does that mean you've figured out your designs so you can win the competition?"

I snort. "Hell, no. I've been busy." I wave my ice cream container at her. "But for now, these are the only two men in my life."

Scarlett's mouth twists into a grin. She doesn't believe me. I guess I don't quite believe me either, but I'm sure going to try.

\*\*\*

On Monday afternoon, I'm in the dean's office, sitting in the conference room. My fellow design students—Megan and another senior, Renee—sit in high-back leather conference chairs. Megan has a laptop in front of her and Renee has her iPad. My yellow legal pad lies on the black-granite topped table. We fill one side of the table. The other side is conspicuously empty. But we still have several minutes before the meeting is supposed to begin.

"Ms. Carter said four o'clock, right?" Megan asks, checking the time on her phone.

"Yes." But I'm anxious anyway. I can see one or two people running late or cutting it close, but all three?

The door opens and three people fill the room. A girl and a guy I don't recognize, and the third person is Reed's girlfriend. Or is she his ex-girlfriend? She's still as energetic as she was the last two times I've seen her. She bursts into the room, her curls bouncing and a bright smile on her face.

The guy's face is flushed. "How is it that you all knew where to meet and we were given the wrong room?"

We give him blank stares until Megan says, "Our advisor told us to come to the dean's office."

"We were told the chancellor's office." His tone softens, but not by much.

"Wait a minute." Renee sits up. "Are you suggesting we told you the wrong location?" Indignation riddles her words. "Why would we change the location and not tell you?"

His eyebrows rise and a sardonic smile darkens his eyes. "As some underhanded attempt to keep us from being part of the committee."

Renee rolls her eyes. "That's the stupidest thing I've ever heard. If I really thought we could get rid of you all by giving you a wrong room number, I would have made sure you were told the date was a day later. Then you really couldn't find us."

"See!" he shouts, turning to Reed's girlfriend. "I told you!"

"Greg," she says. "Don't be ridiculous. Our advisor told us to go to the chancellor's office. It was a simple misunderstanding."

I stand and flash Greg a smile. "Why don't we start over?" I point to my chest. "I'm Caroline Hunter." I turn to the girls seated to my right. "This is Megan Thorn and Renee Rodriguez is on the end."

The non-design students remain standing so I forge on.

"I confess this is new to us and not how our department is used to running the fashion show." I cast a quick glance at Megan and Renee. "But that being said, we're very excited the Monroe Foundation has chosen to partner with us to raise money for the underprivileged children in Middle Tennessee. We're thrilled to be part of a community outreach project."

His shoulders relax.

"Why don't we all sit down and we can all go around and formally introduce ourselves. We can also state what skills we bring to the table to benefit the show."

As they move to their seats on the opposite side Renee places her arms on the table and leans forward. "Forgive me for stating the obvious." Her eyes narrow. "But how can students who don't know anything about fashion design help put on a fashion show?"

Renewed tension fills the room, and I want to strangle Renee. She's voiced her displeasure over the outside involvement multiple times before this meeting. Megan and I have tried to reason with her, insisting we have no say in their addition to the committee and we need to make the best of it. She obviously has her own agenda.

Greg turns to the other girl standing quietly behind him. "See, Wendy? I told you this was pointless." He heads for the door.

I take a step forward and stop his path. Ms. Carter is counting on me, and I need her recommendation with her New York friend. "Wait. Please, don't go. Renee doesn't speak for Megan and me."

Reed's girlfriend places a hand on Greg's arm. "Come on, Greg. This is new for us too. I think we can make this work."

Greg scowls and slinks to his seat.

Reed's girlfriend flashes me a smile and it seems genuine, not a fake sorority girl smile.

Looks like I have an ally on the enemy front.

Everyone sits down, leaving the chair at the head of the table empty.

Reed's girlfriend begins the introductions and her face lights up with excitement. "I'm Lexi. I'm a sophomore and a business major, but I have a special interest in running nonprofit organizations. I've had experience organizing fundraisers and even though this is my first year at Southern University, I'm excited to be included on the committee."

Greg shoots her an annoyed look, then looks at me. "I'm Greg and I'm an accounting major. I'm in charge of the allocation of funds for the program."

Before Wendy even speaks, I realize what the foundation has done. It's ingenious.

Lexi flashes an encouraging smile at Wendy before she speaks. "I'm Wendy, and I'm a senior getting a marketing degree. Last summer I interned for a firm in Memphis that worked on a local nonprofit campaign. Our timing for this particular event is pretty tight, but I think we have time to throw something together before the show next month."

Renee is next, but her mouth gaps before she sits up, her attitude changed after hearing the other student's potential. "I'm Renee, a senior in fashion design. I've modeled in the past and have connections to several girls in the school who have modeled and will probably volunteer their time."

Megan smiles, full of enthusiasm. "I'm Megan, also a senior design student. I'm great at time management and I know some photography students who are interested in shooting the show for their portfolios. I'm sure we can get them to take some preshow photos to use for publicity."

It's now my turn and although I'm bursting with excitement, I'm now at a loss as to what to list for the attributes I bring to the table. I can't tell them all that Ms. Carter suggested me because of my peacemaking abilities. "Uh … I'm Caroline and I'm a senior majoring in fashion design."

I was the one who suggested this exercise, but I hadn't planned on everyone presenting such vital roles to organizing the show. Anything I say at this point will sound lame, but I have to say something. "I'm great at organizing and I work well in groups." *Really? That's all I can come up with?* "I'm looking forward to being part of combining the practicality of the business department with the creativity of the design department." I look around the table. "Perhaps we should appoint someone to be in charge and keep us on task?"

Greg's upper lip curls into a sneer. "And I suppose that person should be you?"

My shoulders stiffen. "Well, no … but we need…."

"We already have a chairman." Lexi looks up from the phone in her hand. "He was sent to the wrong location too, but he's here now. In fact, he should walk in the door at any moment."

As if on cue, the door opens, and I hide my surprise at who walks in the door.

Reed Pendergraft.

# Chapter Five

Why is a mathematics grad student in charge of a committee consisting of business and fashion design majors?

Reed's forehead burrows when he enters the room. He shuts the door behind him and places his hand on the back of the seat at the head of the table. With his white dress shirt, blue tie, gray dress pants, and loafers, he looks like a CEO of a company, not a mathematics grad student. His no-nonsense attitude clinches it.

"Who was in charge of the room allocation?" His eyes scan the people sitting at the table then land on me. He hides his surprise well, one moment of hesitation before his attitude returns.

I suppose he expects me to answer since he's still looking at me, his eyebrows sinking even lower.

"It was a simple misunderstanding, Reed," Lexi murmurs. "Our advisor told us the wrong location and I told you. We're all here now."

Reed and Lexi lock eyes and they appear to have a nonverbal conversation. Reed glowers at her, but Lexi smiles sweetly. After several seconds, Reed's frown deepens, and he sits in the chair and folds his hands on the table in front of him. "Have you begun?"

Everyone remains silent until Lexi, the only person not stunned into silence, speaks up. "We've all introduced ourselves and listed what we bring to the table." She flashes me a smile, and it still seems genuine. "It was Caroline's idea."

Reed's sharp eyes pin me again. "And you didn't think to wait for me?"

Now he's starting to piss me off. "I'm *sorry*. But until approximately a minute ago, I didn't even know you were on the committee. We were only told to show up in this room at four. We didn't know who or what to expect." I'm surprised by my outburst. This is so unlike me, except, apparently, with Reed. Even Megan stirs next to me, probably caught off guard as well.

Reed must accept my answer because he looks around the table again. "I'll need everyone to write their name and contact numbers, schedules, and e-mail addresses so that I'll be able to contact you regarding meeting locations and times if there's a discrepancy in the future. We have a very short time to put this together, and we'll have to put in some long hours to make it happen."

His scowl deepens, and I wonder how his face doesn't pucker in on itself like a black hole. If only I could be lucky enough for Reed Pendergraft to disappear.

Megan releases a tiny gasp.

Reed tilts his head slightly, and his eyes harden even more, a feat I didn't think possible. "I can assure you, Ms. Hunter. I'm not going anywhere."

Oh, dear God in heaven. I said that out loud.

I'm about to die of embarrassment.

"Now, Ms. Hunter, since you are indeed stuck with me until this show is complete, would you be so kind as to allow me to take a sheet from your legal pad and pass it around?" His voice is tightly controlled but the throbbing vein on his temple gives away how angry he really is.

I nod my consent and slide a sheet of paper toward him after I rip it off with shaky hands, my face on fire. What in the world possessed me to say that out loud? I'm usually the epitome of a southern lady in situations like this, and that was *not* ladylike behavior.

What happens over the next few minutes is a blur. I'm lost in my own mortification. I can't believe I made such a mistake. I'm always in perfect control of my reactions. But Reed Pendergraft irritates the shit out of me.

Reed is passing out stapled, multi-page handouts. "In the papers I'm giving you, I've listed the tasks that need to be done, the dates they need to be done by, and a blank spot so we can determine who will complete each task."

We flip through the sheets in silence. The only sound is the rustle of papers and the air conditioning kicking in. Reed is amazingly thorough with every detail of putting together a fashion show, and I wonder where he acquired this kind of knowledge.

After we read the sheets, Reed lists the duties, and we sign up for specific jobs. I might be impressed with Reed's organizational skills if he weren't so controlling.

"Excuse me, *Mr. Pendergraft*." I stress his last name, hoping that calling attention to it will show him the ridiculousness of his formality. "But I was under the impression that this was a committee, not a Marxist takeover."

Lexi's shoulders shake and she finds her lap fascinating.

Reed leans forward. "Ms. Hunter, when I am in charge, I am in charge. If you don't like it, you may leave."

He's issued a challenge, and I'll be damned if I back down. "This isn't one of your classes, where you can boss your students around to feed your monstrous ego. How many souls are sacrificed each day to appease your thirst for fear and cowering? You don't scare me. In fact, I can assure you, *Mr. Pendergraft*. I'm not going *anywhere*."

We have a momentary stare-off, and I can feel everyone's eyes on me. I'm not Scarlett, and I'm used to attention, although it's usually positive. Not because I'm in the middle of some asshole's pissing contest. So I hold my gaze and ignore the unwavering contempt plastered on his face.

Finally, his back stiffens, and he turns his irritation to the rest of the group. "Does anyone else have an issue with the way I'm running the committee?"

I wait for Greg to speak up since he had no problem standing up to me, but the asshole remains silent. I wonder if I'm being unfair. Reed has an intimidating presence, and Greg strikes me as a non-discriminating bully. Bullies back down when threatened by bigger bullies.

The next thirty minutes pass quickly, and my list of grievances against Reed Pendergraft continues to grow. He's a stuck-up Northern snob who looks down on all things Southern, both the region and the university. What the hell is he doing in Tennessee? From what little I know about the math department from Scarlett, Southern University doesn't even rank in the top twenty universities.

So what's Reed Pendergraft doing here?

Reed announces that we'll have another committee meeting on Wednesday at four, and if we can't make it due to other commitments, we can quit right now. When everyone remains silent, he reminds us that our assignments are due then. "That's it for today, everyone may go. Ms. Hunter, I need you to stay."

Lexi remains in her chair as everyone gets up to leave. I'm tempted to go with them, but I'm curious why Reed has asked me to stay. If it's to chastise me again, let him have his fun. I stood up to bigger, meaner bullies than him in high school, and I had much more to lose then. The last members leave the room, and Lexi's gaze shifts from Reed to me and then back again.

Reed taps the end of his remaining papers on the table. "Lexi, you may go."

"No way." She remains in her seat, and Reed sighs. She must have him wrapped around her little finger. It's nice to know that bossy Reed is controlled by someone, but their relationship confuses me.

"Whatever you have to say, I have a right to hear," she says.

Interesting change in dynamics. Maybe Lexi is suddenly the jealous type, and she wants to make sure nothing inappropriate happens behind the closed door.

Reed shoots her a scowl, then turns, his cold brown eyes staring at me. "Ms. Hunter."

I return his stiff tone. "Mr. Pendergraft."

Irritation flickers in his eyes.

I've gotten a reaction from him, and a thrill races down my spine. I'm surprised how much I'm enjoying this exchange.

"Ms. Hunter, I can't have you disrupting the meeting with your fascist comments."

My eyebrows shoot up. "*Fascist*? Which part of me objecting to your hostile takeover is fascist? Do you understand that *you* have invaded *our* program? For years the show has been run by the design department, and this year we've had the business department thrown at us. We're expected to give them equal say. I had my doubts this would work until we all introduced ourselves, and I decided this plan was actually brilliant."

I point my finger at him. "But then you show up and act like you're a dictator. I'm willing to work with the other members *as a committee*—and excuse me if I'm wrong, because I've been led to believe that a committee *is* a democracy—but you came in and bullied the members into silence. Everyone in this room is scared to death to contradict you."

I stand, picking up my notepad and purse. "So if that's your management style, *Mr. Pendergraft*, no thank you. Good luck with that."

His eyes widen, but he doesn't say anything when I stomp to the door and leave the conference room. Raw anger courses through my blood, warming my chest and my face. But pride fills me too. I haven't stood up to anyone like this in years. When I was a kid, I never backed down to bullies. Never let them see my fear and humiliation, even if it was boiling behind a hard expression.

The people who know me now wouldn't recognize Carol Ann Hunter from Shelbyville. When I packed up my life and came to college, my parents never expected me to make it. My mother thought I was uppity since I didn't think their life was good enough for me. I was scared enough to move to Southern. I didn't need their negativity and expectations of failure to remind me of what I risked. So I never went back. Her choice, not mine.

Once I made that decision, I realized I could become whoever I wanted to be. This was my chance at a fresh start. No one here knows I grew up in a trailer park at the edge of town. No one judges me because I ate subsidized lunches. I left that girl and my past with her. I became Caroline, a sweet, soft-spoken girl who Southern boys want to take home to their mommas. Only Scarlett knows my secret here. I never even told Justin, even after two years of dating. I dodged most questions about my past and made up the rest.

For three years I've buried Carol Ann deep inside and for the first time since I drove out of Shelbyville in my beat-up, rusted Ford Focus, she's resurfaced. All because of Reed Pendergraft.

And I don't like it one bit.

Megan is waiting for me in the hall, worry lines crinkling her eyes. "Well…?"

I lift my chin. "I quit."

Her eyes fly open. "No!"

The realization of what I've done hits me full force. This was my shot at boosting my flimsy resume, and I've thrown it away all because of my temper. My future employer won't care that conceited egomaniac Reed Pendergraft ran the whole damn thing. They only want to know I was part of it and what role I played. Reed gave me roles. I just tossed them away. All because of my pride.

I shake my head and grip the strap of my messenger bag to hide my now trembling fingers. "What's done is done. I suppose I should go tell Ms. Carter."

"Maybe you can go back and—"

"No." My answer is firm, hiding my temptation to do the very thing Megan is trying to suggest. Go back and grovel to get my spot back. And as much as I know I should, I can't bring myself to do it.

"Caroline. Wait!" Lexi's voice calls behind me.

I take a deep breath before turning around to face her.

She stops in front of me, her eyes pleading with mine. "You can't quit."

"I think I just did."

"No, I know." She shakes her head and her blonde curls bounce around her face like a shampoo commercial. I want to hate her but she's so damned sweet. "But I'm asking you to reconsider."

I try to contain my shock. Reed's girlfriend is asking me to stay on the committee.

"Why?"

Conspiratorial glee washes over her face. "Because no one talks to Reed that way, and you have no idea how much I loved watching you make him squirm."

Now I'm really confused. Why would Lexi want her boyfriend to squirm? And why would she want *me* to do it? "Look, I'm not sure what—"

"Please." She clasps her hands and brings them to her chest. "Reed really is nice, once you get to know him."

I clench my jaw. "I guess I'll never know since I have no intention of getting to know him."

"You don't have to, just hang in there for a month and continue to stand up to him. I'll stand with you next time and between the two of us, we'll bring him down a peg or two."

I squeeze my eyes closed then open them. "Forgive me for asking—because this is really none of my business—but why would you want me to help you bring your boyfriend down a peg or two?"

Shock covers her face, and for a moment, I wonder if I've crossed a line, although I'm not quite sure how. Then she breaks into giggles.

Irritation prickles the hair on the back of my neck. "I'm not sure what's so funny."

"Reed ... my boyfriend...." She shakes her head and takes a breath.

"Are you saying he's not your boyfriend?"

She gets her laughter under control. "No. He's my brother."

"Your brother?" But it all makes sense now. At Scarlett's party, Reed touched her in a protective way, but there hadn't been anything that suggested they were a couple. Just me jumping to conclusions. And at the club, Lexi was annoyed that Reed was there. Of course, she would be. Who wants their brother cramping their dating life?

She leans closer and lowers her voice. "Reed is used to getting his way, and he's used to bossing people around to get it. It will be fun to watch you work him over."

I'm not sure how Reed became part of the committee that includes his sister, but nothing surprises me when it comes to the chancellor. "Lexi, you seem like a sweet girl." I take a deep breath. "But I'm not on the committee to settle some score for you with your brother. I'm there to build my already pathetic resume."

"Then come back to the committee and do that! And give my brother the opposition he needs."

I shake my head. "I don't know."

An evil glint fills her eyes. "You have to admit you kind of liked it."

I did. And that's the problem. I liked every moment of telling him off. It was like the dam burst free, letting loose all the times I'd bit my tongue and buried my irritation and anger over the last few years. I not only liked it, but I'm desperate for more. I'm not sure I can control the Carol Ann begging to come out.

Even more alarming is the way he makes me feel. Even when we're fighting, an undercurrent of desire flows beneath my skin. My reaction to him is dangerous.

But Lexi's right. I need this for my resume, and the show is in a month. I can endure anything for a month.

Why do I think I'll regret those words?

# Chapter Six

I call Scarlett as I storm across campus to my car. "Why is a math grad student on a fashion show committee with a bunch of business and fashion degree students?"

"Slow down. What are you talking about?"

"Reed is the chairman of the fashion show committee."

"How did that happen?"

"The chancellor."

"Oh."

"Here's the even weirder part: his girlfriend? She's really his sister. And she's on the committee too. How did that happen?"

"I don't know."

I hear the distraction in her voice. I know her schedule, and she's in the math lab, but she knows I wouldn't call her unless it's an emergency. While this doesn't count as a technical emergency, I'm feeling out of control after my encounter with him.

"Perhaps he's there as an outside mediator."

"Not with his sister on the committee. At least I can see why she's there. She's a sophomore business major. Their family connection breaks down all suggestions of a nonbiased tiebreaker."

"Huh."

I shake my head. "I'm sorry. I don't know why I called you. You're working. I'll just talk to you later."

"Caroline, wait." She pauses for a second, and her voice isn't as muffled. She must have moved out into the hallway.

"Do you think you can work with him after what happened Friday night?"

"I don't know." I gnaw on a cuticle on my finger, then stop when I realize what I'm doing. I haven't done that in years, either. "He gets under my skin and irritates the hell out of me. If he's from Boston, why is he even here at Southern University?"

She sighs. "I don't know much about him, but I've checked into him today after what he did to you. He's from the east coast. He went to a prestigious school before he started grad school here this semester, but for the life of me, I can't find out which one, which is really odd. Even more odd is that Southern doesn't rank up there in the best of the best schools for mathematics degrees. Why would he go to an Ivy League school for his undergrad work then come here for his master's?"

"So why *is* he here?"

"I don't know. He keeps to himself, but he seems lonely, so that's why I invited him to my party. Honestly, I didn't expect him to show up. I don't see him much. He runs the math lab this semester, but our hours usually don't correspond. Even when he's here, he doesn't talk to us much."

"Because he's stuck up."

Scarlett pauses. "People always have a reason for what they do."

I'm at my car, but I lean my hip against the side door, brushing back the loose hairs that blow into my face. Don't I know it? I'm not proud of some of the things I've done, but there's always some reason for it, even if it's misguided. "I like the person I've become here at Southern." I finally say. "He brings out the old me." It seems stupid now, that I let him affect me so. And I'm embarrassed I'm admitting this to Scarlett.

"There is no old you and new you, Caroline. There's only you."

Leave it to pragmatic Scarlett to say something so rational.

"So what do you want to do?" she asks. "Do you want to quit?"

"I already quit."

"What?"

I unlock my car door and slide into the driver seat. "He walked in and took over, Scarlett. He came in with an 'I'm better than you attitude' and started bossing everyone around, assigning jobs and being hateful." I grimace. "I may have compared his entrance to a Marxist takeover."

Scarlett laughs. "You're kidding."

"I wish I were."

"So that's it? You're just giving up on your dream? You've been talking about being on that committee since freshman year after you attended your first show. You're going to let one guy take that from you?"

I'm so glad I coerced Scarlett to room with me freshman year. I truly don't know what I would do without her. Our conversation reminds me how much I miss seeing her every day. "No. Lexi convinced me to stay on the committee. She said Reed isn't used to people standing up to him, and she wants me to stay and help put him in his place."

"Why would she do that? She doesn't like him?"

"No, that's not it. She obviously loves him. I suspect it's a sibling rivalry thing. But I don't want to get caught in the middle of it."

"So don't. Do your job and ignore him."

"Easier said than done."

"Caroline. You think the person you were before is slipping out, but you've grown. You've changed. She's in there; she's just evolved. Give yourself more credit."

"You weren't there, Scarlett. You don't know what I said and did."

"It couldn't have been that bad if his own sister witnessed it and asked you to reconsider your resignation."

"It was bad."

"Okay. Then consider this a challenge to your personal growth. You've faced adversaries and haters in the design department. And you know you're bound to face it in the real world when you get a job. Creative people tend to get jealous."

While I'd love to argue with her, she's right. "Yeah."

"Good." I hear the smile in her voice. "I'm proud of you. You can do this, Caroline. *You* are in control of your reactions."

"Easy for you to say since you don't work with Reed much."

"If you like, I can talk to him about you. Convince him you're not so bad."

My heart stutters. "Don't you dare!"

"I'm joking. But I'll try to get to know him a bit better. Maybe I can give you some insight to help you get along with him."

"All right. But don't be too obvious."

She chuckles. "I'll be discreet. Now I have to get back in the lab. But call me if you need to talk later, okay?"

"Thanks, Scar."

I go home and take a nap then grab some dinner and head to the design studio. I haven't the vaguest clue what to do for my project, but I need to figure it out soon. I'm not surprised to find several students already working on projects. Now that I've presented the dress I was working on last week, I have four weeks to come up with ten completed designs, as well as plan the show. I'm feeling the pressure of the looming deadline, but it doesn't jog any ideas loose as I sit with my sketchbook and pencil. I end up sketching a dozen ideas, but none of them grab my interest. After I spend ten minutes staring out the window, I decide I'm not getting anything accomplished here, but I'm not ready to go home either.

Instead, I head to The Higher Ground, the campus coffee shop. It's open until eleven and I need to study for my U.S. government test. I order a coffee but resist a muffin and find a table for two in the corner. This isn't the best place to study. The coffee shop is usually full of socializing students in the evening, not studious ones, but I don't feel like leaving campus and I hate the library. Thankfully, I'm good at tuning out the rest of the world, a necessary skill learned in a mobile home full of kids my mother babysat at night after her day job. I'm so zoned out that I'm startled when someone plops in the chair in front of me and drops her books on the table.

"Hi."

I jump in my seat and look up into Lexi Pendergraft's perky face. I resist a groan. "Hi, yourself."

"Studying?"

I glance down at the open government book and my laptop. "Yeah."

"My brother's not that bad, you know."

There's no holding in my groan this time. "I'm sure he's not."

She leans forward, her palms flat on the table, and her voice lowers. "He has his reasons for being how he is, but I assure you, once you get to know him, you'll discover he's all bark and no bite."

"No bite?" I scoff. "I find that hard to believe. He seems like he's used to biting a lot." The thought of him biting me brings a surprising twist in my stomach. *No, Caroline. You do not want Reed Pendergraft to bite you. Focus.* But my pep talk doesn't appease the stir of my hormones.

Lexi grimaces. "Okay, he does bite a little, but again, he has his reasons."

*Not helping.*

I resist the urge to take a deep breath. "Every time I've seen you, Reed was close at hand. How much time do you actually spend with him?"

She looks down, squirming slightly in her seat. "A lot."

This girl confuses me. She might be a college sophomore, but she seems to have the maturity of a high school girl. Hell, I had more maturity in high school, but then I'm not a good judge. "Lexi, you seem like a nice girl, and while this is none of my business, I feel the need to make a suggestion." I pause. "How old are you? Nineteen? Twenty?"

She glances up, her eyes wide, and she sits back in her seat, suddenly wary. "Eighteen."

"Eighteen? Really? Wow." But it explains a few things.

She lifts a shoulder into a self-conscious shrug. "I graduated early."

"That's okay." I look into her eyes. "The point is that you're in college now, and perhaps it's time you cut the apron strings to your brother." I wonder the wisdom of this since I have to spend the next four weeks working with her, but for some bizarre reason, I feel the need to help her. Maybe it's because I like her, and I don't think she should let a jerk like Reed run her life, even if he is her brother. *Especially* since he's her brother.

Her gaze turns to the window. "I know." She faces me again, plastering on a forced smile. "I'm sorry to bother you. I'll let you get back to studying."

As she starts to get up, I reach across the table and grab her hand. "Lexi, wait." She seems so young and lost. Some protective instinct I didn't know I possessed kicks into gear.

She sits back down, wary again, not that I blame her. She and Reed might have some weird *Flowers in the Attic* type thing, but I like her in spite of myself.

"I'm sorry. I shouldn't have said that. I really like you. Let's forget your brother. We're going to be working together so let's get to know each other." Maybe I can find out more about Reed if I find out about Lexi. They *are* siblings. I feel a bit devious—okay, a lot devious—but I'm curious about Lexi too. It just happens to kill two birds with one stone.

Lexi smiles, but she's still cautious. "Okay."

"You said you transferred here. Where did you go to school before?" If I can find out where Lexi went, than maybe I'll figure out Reed's school. Why I care is beyond me.

Uncertainty flickers in her eyes. "Out East."

Strange. That's the same vague answer Reed gave me. "Which college?"

Flashing a smile, she looks down at my book. "U.S. Government? Isn't that usually a lower level course?"

She's dodging my question. My curiosity is piqued, but I let her change the subject. "I know, but I've always hated anything to do with government so I kept putting it off until I couldn't put it off any longer. Not if I want to graduate." I laugh. "Which I do. So here I am." I wave to my book.

Her eyes widen again. "You hate government?"

She makes it sound like I've announced I hate chocolate. "I'm a fan of government as opposed to anarchy, but I'm not a fan of studying it."

"Oh."

Talking to her is harder than I expected. Still, there's a universal topic that all girls relate to. "Do you have a boyfriend?"

She gives me a sly smile. "No."

I cock my head and grin. "But there's someone you're interested in. Who is he?"

Her eyes narrow, but her lips twitch as she fights her smile. "I never said there was."

"Please. It's all over your face." I lean forward. "So who is he?"

Looking down at the table, she twines her fingers together. "He's in my biology class."

"So?"

She shakes her head and looks up at me. "It's nothing. I need to focus on school this year. I'll worry about boys later."

"That sounds like something my friend Scarlett would say. Before she met the love of her life. Now she's crazy in love, and they're living together."

Her lips purse. "My family would never approve."

"I'm not telling you to move in with a boy, Lexi. I'm telling you that you never know when you'll find love. You may not think you have time for it, but it seems to find you whether you're looking for it or not. You're in college. You're supposed to have a dozen boyfriends."

"Have you had a dozen boyfriends?"

My smile fades. "I've been on over a dozen dates, but only a few boyfriends."

"Do you have a boyfriend now?"

It's my turn to look down. "No."

"Really," she states matter-of-factly.

"You sound surprised."

"It's just that you're just so pretty and smart. The way you handled the meeting…." I'm grateful she leaves my conflict with her brother unmentioned. "I'd think you'd have guys lined up."

"Well, thank you." I swivel my head looking around and laugh, hoping it sounds playful and not desperate. "I don't see any lines."

"So you want one? A boyfriend?" Her tone is still expressionless. I feel like I'm being interviewed.

"I've got a busy year before I graduate. I don't exactly have time." I shrug. "But you're only a sophomore. Plenty of time to try out all the Southern University boys."

"Oh no. I need to get settled here first. Reed would have a fit." The line sounds rehearsed and gives off a Stepford vibe.

There's an awkward silence, and she cringes like she regrets mentioning him. She frowns, then a soft smile covers her face. "Maybe I'll try it anyway."

"Good girl. You're only young once, and dating is part of your college experience." I feel like a college admissions advisor.

She folds her hands on the table, her posture perfectly erect. "Do you have any idea what you plan to do with your degree when you graduate?"

"Um. No. But I'm hoping to come up with a great line for the show. My advisor's friend from New York is coming to the show and has promised to pick one student to work in her design house after we graduate."

"Do you have your designs figured out?"

I sigh. "No."

She studies me, and I realize the tables have been turned. Who am I kidding? The tables were turned the moment she asked me if I have a boyfriend.

"Do you have a signature look? A specialty you focus on?"

"No." I pause. How can I be a senior and not have a focus? But I do, I just don't use it in my classes. "Well ... there is something."

Her eyebrows lift. "Don't stop there."

"It's not something I do in class. Just for myself." I grip my coffee cup. "I repurpose thrift store finds."

She watches me, waiting for more information.

"I buy clothes in thrift stores, but I don't usually use them as they are." I shrug. "Sometimes I do, like a really classic piece, but most of the time I either embellish it to make it more contemporary or I'll use parts of several items and put them together to create something entirely new."

"So each piece is one of a kind."

I hadn't thought of it that way. "Yeah, I guess they are."

She glances at my clothes. "What about what you're wearing?"

"The skirt is a thrift store find." I smooth the wrinkles from my lap. "I added a ruffled edge to the hem, but this"—I wave to my front—"is a Target t-shirt and a thrift store cardigan."

"Do you make many of these outfits?"

"Most of my clothes are my hybrid creations."

"Hybrid creations … I like it." Her eyes narrow. "So why haven't you used your hybrid creations in your classes?"

"Because they aren't real designs, Lexi. They're repurposed clothes."

"There's nothing new under the sun, Caroline. Everything has been done before. It's just your own take on it. Your hybrid clothes aren't any different."

I narrow my eyes. "Why the interest in my designs?"

She gives me a mischievous grin. "I've read my share of *Vogue* magazines."

I don't believe her, but I won't be the one to call her on it. Otherwise, what's to stop her from asking why I scavenge thrift stores?

A cell phone rings and guilt washes over her face as she pulls her phone out of her purse. She looks at the screen and grimaces. "I have to go. Thanks for talking to me."

"We should do this again."

She silences her phone and looks at me in surprise. "Really?"

"Yeah." And after my initial doubt about her, I realize I like her. "Maybe we can figure out something after our next committee meeting."

"Okay." She looks up at me and grins, but it's tight like she's nervous. "I'd like that a lot."

"Sounds great."

She waves and heads for the door as she lifts the phone to her ear. Her voice lowers and a serious expression replaces her smile.

I'm going to help Lexi break free from her brother's hold.

While I watch her walk away, someone else sits down in her seat. I look up, surprised to see it's Brandon, a guy from my history class last semester.

"You're Caroline, right?" he asks.

"Uh, yeah." I tilt my head.

He points to his chest. "Brandon McKenzie. We had history together last spring. How's your semester going?"

I study him before I answer. "Good."

He grins. "You look surprised about something."

"It's just that you never spoke to me the entire semester. I didn't think you even knew I existed, let alone knew my name."

He leans back in his chair. "Oh, I knew your name all right." Brandon gives me a playful grin. "But my girlfriend who also took that class was the jealous type."

"And what would she say if she knew you were talking to me now."

"I doubt she cares since she's now going out with someone else."

We stare at each other for several seconds and he laughs. "This is kind of awkward, huh?"

"Yeah," I smirk. "Kind of."

"I think I know how to remedy this situation."

"Do you now?"

"It's only awkward because we don't know each other very well. Go out with me on Friday night, and we can fix that."

I shake my head and glance at my phone to stall. I'm supposed to be taking a break from guys to concentrate on my project. Going out with Brandon, no matter how cute he is, is not working on my designs. I cringe. "I'd really like to, Brandon—"

He holds up his hands. "Don't say *but*! Don't say it."

"B—"

He clamps his hand over my mouth with a playful look in his eyes. "Don't. Say. But." He slowly lowers his hand as if he's ready to raise it again if I attempt to say the word.

"All right I won't say … that word, *however*—"

"Do you have a boyfriend?"

I lean back. "What?"

"Yes or no. Do you have a boyfriend?"

"No."

He laughs. "See? That wasn't so hard. Do you have plans on Friday night?"

I should lie. Something about this guy screams trouble, but he's incredibly good-looking and he definitely has charm. What if Brandon is *the one*, and I never knew because I didn't give him a chance? I grin. "No."

"Let's see, you don't have a boyfriend and you don't have plans Friday night. It sounds like you are destined to go out with me, Caroline."

"Just like that? I don't see you for months, you never even acknowledged my presence before, and now you drop in a chair in front of me and ask me out?"

"I want to get to know you. Asking you out seems the best way to achieve that goal."

I lift my chin in challenge. "I have a project I need to work on."

"What is it? Maybe I can help you with it."

I shake my head and laugh. He is persistent. "I don't think so, unless you're a fashion design major, and I missed you in all my classes. Or you secretly watch *Project Runway*."

He twists his lips into an over-exaggerated grimace. "Busted. I watch it every Monday."

"Thursday."

"I record it and watch it on Monday." Brandon leans forward, his face dangerously close to mine. "See? We can go out to dinner, and I can help you with your project."

"I don't think so."

"Why? Am I too unattractive for you?" he asks teasingly. A guy like him knows he's good-looking, and he definitely knows how to use it to his advantage.

"Yes, Brandon. That's it." I laugh and close my government book, then stash it in my bag. "You are too hideous to be seen with in public. I can hardly stand sitting here with you."

Brandon stands when I do. "How about I wear a paper bag over my head?"

My eyes narrow. "Why are you so eager to go out with me?"

My question stumps him for a moment. "Because I wasted too much time already. I couldn't ask you out last spring because of my girlfriend."

"Good thing for all of us." I mutter.

"And then after we broke up, I kept thinking about you but had no idea how to track you down. I couldn't believe my luck when I saw you sitting here."

His explanation sounds plausible.

"Come on, Caroline. Take pity on a poor guy. Say yes. It's one date."

I have to admit, my defenses are crumbling. He is persistent, and I admire that quality in a man. The fact he's cute doesn't hurt. "Okay."

A huge smile spreads across his face, and he pulls out his phone. "Give me your number. I'll text you then you can text me your address so I know where to pick you up."

Something tells me not to give it to him, but then I remember how I was lusting after Reed before Lexi showed up. Maybe I need a date to get that guy out of my head. After I tell Brandon my number, he shoves his phone in his pocket. "I'll pick you up at seven, and we'll go to St. Thomas Grill."

"St. Thomas Grill?" It's got to be the most expensive restaurant in town.

"Nothing but the best for you." He picks up my hand and kisses my knuckles, then just as quickly drops it and bolts out the door.

What the hell just happened?

Turns out I haven't turned my back on guys after all.

# Chapter Seven

I stand outside the conference room in the dean's office, my stomach twisting with dread. I'm not afraid to face Reed. I'm more afraid of how I'll react.

I'm only a few minutes early because I wanted as little awkward time with Reed as possible. When I walk in the room, everyone is present except for Renee and Wendy. Reed sits at the head of the table, tapping his fingers on the tabletop. Lexi is next to him and offers me a reserved smile as I take a seat several seats away from Reed. I plan to keep my mouth shut at this meeting, so perhaps staying physically as far away as possible will help.

The two other girls are moments behind me, and Reed wastes no time starting the meeting.

We all report on the jobs we were assigned. Wendy tells us that she has several graphic design students competing to make a logo for this year's event. She plans to bring their final concepts to the next meeting. Lexi reports that tomorrow she plans to meet with the head of the local charity that the Monroe Foundation will make donations to. Megan announces that she's lining up female and male models, but she's still working on the children. She's waiting on the design students to let her know what type of models they need.

A cold sweat dots my forehead. I'm no closer to making my designs than I was last week when Ms. Carter announced the theme. If I don't come up with something soon, I'll never have time to complete construction of all the garments.

"Do you care to share anything with us, Ms. Hunter, or do you plan to stare at the wall the rest of the meeting?"

*Shit.*

I clear my throat to give myself a moment to recover. Of course he'd call on me during the few moments I became distracted. "I've gotten bids from two companies for runways. We've used a carpet on the floor before, but our attendance has always been on the skimpy side. With the extra media and marketing push"—I glance at Wendy—"I expect we'll see a marked increase in attendance. I think we should move up to an elevated stage so the audience will be able to see the models."

The group nods but Reed frowns. "And what is the increase in cost?"

"Several thousand dollars but—"

"Do you make a habit of spending other people's money so freely?"

My mouth drops. I quickly close it as I push down my billowing anger. I refuse to lose my cool this time. "I haven't spent anyone's money, Mr. Pendergraft. I've merely stated my thoughts on the matter. If you'd let me finish, I will tell you the estimated costs to set up the runway with the elevated stage and without."

Reed sits up taller and his chin rises. "Then by all means, continue."

I give them the estimated costs from both companies with both options.

Lexi looks around the table. "It makes sense to go with the elevated stage, if you think about it. And with Wendy using graphic design students for the logo and banners, we'll save money that we can use for the venue." She glances back at Reed, as though she's trying to convince him. "Since the

Monroe Foundation has lent us their name and money, we need to make sure our presentation is quality."

He merely stares at her with his expressionless face.

Surprisingly enough, Reed calls for a vote—score one for democracy—and the outcome is unanimous to go with the elevated stage and with the higher bid because that bidder's stage seemed to be better constructed. Reed abstains from voting since he's the head and the designated tiebreaker. I'm partially surprised he didn't overrule the vote anyway.

Before he dismisses the meeting, Reed assigns more tasks and announces we'll meet on Friday. The words have barely left his mouth, and he's immediately up and out the door. I suspect he doesn't want a repeat of our last meeting.

Greg doesn't waste time following Reed out of the room. I'm sure he's wondering how he got stuck in this sea of estrogen. Megan and Renee fall into step with Wendy as they leave the room discussing ideas they have to get the word out on campus.

Lexi stands next to her seat, waiting for me. "As I mentioned, tomorrow I'm going to see the director of the Middle Tennessee Children's Charity." She pauses. "I was wondering if you'd like to go with me?"

"Sure, but why me?"

She tilts her head with a half-shrug. "You just seem like you'd have an affinity toward the organization."

My heart stutters. Does Lexi know about my past? How could she?

She must see my momentary shock. "It's just that with your hybrid designs, it's something underprivileged girls could do to spiff up their own wardrobes."

Instead of making me feel better, her assessment hits too close to home.

She senses my hesitation. "It will look great on your resume if you have direct involvement with the organization."

I doubt this is true, but Lexi really wants me to go with her. Everything in me screams to tell her no, but I can't bring myself to do it. "Okay, what time is the meeting?"

Her face lights up with excitement. "Tomorrow at four. Can you get away then?"

I nod. "I have an open lab tomorrow, but I can get away." Especially since I haven't come up with any designs to work on.

"Great! How about we meet at the statue of Andrew Jackson at the edge of the west student parking lot, at three forty-five. We can go together."

"Sure."

"About last night." She pauses. "I know I'm too dependent on my family."

I shake my head. What had I been thinking? Lexi's life is none of my business. "I'm sorry. Forget I said anything. I was totally out of line."

She stops and turns to me. "You were right, but I'm not sure I'm ready to lose their support yet. That's part of the reason I'm here, though. To learn to be a bit more independent."

If this is more independent, I'd hate to see what it was like before. My phone vibrates in my purse, and I pull it out. "It's me today." I laugh, but the smile falls off my face when I see the number. Ice water flows through my veins. I consider not answering, but I haven't seen that number on my caller ID in over three years. "I'm sorry ... I have to take this."

"Of course!" Lexi waves and continues toward the stairwell. "See you tomorrow!"

I lean my back against the wall and take a deep breath, unsure if I'm ready to face what's on the other side of the phone. My curiosity wins out. "Hello?"

"Carol Ann."

My mother's voice slams into my head, taking every ounce of confidence I've built up since coming to Southern. "Yes." My voice is tentative. How did she get this number? I changed it when I moved away.

"It's your momma."

I want to say *I know*, but my mind is too muddled.

"I'm sick, Carol Ann."

My breath sticks in my chest. My mother is the healthiest woman I know. When I was younger, the few times she was sick she went to work anyway. Her philosophy trickled down to her children. The Hunter children didn't stay home from school unless they had a fever over one hundred and two.

"I didn't want to call you, but your father insisted." Her voice has always been gravelly from years of smoking, but there's a raspy tone I'm not used to hearing. My father's voice is muffled in the background, encouraging her to continue. "They say it's not good. I only have a couple of months."

I'm not sure what to say. I'm standing in the busy hallway of the administration building, students streaming past me, and my mother has just told me she's dying. I know I should feel something, but there's nothing.

"Your father thought you should know."

"What is it?" That's an odd way to ask, but it's the first thing that pops into my head.

"Lung cancer." She laughs, but it sounds like a bark when she starts to cough. "Guess you were right after all."

Back in fourth grade, we learned about the dangers of cigarette smoking from our DARE officer. When I went home and begged my mother to stop smoking, worried her lungs would turn black like the ones in the photos he showed us, she told me to mind my own damn business. My feelings had been hurt for days, and I'd be justified to say *I told you so*, but the words stay deep in my chest.

"Okay." I know I should say something else. Feel something else.

"All righty then. That's it." And then there's silence. She's hung up.

I stay propped against the wall, not trusting my now shaky legs. Of course, she'd call me out of nowhere in the middle of the day and drop this bombshell on me. She hasn't said the one thing I've been waiting to hear since the day I drove out of Shelbyville: *I'm sorry.*

But she'll never be sorry. She may have admitted I was right about smoking, but she'll never admit that she treated me like dirt when I left home.

The truth hits me now, why I feel nothing at her news. She may be dying now, but she's been dead to me for three years.

# Chapter Eight

When I walk across campus at three forty-five, I see Lexi standing next to the eight-foot-tall statue of President Andrew Jackson. Other than country music, he's Tennessee's claim to fame. Southern has several images of him scattered across the campus.

Lexi wears a classic gray tweed skirt and jacket, an ivory blouse underneath, and a pair of three-inch-heeled black pumps. Her blonde hair is pulled into a French twist. I considered going casual so I'm now thankful I went with a business look as well: a silk blouse with a wool skirt and my suede boots. I'm also thankful I added a cardigan because there's a nip in the air. Fall has finally arrived, bringing rain clouds to the west with it.

She casts a wary gaze into the parking lot then looks back toward the campus. A smile spreads across her face. "Hi. Thanks for coming."

"Thanks for inviting me." Now that I'm closer, I can see her suit is made from high quality wool and has a tailored fit. Her bag is soft leather, and her shoes obviously didn't come from Payless. Lexi's attire reeks of money, but her clothes are extremely conservative for an eighteen-year-old. "I love your suit. Is it Chanel?"

She grins, but it falters a bit. "Yeah, I suppose you would notice since you're a fashion major."

I tilt my head and study the cut. "It doesn't look vintage so it had to cost a fortune. Where did you find it?" Most college students could never afford a suit like hers.

Her eyes shift to an approaching car. "A friend gave it to me last year. At my old college."

She's acting strange, but I don't want to pry. Perhaps she's embarrassed that she's wearing hand-me-downs. I hate admitting my clothes are mostly thrift store finds, even if I usually repurpose them.

An older sedan pulls up to the curb and Lexi walks toward it. "There's our ride."

I follow her, confused, as she opens the back door and stands next to it. "Come on, we're going to be late."

I start to slide into the backseat when I see who's sitting in the driver seat.

Reed.

In my shock, I gasp and start to get out of the car, but Lexi is climbing in, pushing me back inside and shutting the door.

"Okay, Reed. Let's go."

Reed grips the steering wheel, staring straight ahead. "Lexi." Her name is a rumble.

"Reed, we're going to be late and you know how much you like to be prompt."

His jaw tightens as the car pulls away from the curb toward the parking lot exit.

I finally come to my senses. "What the—"

Lexi turns to me, beaming. "Caroline, tell me about your project."

I have no idea why she's so happy. She knows how rude her brother is during our meetings, but does she have any idea her brother humiliated me a week ago? Lexi seems like a sweet girl, so I suspect not. She's probably one of those girls who has a hard time believing anyone, especially her brother, can do something terrible. I have two choices: One I can throw a huge fit and insist Reed stop the car; or two, I can pretend his presence doesn't bother me at all. I decide to go with option two. Reed's behavior in the meeting and at the bar was to get a reaction from me, and I fell right into his trap. I'm not making that mistake again. Ignoring him, or worse yet, being nice to him will drive him crazy. I can't quite bring myself to be nice, so I choose the second option.

But the question about my project sends anxiety skating down my back. I've made no progress. At all. I still haven't come up with a commonality to tie all my pieces together, or even tie into the theme of *Everyday Living*. Not that I have any pieces to tie together. I have nothing. "It's still in the planning stage."

"Sounds like you're stalling," Reed mumbles.

Lexi's eyes narrow. "Who are your favorite designers?"

I'm not sure if she's asking to intervene or if she's truly interested, but I'm eager to avoid a confrontation with Reed. My ire has been stoked, my irritation simmering to a low boil. "I like classic designers: Caroline Herrera, Chanel of course."

"How original," Reed mutters just loud enough for me to hear.

Ignore him.

"But I love the delicateness of Alberta Ferretti's designs and Matthew Williamson's use of color."

Lexi's eyes widen. "I'm surprised. Matthew Williamson has more of an edge."

I stare at her for a moment. "You know about designers?"

She blinks, then gives me a sly smile. "What can I say? I like *Vogue*."

"For the pretty pictures." Reed drones.

"Why did he come?" I snap.

Now Lexi looks worried. "He's our ride."

"I have a car in perfect working condition." But that's not entirely true. The car is twelve years old and barely on life support. I'm replacing a quart of oil every other day and the brakes are sketchy. I pray it lasts until I graduate and get a job. If I get a job. All the more reason to keep my mouth shut and ignore Reed's taunts.

Lexi shoots an annoyed glance to the front, but Reed stares straight ahead and doesn't notice.

Why in the hell is he here? I realize the only time I've seen Lexi without her brother is last night in the coffee shop. I've heard of close families, but this borders on creepy. Why would she want to spend so much time with him when he's a total ass?

Lexi turns toward me. "What made you want to go into fashion design?"

I give her my standard answer. "Clothing is an expression of people's personalities and designers can help draw those nuances to the person's exterior." It sounds pretty and most people are impressed, even my advisor. But the fact is that it's a lie.

I've given the explanation so many times I've begun to believe it myself, but after my conversation with my mother, my entire world seems to have shifted off center. Not enough to shake up my life, but enough to throw everything off.

"People actually believe that?" Reed asks.

"Reed!" Lexi's voice is harsher than I've heard from her, but Reed doesn't seem to notice.

My shoulders straighten and I look into the rearview mirror so I can see his face, even if he's not looking up. "And what do you have trouble with, Mr. Pendergraft?"

*"Draw nuances of a person's personality to their exterior?* It sounds like something you'd find on a freshman college entrance essay."

"What? And I'm sure you have some perfectly logical reason as to why you want to get a graduate degree in mathematics?"

"Of course, I do."

"And it is...?" I lift my eyebrows and glare into the mirror. Reed's gaze lifts and I lock eyes with his in the reflection.

His focus returns to the road. "I like the logic of math, and I think the world needs more logic instead of fluff answers such as drawing nuances of a person's personality."

I'm surprised I'm not hurt by his rude behavior, but I'm too furious for hurt feelings to rise to the surface. "The world needs more beauty and kindness, not rude behavior thinly disguised as logic."

Lexi's face pales and I'm sure she regrets bringing me along.

Strangely enough, Reed remains quiet for the next few minutes until he pulls into a small parking lot in front of a series of houses that are painted the same dark tan with black shutters. Yellow chrysanthemums fill neatly tended flowerbeds in front of the houses. A sign in the yard reads: *Middle Tennessee Children's Charity.*

Reed wastes no time parking and jumping out of the car before Lexi and I get our doors open. Not that I'm in any hurry to get out. I need to pull myself together before I go inside and meet the director.

Lexi senses my hesitation. My hand stretches across the cracked leather of the backseat and Lexi's hand covers mine. "I'm sorry. I know he can be rude, but he's not usually this bad." She sighs. "You seem to bring out the worst in him."

I laugh, but it's more of a snort. "Lucky me."

"I'm sorry."

I pull my hand out from underneath hers. "Stop saying you're sorry. He's the ass. How does that make *you* responsible?"

She wrings her hands in her lap. "I invited you … and he came…."

"Lexi, stop. I was happy you invited me. Now let's go inside."

I'm not really ready to go in, but what I need is a few minutes to myself, and that isn't happening. I push my door open.

I refuse to let Reed ruin this for me. When Lexi first asked me to come, I hesitated because of the painful reminder of my past. But my phone call with my mother yesterday made me realize there are other children like me. Children determined to escape their beginnings and make something of themselves. If I can be part of something that gives them the courage to do that, then I need to take it.

Reed holds the door open, wearing the same stuffy expression he wears when he conducts our committee meetings. He ignores me as I brush past him, and I'm thankful. Telling him off in front of the charity's director would likely be frowned upon.

The walls of the entry and long hall leading to the back of the house are covered in photographs, but before I have a chance to examine them, a woman emerges from a doorway off the hall.

Lexi takes a step forward and offers her hand. "I'm Lexi Pendergraft. I have an appointment to see Ms. Marshall."

The woman smiles and shakes hands. "That's me, but everyone calls me Evelyn."

Lexi turns to the side and gestures toward us. "This is Caroline Hunter and Reed … Pendergraft. They're both on the committee."

Lexi may be a bubbly college sophomore on campus, but at this moment she's in full-on business mode. She speaks with an air of confidence that some thirty-year-olds don't possess.

Evelyn shakes our hands. "Pleased to meet you both. Why don't we go into my office?"

We follow her into a room that looks like it was once a dining room. Her wooden desk is at an angle and clutter-free. Photographs of children cover the walls. Two chairs sit in front of her desk, and an overstuffed chair takes up the far corner of the room. Lexi sits in front of the desk, and I hesitate. Reed stands by the door and gestures to the chair next to Lexi with a sardonic smile.

Evelyn and Reed take their seats and Evelyn rests her forearms on the desk and leans forward. "We're honored the Monroe Foundation chose to donate to our organization."

The photos on the wall drag my eyes like magnets. Some are of children on a playset. Others are of children bent over homework or reading books.

I expect Reed to answer and take charge like he does in our committee meetings, but he sits back and crosses his legs. Lexi lifts her chin as she asks Evelyn, "What is the greatest challenge your nonprofit faces right now?"

"The economy has hit this area hard, and unfortunately we have more needs than resources." She twines her fingers and leans forward. "Many children are in need of the basics like school supplies and clothing. We've set up programs to distribute free school supplies at the beginning of the year to children in need, and we have a Christmas program that provides gifts to struggling families. But there are so many needs that aren't being met. Health and dental care. Even something as simple as clothing that is new and fits can make the difference between social acceptance and ridicule, especially in middle school.

"We've done our best to meet the demand, but there are more children than we have resources. It breaks our hearts to turn children away, but we've been forced to this past year." A frown tugs at the corners of her mouth. "That's why the Monroe Foundation's generous offer is a godsend."

Lexi sits primly in her seat with her hands folded in her lap. "The committee will do everything we can to help The Children's Home." Her tone is businesslike, and I wonder if what Evelyn has said has soaked into her head because I'm on the verge of tears. Evelyn's words have swept me back ten years to the girl in Shelbyville who wanted desperately to fit in but was ostracized because her wardrobe came from Goodwill.

Evelyn and Lexi talk for the next ten minutes about the organization before Evelyn stands. "Well, let's check it out, shall we?"

Lexi and Reed stand, and I realize I've missed where we're going, reminiscing. Evelyn leads the way, and I follow Lexi down a hall toward the back of the house. The walls are filled with more photographs.

One in particular pulls me closer. The photo is of a girl who looks like she's about eight with blonde curls and blue eyes. Her face is too thin, but it's her eyes that suck me in. She looks so haunted and beaten down. The girl looks so much like me in third grade that I freeze.

"Caroline?" Lexi asks.

I glance away from the photo and notice the three of them watching me.

# Chapter Nine

"I'm sorry. Did you ask me a question?" My voice shakes.

Evelyn gestures to the wall. "I said that I see you're drawn to the photos. Our charity has helped children all over middle Tennessee for over two decades. We've collected photos over the years."

The blood rushes from my head. *We've helped children all over middle Tennessee.* "How far south does your assistance extend?"

"A little past Shelbyville."

The truth hits me square in the face. The girl in the photo is me.

Evelyn and Lexi continue down the hall, but I stumble backward into Reed's chest, and he catches my elbow. "Are you okay?"

I nod, but I can't stop staring at the photograph.

"You look like you're about to get sick." His voice softens, with only a hint of gruffness.

I feel lightheaded, but I refuse to let him, of all people, see me flustered. "I'm fine."

"You don't look fine."

"I'm—"

Reed steps in front of me and looks toward the back of the house. "Caroline is fascinated with the photographs so we're going to examine them for a minute or so. We'll follow you in a moment."

Lexi turns and gives us a curious glance.

"Are you sure?" Evelyn asks. "I'd be happy to wait."

"You go ahead," Reed says. "I know how eager Lexi is to see the tutoring center."

"Yes, that's right." Lexi chimes in.

"Well, if you're sure…." Evelyn seems unconvinced.

"Have I mentioned how excited I am to meet some of the children we'll be helping?" Lexi takes Evelyn's arm and leads her out the back door.

Reed's lowered voice interrupts my thoughts. "Caroline, do you want to sit down or get some fresh air?"

I want to tell him neither, but the photo has shaken me up more than I want to admit. I need to catch my breath. "Outside."

He leads me out the front door and to a chair on the porch. I'm embarrassed when I sit and clutch the sides of the chair. Why am I reacting this way? I've put my past behind me. That little girl in the photo isn't me, not anymore. Perhaps it's my mother's phone call on top of the uncertainty about my future, but the once-familiar feelings of hopelessness and desperation claw their way to my consciousness. They've been buried for so long that they burst forth in a frenzied panic and I fight to regain control.

To his credit, Reed doesn't ask questions, and he doesn't hover either. He stands on the other side of the porch, his hand on the railing as he watches the traffic. His dark brown hair blows in the breeze, and his cheeks pinken from the air that has turned colder in the short time we've been outside. As if he reads my train of thought, he slips off his jacket and moves toward me, placing it over my shoulders.

My mouth drops. "Reed, you don't—"

"I know you find this difficult to believe, but I am capable of being a gentleman."

"I…." but I stop." I don't have the energy to argue with him. "Reed, you don't have to give me your jacket. I'm fine."

"You're shivering, and I'm from Boston. I'm used to the cold. This is nothing."

I'm shivering but it's not entirely from the cold. This is the first time in three years I've come face to face with my past, and I'm not handling it well. I'm not as strong as I think I am. That alone is unnerving. I fall silent, surprised when Reed continues to stand next to me.

He clears his throat, keeping his eyes on the street. "Most people would ask you what's wrong or what happened to make you react this way, but you and I hardly know one another, and after some of our recent interactions, it seems presumptuous to ask." He shifts his weight. "When you're ready to join Lexi and Ms. Marshall, we'll go. Until then, I'll wait with you."

His voice is gentle, and I'm grateful he doesn't pry. I wondered how I would explain if he asked about my reaction, so now I'm off the hook. But for some reason, I'm worried about what he thinks. Why I'm worried what Reed Pendergraft thinks is beyond me.

After a minute of convincing myself that the past really is locked behind me, I stand, grateful I'm now steady on my feet. "I'm ready."

He nods and opens the front door. I stop in the doorway and look up into his face, prepared to thank him. But instead, my breath catches, and my heart begins to race. His eyes are a rich shade of dark chocolate. My gaze lowers to the curve of his jaw and then over to his mouth. I resist the urge to reach up and run my finger along his bottom lip, no matter how tempting it is. His dress shirt stretches across his broad shoulders and for a brief second I wonder what he looks like underneath his clothes. I'm lost in my daze, but somewhere in the back of my head, something tells me that touching him would be a bad idea. I just can't remember why.

His mouth parts as his breath shallows. I find myself leaning closer to him before I get a grip. Then I remember why caressing Reed Pendergraft's lips is a bad idea. He's an asshole.

This man makes me look like a fool for sport.

I take a step back. "Good try with the nice-guy routine."

Annoyance flickers in his eyes, and his jaw hardens. "Are you going to ogle me all day or can we rejoin the others?"

I walk past him into the hallway, grateful for the rush of anger that replaces the lust, despite the fact that my nerve endings are on fire. "*Ogle you?* Don't let your fantasies slip into reality, Reed."

"*Fantasies?* You think I'd fantasize about *you?*"

I refuse to physically react to his putdown even if it stings and reminds me of last Friday night. I try to get away, but he blocks my path, his eyes blazing.

My hormones kick into high gear, sending a fresh wave of lust through my blood, even stronger than before. "You shouldn't make it so obvious, Reed." I taunt him.

He moves closer, forcing me to step backward toward the wall, anger burning in his eyes.

"We both know you want me." My voice is husky and sounds foreign to my ears. I've never so wantonly tried to seduce a man before. Good southern girls aren't the seducers. They're the seducees.

"Don't flatter yourself, Caroline." But he moves closer, his voice lowering.

I'm not sure why I'm tormenting him this way. The truth is I'm tormenting myself just as much if not more. My back is pressed against the wall, a picture frame digging into my shoulder blade, but I stare up into his eyes, wanting him more than I've ever wanted anyone.

His hands are on the wall on either side of me, and he leans closer, his mouth inches from mine. He's agonizingly close, and I wonder if he's planning to tease me again like our near-kiss on the dance floor. But just when I'm sure he's about to pull away, he groans and his mouth captures mine. I wrap my arms around his neck and press my chest to his, opening my mouth to his demanding tongue. His hands reach around my back and pull me away from the wall, splaying across my shoulder blades, tugging me tighter to him. My knees weaken, but Reed holds me close as one of his hands moves up into my hair, tilting my head to give him better access.

Just as abruptly, his head rises, his eyes burning with raw desire. Then horror slides across his face, and he drops his hold.

Without his arms holding me up, I'm not sure my legs can support me. I step back into the wall while I catch my breath and try to figure out what the hell happened.

I have never lost control like this, not even with my ex-boyfriend Justin. And I dated him for over two years.

"That was … wrong." Reed finally says. Thankfully, he looks as shell-shocked as I feel.

"Yes, very wrong." It's wrong to detest someone so much yet want to do him right here in a public hallway.

"We can't let this happen again." But he looks like he's trying to convince himself more than me.

"No. We can't … do that again." But mostly because I don't trust myself with him. Obviously this man not only makes me lose my temper, but also makes me want to lose my panties. "We need to find Lexi."

Hearing his sister's name changes his entire demeanor. His lust evaporates and anxiety and irritation replace it. "Yes, we *do* need to find Lexi. I've wasted too much time as it is."

There's the man I've learned to loathe. "Did you seriously call what we just did 'wasting time?'"

He straightens his tie. "Clearly nothing productive came of it, thus it could be considered a waste of time."

It takes every ounce of strength within me not to kick him. "Don't worry, *Mr. Pendergraft.* I won't be wasting your time again."

His stern expression wavers. "Good."

I stomp down the hall to the back door, my heels clacking so hard against the wood floor I'm surprised I don't dent the floorboards.

Reed follows behind me and reaches around to push the door open. I bat his arm away. "A little late to be playing the gentleman now, isn't it?" When I stomp down the steps and look around, trying to determine where we're going, I noticed Reed's cheeks blush.

Reed Pendergraft blushing?

He looks sheepish as he glances down. "I'm sorry. That was ... unlike me. I assure you that I don't normally attack random women like that." He clears his throat, his face now red.

I'd give him kudos for forging ahead if I weren't so furious.

A scowl darkens his face. "I'm not sure what came over me. I won't it happen again."

I should confess that I'm not sure what happened with me either, and I'd be lying if I said his announcement didn't fill me with disappointment. But instead, I grasp onto one of his phrases, because anger is safer than the wanton lust flowing through my veins. "Random women? You're calling me a *random woman?*"

Confusion fills his eyes before he realizes what I'm talking about. "It's not how it sounds."

And while I know that, I don't really care. I need to vent these strong emotions somehow, and if I can't make out with him, I'll verbally attack him instead. "How many women are you in the habit of kissing anyway?"

"Not many. I'm usually more selective." His anger returns. His hands fist at his sides.

"Was that a slam against my character?"

He takes a step toward me, and we're less than a foot apart. "Should it be?"

Reed looks like he's about to kiss me again, and to my shock, or maybe not, I want him to.

But I can't forget that he made a fool of me before. Who's to say he won't do it again? I take two steps back and swivel my head around, trying to figure out where Lexi and Evelyn went. I need a chaperone, and I need one quick before I do something I'll regret. "Where are we supposed to go?"

I expect a sharp retort, but the fight seems to have left Reed as well. "We need to go to the building on the left." He waves his hand toward a house. "It houses the afterschool program."

As I walk the concrete walkway behind the houses, I try to pull myself together. My reaction to Reed is a combination of hormones and seeing the photo of myself. I'm emotionally vulnerable. All the more reason to stay away from him.

When we reach the door, Reed lightly touches my arm. "Caroline, wait."

I shiver from the cold, but Reed blocks the wind. The heat of his body draws me toward him, and I can't resist looking up.

He lifts his hand toward my face and as he leans closer, I'm mesmerized by his dark brown eyes. I wait for him to kiss me, but his fingers brush my hair on the back of my head. "Your hair was messed up," he murmurs, his lips a mere six inches from mine. His fingers tangle in the strands, and he slowly rakes them down, taking longer than necessary, yet I can't seem to find the will to stop him.

"Thanks," I finally say.

His gaze has fallen to my lips. He leans closer, but the door opens, and he jumps back as though he's been caught doing something he shouldn't be doing.

Which of course he has.

Evelyn's back is to us as she faces into the building. When she turns around, she's missed our strange behavior.

"Oh, there you two are. I was about to send a search party out for you," she laughs.

Reed gives her his stick-up-his-ass smile, not that she notices. "No need. We spent a lot of time checking out the photos."

"Well, come in." She pokes her head outside to look up into the sky, then backs out of the way for us to come in. "I do believe it's getting colder."

Reed studies me. "Funny, I hadn't noticed." Then he motions for me to go in.

That's the first time he's actually acknowledged that I do something to him, even if his body—and his mouth—has told me otherwise.

I follow Evelyn into a 1970s-era kitchen, gold appliances and all. She stands in the middle of the room and holds out her hands. "Since our headquarters are here in Greensboro, we have on-site services. We have the children dropped off by bus for our afterschool tutoring program. In other areas where we have a tutoring program, we usually run the program on the school property. With the Monroe Foundation donation, we're hoping to open more programs, especially in more rural areas where state funding is stretched to the limit." She looks over her shoulder as a young woman comes in and grabs several small paper cups and a pitcher of juice from the refrigerator. "We also provide snacks. They're usually starving after school."

We follow her down a hall to a room with a table and several children that look to be ten or eleven years old. They're huddled over papers and notebooks. A college-aged woman sits at the table with them. She looks up and smiles.

Evelyn stands in the doorway. "We're fortunate that Southern's school of education sends students to help with our kids."

Evelyn continues down a hall to what looks like it used to be a large bedroom. A teacher kneels down on the floor talking to a small child. There are about ten other children in the room, some sitting at tables working on homework. Others play with board games or work on puzzles. "This is the room for our first- and second-graders." I walk into the space, suddenly transported back fifteen years, to a particularly rough financial time when my father was laid off for twelve months. That year my older brother and I went to a program exactly like this.

My stomach knots at the memories. "You have one of these programs in Shelbyville."

Evelyn beams. "Yes, they were one of our pilot sites."

That's how they have a photo of me.

Thankfully, I don't react like I did with the photo.

A little blonde girl slams her pencil on the table and drops her head over her paper. I kneel next to her and to see what's frustrating her. She's working on subtraction problems, and she's gotten several wrong. Her name is written carefully at the top of the paper—Desiree.

"Subtraction's hard, huh?" I tilt my head to get a better look at her, but her hair falls around her face.

Her head bobs, but she keeps her gaze down.

"My name's Caroline. Can I have a look?"

Her fingers splay across the sheet and she slowly slides it toward me.

"Do you use a number line?"

"I forgot it at school." Her voice is muffled.

"We can make you a new one."

I look up the teacher in the room. "Do you have a scrap piece of paper I can use?"

She gets up from the table. "Sure."

Reed fills the doorway, his face expressionless as he watches me. Evelyn stands inside the room and looks like she's ready to move to the next room.

"You go ahead," I say. Lexi is the integral part of this meeting. I'm just a tagalong. "I'm going to stay here with Desiree for a little bit if that's okay."

Evelyn smiles. "Yes, of course, dear. I love that you've made a connection with the children." Reed takes a step into the hall to let Evelyn out, but he hesitates in the doorway and looks torn about leaving me behind before walking down the hall. While the hormonal part of me is disappointed to see him go, the rational part of me is glad.

The tutor hands me a piece of paper. "Thanks for helping out. The program has gotten more kids this semester and we're having trouble helping all the children."

"Glad to help."

The tutor turns her attention to the boy next to her.

Desiree is still hiding behind her hair so I start to make a number line, making twenty tick marks.

"I wasn't very good at subtraction, either," I say as I start to number.

The little girl stays silent, but her face has lifted more so I can see her cornflower blue eyes.

"Do you know what's funny?"

She shakes her head, her eyes wary.

"I do all kinds of subtraction now, and I like it."

"You do?"

"Yep." I give her a big smile. "Did you know I go to school too?"

She shakes her head.

"I go to college. Guess what I'm going to be when I graduate?"

The girl sucks one side of her lower lip into her mouth before she says, "A teacher."

I shake my head. "Uh-uh. I bet you'll never guess."

"A doctor." Her voice is bolder, and she's looking directly at me now.

"Nope. A fashion designer. Do you know what that is?"

She shakes her head, looking embarrassed.

I lean closer as though I'm about to share a secret. "Well, a fashion designer makes clothes for people to wear, but it's so much more than that. They decide the fabric and color of the clothes, and how it should be cut out of the cloth. They can help people feel good about themselves by making them something beautiful to wear."

She's still silent, but she's listening intently.

I write the last numbers on the line and place it in front of her. "But measurements are important. You have to make the clothes fit the person's body or it doesn't look right. Moving a seam just a tiny bit can make the difference in a person looking just okay or beautiful."

Her eyes widen. "It's like magic."

I smile. "It sounds like it, doesn't it? But it's really math. Knowing how to add up the measurements and subtract them is the trick of it. And it all starts here." I tap on the paper with her subtraction problems.

We work on the problems for several minutes, using the number line and Desiree is more confident when we finish. "I get it now." She offers me a shy smile.

"Good. It just takes lots of practice. And do you know what?"

She shakes her head, her gaze on me.

"Maybe you'll like math so much you'll study it in college like my friend Scarlett." I look up at the doorway. Reed is standing on the threshold watching me with an unreadable face. I have no idea how long he's been there. "And my friend Reed."

His eyebrows lift in surprise.

Scarlett would choke if she could hear me right now. I've done nothing but tease her about her math-geek status and here I am suggesting this little girl consider it for a major. "Math is really important. You use it for everything, and it's pretty easy once you get the hang of it."

"But you make people beautiful." Desiree says. "I wish you could make me beautiful."

A lump forms in my throat and I try to swallow it to answer. "Oh, Desiree. You're already beautiful." But I know what she's saying. I was her years ago. I see her faded and worn jeans. Her stained T-shirt that's been worn many times.

"Why do you want to be a fashion maker?"

"A fashion designer?" I could give her my pat answer, the one Reed made fun of, and she'd never know the difference. This little girl was me. She deserves the truth, but Reed is standing in the doorway listening to everything I say.

I brush her hair from her face and wipe a smudge off her cheek with my thumb. "Once upon a time, there was a little girl who didn't fit in with all the other kids. She felt ugly while all the other girls were pretty and wore pretty things."

"Did the little girl get pretty dresses too?"

*No, the little girl didn't*, but I can't tell Desiree that. She's waiting for me to give her a fairytale ending, but there isn't one. The little girl didn't find a prince. She didn't become a swan. She went off to college with the hope of scoring a rich boyfriend/husband and ended up alone. The major she picked was mostly because it was what she already knew. Already loved. And now she was scrambling to figure out what to do with it. I can't tell Desiree any of this, but I can empower her. "She learned to make them herself."

Her eyebrows scrunch together as she thinks about what I said. "Like she's her own fairy godmother?"

"Yes, exactly." I take a breath. "The pretty girls in my story, they may have worn pretty clothes and had pretty hair, but they weren't pretty on the inside, Desiree." I tilt my head down to look in her eyes. "They're pretty packages with nothing but fluff and jealousy inside. There will always be people who tell you that your clothes are ugly or that your car is old and rusted. That your house needs to be painted or your shoes have holes, but those people will never be your friend. Not even if you get all the pretty things they have. Real friends don't care about any of that and they love you for *you*."

She looks unconvinced. "But I still wish I had a pretty dress and looked like a princess."

"Of course you do. All girls do." I laugh. "Do you know what? If you try really hard with your math homework for the next week, *I'll* make you a pretty dress."

Her eyes widen. "You mean it?"

I smile. "Yes."

The other girls at the table have remained quiet but now burst into shouts.

"I want one!"

"Me too!"

What have I started?

Even as their excited voices shout in my ears, I realize this is the answer to my problem. I can create a children's line and maybe I can use actual children in the center as my models. It's the perfect blending of the event and the cause.

Reed moves next to me. "Caroline, a word, please." It's a demand, not a question.

I stand and turn to face him, already knowing his concern. "Reed, I know you think it's a lot to promise to make them all—"

He grabs my arm and pulls me into the hall. "You can't toy with these children's hopes."

"But if I can use them as models in the show then—"

His eyes fly open. "*You can't use them as models for the show!*"

Anger tempers my excitement. "Why in the world not?"

"Haven't you heard of confidentiality? Do you really want these children to be paraded on stage? It would be like them wearing signs that say *I'm a charity case.*"

While I understand his concern, I'm not fond of the derision he uses. "And are you saying these children aren't worthy of being in the show because of who they are and where they come from?"

"Of course not!" But his tone reeks of backpedaling instead of conviction.

"Did it ever occur to you that these little girls might feel better about themselves if they were models on a runway? That for one day, they'll feel pretty and special. They'll be the envy of the mean kids in their class instead of the other way around?"

"Well, no…."

"We don't have to announce that they receive help from the organization. No one has to know. They could be children from the rich side of town."

"I never thought…."

"No." I swallow my disappointment. One hot kiss and some lustful looks, and for some reason, I forgot he was the arrogant ass who thinks the worst of me. "It's obvious you didn't." I walk around him. "Now if you'll excuse me."

I've left five little girls in the room who want me to make them pretty clothes. Now I need to see what I have to do to make that happen.

# Chapter
# Ten

Evelyn is delighted by my plan, but Lexi is even more so.

When we leave the office and head out to the car, Lexi loops her arm around mine. "I knew bringing you would be a good idea! I hoped it would spur your creativity, seeing firsthand the organization you were helping raise money for. I just never imagined it would be so literal."

Reed is waiting outside, his backside to the car as he watches the street. He's wearing a scowl, as usual, but damned if he doesn't look good wearing that too. I stuff my wanton feelings down. What the hell is wrong with me? Lusting after a jerk. I've never been one of *those* girls, and I don't intend to start.

"Well, nothing's for sure yet." I need to focus on my project now that I have inspiration. "Evelyn has to get the parents' permission."

"But that was a fantastic idea for you to use the children as models for the other designers too."

I shrug. "They need child models, so I figure why not?"

"Have you got a style or color to tie your collection together?"

"Not really. I want to sit down with my sketchbook and play around with some ideas first."

As we approach the car, Reed opens the passenger door and stands next to it. I have no intention of sitting in front next to Reed, but Lexi sneaks around to the driver's side and climbs in the back. Reed's eyes flash with alarm, and I'm not sure if I should be happy he's as freaked out as I am by the idea of sitting next to me. But to protest and sit in the back would not only be rude, it would look like I can't handle sitting next to him. I have no intention of letting him know he's gotten under my skin.

I give him a tight smile. "Why, thank you, Reed. You really can be a gentleman when you want to." I slide into the seat and he shuts the door without a retort.

We drive back to campus in tense silence. Reed keeps both hands on the wheel. I don't know whether it's because he feels the need to strangle something or whether he's trying to keep from touching me. Or both. Neither is good.

"Reed." Lexi's voice interrupts my thoughts. "I need you to drop me off at the bank."

His head jerks up. "The bank is a good ten minutes from where we are now. The opposite direction from the campus."

She leans forward, her hand resting on the seat next to his shoulder. "I forgot to mention I had an appointment with one of the investment bankers at five-thirty."

"It's five-fifteen now. There's no time to take Caroline back and drop you off at the bank."

"Then drop me off and take Caroline back to campus."

Reed hesitates.

"For heaven's sake, Reed." She groans. "I know you don't have any more classes today. What's the big deal?"

"Reschedule your appointment."

"I can't. It's for a class project and I have to bring my notes to class tomorrow."

I suspect she's lying. For all her cheeriness and fluff, Lexi doesn't seem the flighty type, especially after seeing her in action today. If she really had a meeting, she would have already made prior arrangements for me to get back to campus.

She's either lying about her appointment or she's purposely set it up for Reed and I to be alone.

Lexi's matchmaking, and I don't like it one bit.

And neither does Reed. He shoots an anxious look in my direction then up to the mirror to look at her. "Lexi, you live by your Google calendar. You're telling me that you just now remembered your appointment?"

She shrugs with a smug grin. "What can I say? Everyone makes mistakes sometimes. Even *you*, big brother."

I can see Reed wants to call her on it. *I* want him to call her on it. But he grumbles under his breath and turns at the next intersection—away from campus.

"Wait." I say before I come up with a reason why this won't work. I could say I have a class but both Reed and Lexi have a copy of my schedule. We all shared them the day of our first meeting.

Reed turns to me and lifts an eyebrow.

I sink back into the seat and release a heavy sigh. I'm being ridiculous. We're adults here, albeit, barely. I can sit in a car with him for twenty-five minutes, fifteen of them alone with him. I'm mature, mostly. I can do this. "Never mind."

Lexi sits back in her seat and begins to talk about the nonprofit and ideas that came to her for future fundraising.

I look over the back seat to glance at her. "You really love this, don't you?"

"Yes. I feel like I'm actually accomplishing something other than…." Her voice trails off as her eyebrows knit.

"Other than what?" I prompt.

"Other than going to classes. Do you ever feel like you've spent your whole life in school and you're dying to get out?"

Right now, school is the only security I feel. The big bad world scares the hell out of me, but I'm not going to tell her that. Not in front of Reed. "Yeah, sometimes I do."

"So when I get to do something like this fundraiser, I feel like I'm making a difference. I'm helping someone."

I can't think of the last time I felt like I made a significant difference in anything. Perhaps I'll find it helping the kids at the tutoring center. Still, I'm not naive enough to think one pretty dress and an afternoon on a runway are going to change these kids' lives, but at least it's something.

"So you've helped with other fundraisers before?" I ask.

"Tons."

"How did you find so many opportunities? You're only a sophomore in college."

Her smile falters.

"We grew up in Boston." Reed interjects. "All you have to do is toss a rock across the street and you'll hit a nonprofit. Lexi was part of a high school club that worked with charities."

"Huh." I'm trying to decide if my brother knew anything about my high school activities, let alone hang out with me. I haven't seen him since the summer I left. Last I heard, he took off for L.A. with his rock band.

"So you haven't done charity work before?" Lexi asks.

"No." I'm fairly certain receiving charity isn't the same thing. "Where did you go to high school?"

They both remain strangely quiet until Reed answers. "We went to a small Catholic school."

Why is Reed answering such simple questions for his sister?

"So you're Catholic?"

His eyebrows twitch. "Do you have anything against Catholics?"

"Well, no…."

I clamp my mouth shut. This conversation has derailed, and I don't see the point of trying to fix it.

Reed pulls into a parking lot of a three-story building and parks at the curb. "What time is your appointment over, Lexi?"

"This is a meeting, not a therapy session. There isn't a predetermined end time."

A therapy appointment is an odd comparison.

He grunts in frustration. "An hour?"

She grins. "An hour should be sufficient." She opens the car door. "Why don't you two go get something to eat while you wait for me?" Then she jumps out and runs into the office building.

"I think we've been set up," I say as I watch her disappear behind the revolving door.

"Yeah." Reed sounds as thrilled as I feel.

"No offense, but I don't have time to hang out with you for an hour." Not that part of me doesn't want to. Maybe I should just give in to temptation and get him out of my system. Isn't that what Tina does? Has her fun with a guy and moves on. But Reed doesn't seem like fling material, and I'm not that kind of girl. Not to mention we still have three weeks to work together. No, giving into temptation is the worst of worst ideas.

His shoulders tense.

As he drives to the parking lot exit, and I realize how rude my statement sounded. I sigh and rub my forehead. "Reed, we have to work together for several more weeks, and we both know that something happened between us." *Something happened between us.* Talk about the understatement of the century.

Thankfully Reed doesn't call me on it. He doesn't say anything, just hangs onto the steering wheel for dear life.

"We can ignore that something happened and fight this … feeling we experienced." I can't bring myself to say attraction. "Or we can address it and meet it headlong."

Reed smirks. "And how do you plan to face it headlong? You're not proposing we get it out of our system, are you?"

I'm tempted. Lordy, I'm tempted. "Don't be ridiculous. Of course, not. It's been awhile since I've had a boyfriend—"

"You could have fooled me with your date last week."

"That was one date, and we both know how well that went. And besides, when you asked me out, you said you hadn't met many people yet. Wasn't that your reasoning for asking me out?"

"Caroline." He sighs. "Sometimes I'm socially inept."

"You think?" I try to keep a straight face, but I can't help laughing. "The high and mighty Reed Pendergraft admitting he's imperfect. I do believe that's the eighth wonder of the world." I tap my chin with a finger. "Or is it a sign of the apocalypse?"

To my surprise, he actually laughs. "Are you calling me the Antichrist?"

I laugh again. "I wouldn't go that far."

"Then maybe you could have a chat with some of my Algebra 101 students and convince them otherwise." He laughs. "But then again, maybe it's better if they have the fear of God in them."

"Or in this case, I think you mean fear of Satan."

"True enough." A dazzling smile spreads across his face, and I realize this is the first time I've seen him actually smile. Sure, I've seen smirks and sarcastic grins and plenty of derisive looks, but Reed actually looks happy.

Could it be that he's so cross all the time because he's unhappy?

Is it my business if he is?

But now that the seed has been planted in my head, it takes root like a fast-growing weed. I like this side of him, even if it's only a glimpse. But seeing a side of Reed that I like to go with the hot chemistry we share is dangerous territory. "We've gotten off point."

"Have we?" he asks, trying to look innocent.

"It's obvious that there's something between us, but the truth is we have nothing in common."

"Don't you mean I don't have a big enough paycheck?" His cold tone is back. Damn my mouth.

"I was out of line to say that at Scarlett's party. I didn't mean it." I lean toward him and the musky scent of his cologne fills my nose. I fight the urge to move closer. "You had just suggested that we go out because you were desperate. I was hot and cranky. Not a good combination for me. Throw in hungry and you have the trifecta of bitchiness. I'm not proud of it, and I'm truly sorry I said it."

He's silent for several seconds. "Apology accepted. I have to admit, it was probably the worst pickup line in history."

I laugh. "I suggest you mark it out of your playbook."

He waves his hand in the air. "Consider it gone."

"I hope we can get along for the rest of our time working together. You're kind of fun when you take the stick out of your ass."

"Do you realize your accent is thicker when you curse like that?" His grin broadens.

"What's that supposed to mean?"

"I like your drawl."

"You could have fooled me. I think your observation of my accent the night of Scarlett's party was neutral, with a hint of insult."

"Let's just say you weren't the only cranky one that night."

"Why were you cranky?"

"Do you really think that's any of your business?" His words are confrontational but he looks amused.

"I told you my reasoning."

"Yeah, you were hot. Hot for Dylan."

"You're not being fair. I'd wanted to go out with Dylan for months. I'd only met you and you practically compared going out with me to folding your laundry."

His usual seriousness returns, but he's not confrontational. "There's more to the Dylans of the world, Caroline. Be careful."

I should be insulted over his lecture, but he sounds genuinely concerned. "I'm not a virginal maiden, Reed. I've had my share of worldly experience."

"But not with guys like him."

"And what exactly do you mean by guys like him?"

"Looks, money, charisma."

"You make it sound like a bad thing."

"Caroline, I'm serious." And he is. A part of me hopes that it's jealousy rearing its ugly head, but I can see that's not it. Worry lines crinkle his forehead. "How many guys have you dated that came from old money like Dylan?"

My eyes narrow. "How do you know Dylan comes from old money?"

"How do you?" His condescending tone has returned.

I lift my chin. "It's common knowledge on Southern's campus."

"Not *everything* about people is common knowledge." We're both quiet and then Reed grins. "Case in point: if the fact that heat makes you irritable had been common knowledge, I never would have risked asking you out."

"True enough."

Reed pulls into the student parking lot. "Tell me where your car is, and I'll drop you off."

There's no way in hell I'm letting Reed see my clunker car even if his isn't that much better than mine. "Thanks, but I'm inspired to start working on my designs for the show. I think I'll head over to the design lab for awhile."

He pulls up next to the curb, Andrew Jackson's granite likeness watching over us. "What I said before." He pauses and runs his hand over his head. "I'm sorry. I didn't mean it."

I lift an eyebrow. "Which part?"

"I … uh…." he stutters. "Insulting you."

"That narrows it down to about twenty incidents."

He cringes.

"Don't worry. I'm teasing. I've realized that you have a way of insulting people without even trying."

He looks guilty, and his mouth opens to say something then closes.

"It's a gift. You should be proud." I look into his eyes with mock seriousness. "But wield your power carefully."

An ornery glint fills his eyes. "I'll keep that in mind."

He turns toward me and his playfulness slides off. His eyes darken as he inches closer.

I'm pulled toward him.

His mouth parts, and my gaze is drawn to it, thinking about our kiss earlier. I suddenly want to lick his bottom lip. I want to take off his shirt and see what's underneath. He hinted he didn't have abs like Dylan, but I doubt he's flabby either, despite the loose dress shirts he wears. Perhaps it's the way his pants hang from his hips.

I want to go out with him and do so, so much more than I ever let myself do on a first date. Or my first five dates.

But Reed and I together are a bad combination, the money issue aside. We're like fire and ice. Sure, that's fun now, but soon enough the newness wears off and if you're lucky, all you're left with are heated arguments and an empty, loveless marriage. If you're not lucky, the police and domestic disturbance charges are involved. No, Reed Pendergraft is off limits. I need to remember that.

The playfulness has left his face, and his eyes are on my lips again.

*Just one taste....*

No. "What happened today was a mistake." I blurt out.

Confusion scrunches his face before he realizes I mean our kiss.

"Reed, I'm actually beginning to like you. And we have to work together on the show. Can you imagine how tense it would be if we went out and it went horribly wrong? We think it's bad now. You know, hell hath no fury like a woman scorned, and all of that." But it's his reaction I'm most worried about.

He hesitates, still looking in my eyes, as though he's searching for something. Finally, he turns to face the windshield. "Yes, you're right. We're incompatible."

I'd expected him to protest or try to convince me otherwise. He wasn't supposed to *agree* with me. "Yes, we would be a disaster."

Before I change my mind and attack him, I open the door and scramble out of the car, eager to get some distance between us.

I walk across the campus, fighting the cold wind, and I'm certain of one thing: Reed and I are the biggest liars in the world.

# Chapter Eleven

I'm standing in front of the bathroom mirror, jostling for space with Tina. It's times like this I miss Scarlett even more than ever. She rarely spent time in front of the mirror. The space was usually all mine.

"Who are you going out with?" Tina asks, swiping mascara on her lashes.

"Brandon McKenzie."

"Don't know him." She shrugs.

"And who's your date?" I'm not sure why I'm asking. The odds are five-to-one that she'll never go out with him again.

She gives me a mischievous grin then fluffs her short brunette hair. "This one's different than my usual dates. I'm going out with a grad student."

A ball forms in the pit of my stomach. "Oh, really?" I try to sound casual. Surely, I'm wrong. Tina never dates guys from the math department. She says they're all geeks.

"I even broke one of my rules for him." She pulls the hem of her shirt down, exposing more cleavage. "He's a new grad student who moved here from out East. And he is *hot*."

I'm so disgusted that I can't bring myself to ask her who her date is. I know. I'm not disgusted with Tina. Good for her for bagging a grad student. I'm disgusted with the high and mighty Reed and his lectures about who I'm going out with when he stoops to going out with Tina.

Tina and I have a tenuous relationship at best. Granted, she has tough shoes to fill. Scarlett and I are best friends, and Tina has no illusions of getting that close to me, not that she wants to. She has her own friends who she parties with every weekend and occasionally on weeknights. But lately, her behavior has gotten wilder and more out of control. I'm surprised she hasn't flunked any classes yet, but midterms are approaching.

She puts her hand on her hip and juts it out, her eyebrows raised. She's waiting for me to say something.

"That's awesome."

She misses my sarcasm. "I know, right?" She bumps into me as she leaves the bathroom.

I stand in front of the mirror, staring at my reflection. I look good, but I know I'm pretty. I'm naturally blonde. I have blue eyes and high cheekbones. My looks garnered me lots of attention back in high school, especially after several jealous popular girls spread rumors that I was a slut. But it's different now. No one knows my past, and I'm careful to wait a minimum of five dates before I have sex. My reputation is important if I want to marry a boy from a good family. I'm careful to preserve it.

After my past experiences, I always get nervous before a new date, worried the guy will turn out like half my dates in high school, and Dylan last week. Or now that I think about it, like most of my dates over the last few months. Do guys think because I'm a senior now that I'll just hop into bed with them? But my nervousness has never stopped my excitement before a date, the ball of nerves that twines in my stomach. So why am I not excited now? Brandon's cute. He's witty. I don't know if he has money, but I don't care.

Because if I'm honest, I want Reed to go out with me, not Tina.

*Oh, Caroline. You had your chance. Besides, it would never work out.*

The doorbells rings, shaking me out of my musings. I hope it's Brandon, but only because I can't handle seeing Reed right now. But then again, when can I handle seeing Reed?

It's my lucky night. Brandon walks into the living room wearing a dark suit and black tie. His dark hair is styled and he looks good. Very good. His eyes scan my body, but not in a leering way like Dylan. I'm not surprised he's looking. When he told me we were going to St. Thomas Grill, I pulled out my black cocktail dress. The spaghetti straps show off my shoulders and the dip in the front shows cleavage without making me look like a slut. The skirt is flouncy with Georgette ruffles—enough to add a bit of whimsy but not enough to make me look hippy. I'm wearing strappy black heels that show off my red polished toes. I hold my black velvet wrap in one hand and my vintage beaded purse in the other.

Brandon shakes his head in wonder. "Caroline, you look beautiful."

I smile. "You look quite nice yourself." Maybe this night's going to work out after all.

Brandon watches me in silence for a moment before he startles and reaches to take my wrap from me. "Here, let me help you with that."

Tina stands next to the open door, and the smirk on her face tells me she's about to make some smartass remark. The guys she goes out with usually don't even open the door.

And then Reed shows up.

And damned if he isn't drop-dead gorgeous.

He's wearing a pair of jeans and fitted T-shirt with a leather jacket. His shirt clings to his chest and stomach and it's obvious that Reed Pendergraft doesn't have an ounce of flab on him.

I realize I'm gawking at him, but he's staring at me too and it's not the look of a merely curious man.

Tina hangs on the door, her head swiveling from one of us to the other. "Do you two know each other?" She flicks her wrist, pointing at me, then Reed.

"I was about to ask the same thing," Brandon says, draping the wrap around my shoulders, then pressing his arm around my back. Brandon has staked his claim. Thank God human males have evolved past peeing to mark their territory.

"I ... uh...." I stutter.

Tina's eyes narrow at me. "How do you know a grad student in the math department?"

"Scarlett's party," Reed says.

"Yeah, okay." But she doesn't seem convinced. "I didn't realize you came to the party, Reed."

Reed's eyes are still on me. "I wasn't there long."

No, I made sure to run him off. What the hell was I thinking?

"And now we're on the fashion show committee together," I add.

"You're on the fashion show committee?" Brandon asks. His hand rests on the bare skin at the bottom of the wrap. He's invading my personal space. I find it suffocating and wrong with Reed this close. But to shake Brandon off at this moment is a very bad idea.

Reed's eyes take on his trademark Death Star laser-glare. To his credit, Brandon doesn't back down.

"I was appointed by the chancellor as the committee chair."

"But you're a mathematics grad student."

Tina leaves her door-guarding post and walks past us, patting Brandon on the cheek, "Don't think too hard about it, dollface. You might hurt something."

Brandon frowns but ignores her.

I have to get out of here. Twisting around, I look up at Brandon. "Shouldn't we be going?"

"Yes." And he takes a step forward, yet Reed remains on the threshold.

"Where are you two headed?"

I start to answer, but Brandon jumps in. "I'm not sure that's your concern."

Reed's eyes rest on my face. I'm not sure what he wants from me, but I know I need to get out of this room before I do something I'll regret. Like throw myself at him. And the way Reed's looking at me, I don't think he'll stop me.

"Reed." My voice is soft and pleading. "Please."

He swallows then steps backward out onto the walkway outside our apartment.

Brandon keeps his arm around me until we get downstairs and he opens the passenger door to his BMW.

Brandon McKenzie has money.

This should make me happy, but the only thing I can think about is Reed and how good he looked, and the raw hunger in his eyes. I should be embarrassed. It's obvious Brandon and Tina saw it too, but I'm not. I'm incredibly turned on.

Reed Pendergraft wants me.

"Earth to Caroline." Brandon interrupts my thoughts. He's already left the parking lot and we're driving down the road. I've zoned out for several seconds.

I turn toward him and try to smile. "I'm sorry. Did you ask me something?"

"I asked if you and Reed have dated."

"What?" I shake my head. You can't call making out in the hallway of a nonprofit dating. "No. We haven't. Besides he just moved here from the East Coast."

"And you know this, how?"

"He told me when we were introduced at my best friend's party." I know how bad this looks and I need to try to salvage the evening. "He came to Scarlett's party, but he was rude, and I was rude back, and it's all so stupid now. But since we're on the committee together, we've set up unspoken rules to get along. Especially after our shaky first meeting."

Brandon remains unconvinced.

"In fact, I quit because of Reed. He's the most infuriating ass—" The phrase *the lady doth protest too much* floats into my head. "We don't get along, let's leave it at that."

Brandon turns to face me. "You quit."

I shrug. "For about five minutes. Until someone on the committee reminded me how great being a committee member would look on my resume. So I stayed, somewhat against my better judgment."

"How can being on the committee help your resume?"

"Every fall, a designer from New York comes to the show and chooses a student to work in her house for a minimum of three months. The designer is a friend of my advisor so the design students on the committee have a better shot at winning a job at a fashion house in New York. I stayed on because I decided I wasn't about to let a rude person keep me from reaching for my dreams."

Part of me is frustrated that I have to explain myself, but I know what he's asking. *Did I stay because of Reed?* At *that* moment, I can honestly say I didn't, but I can't say the same thing now. Still, Brandon is nice and courteous, unlike Reed, even after dealing with Reed and my reaction to him in the apartment, which is embarrassing when I stop and let myself think about it. No, Brandon is a seemingly nice guy who is still interested despite our rocky start. I need to give this my full attention.

"So that's your big goal after graduation? To move to New York?"

"Honestly? I don't know. This year kind of snuck up on me and now I'm scrambling to put a life plan together." The whole situation is depressing. I don't really want to move to New York City alone, but I need some goal, some challenge. It seems like a big one to shoot for. "Enough about me. I want to hear about you. What's your major?"

He shoots me a grin. "Pre-med."

I sit up straighter. "Wow. That must be a tough course load. You're a senior, right?"

He nods.

"So when do you find out that you got into med school?"

"My application to Vanderbilt isn't due until the end of the month. I'm applying to a few other places as well, but in my case, it's a given I'll get into Vandy. My father is a renowned cardiothoracic surgeon and went to med school there. With his pull, I'll get in."

"Doesn't that bother you? That you pulled strings to get in?"

He shrugs. "Not really. That's how life works."

I study him to see if it's false bravado, but his opinion seems genuine. I can't imagine living that way, but then again, I've scraped for everything worth having in my life. No one's pulled strings for me.

But it occurs to me that Brandon comes from a family that's well off, and he's on a career path to potentially earn a lot of money. I've spent the last year looking for the man next to me, and I'm still stuck on Reed.

*Forget about Reed.*

When we get to the restaurant, Brandon is a perfect gentleman, opening doors, walking on the outside of the sidewalk next to the parking lot.

"You went to cotillion," I say as he opens the door to the restaurant.

He grins, amused. "What gives me away?"

"Your impeccable manners, for starters."

He winks. "And you haven't even seen my foxtrot yet."

I can't help laughing. He really is amusing.

When I was in the seventh grade, I went to my one and only cotillion and thought I'd entered a fairytale land. The boys wore suits and the girls wore pretty dresses. Mine was borrowed, of course. A friend of mine took me along and loaned me her dress. And for two hours I had a taste of what it was like to live somewhere other than in the Land of Nothing. But those two hours were all it took to show me the goal to which I needed to aspire.

Of course, when my mother found out where I'd been, she was furious. "We ain't those highfalutin' people, Carol Ann. The sooner you wise up, the happier you'll be."

Part of me still desperately wants to prove her wrong.

Brandon's made reservations and the hostess seats us when he gives his name. The restaurant is dimly lit and tealight candles flicker in glass centerpieces.

He orders a bottle of wine. The sommelier opens the bottle and lets Brandon smell the cork before the he pours the wine into our glasses. I'm in awe. I've only seen this done on TV or the movies. My old boyfriend was lucky to be able to afford Red Lobster, not that I complained. We're in college. My end game has always been life after graduation.

Brandon charms me all through dinner and after we order desert, I clasp my hands and rest them on the table. "How is it that you're not with your girlfriend anymore?"

He grimaces. "She found someone else."

I try to contain my surprise. Brandon seems perfect, but now I wonder what hidden flaw sent his girlfriend running off with someone else.

"She found a girlfriend."

"Ouch." But this news makes me feel better about him. Contrary to what some idiots think, there's no way he drove her to it. It means he might be perfect after all, even though I know there's no such thing.

"So what specialty do you want to study?" I ask, licking chocolate mousse off my spoon.

He's watching my mouth, and I can't help comparing my reaction to him with my reaction to Reed. If Reed were watching me lick this spoon, my panties would most likely evaporate. But while I like Brandon watching me, it's more in terms of victory. He's interested. Score one for me.

So what the hell is wrong with me? Brandon is everything I'm looking for, but I've spent most of this dinner fantasizing about Reed standing in the doorway of my apartment.

*Picking up Tina*, I remind myself. He stood in the doorway of my apartment picking up Tina. Not me.

Why am I focusing on a destined-to-be-middle-class college professor?

Brandon leans forward with a serious expression. "I've failed you."

My breath sticks in my chest. Has he read my mind? Did I say what I was thinking out loud? "How so?" I force out.

"We've spent the last hour without once discussing your project." He reaches into his suit coat pocket, pulls out a folded piece of paper and sets it on the table. "Now keep in mind, I didn't know what kind of look you were going for, so this is just a first attempt."

He unfolds the white paper and spreads it open. He's drawn stick people with triangle dresses and rectangle pants. "I thought maybe you could go with a geometric theme." He points to one figure wearing a triangle on top of his head. "I even added an accessory here."

I cover my mouth to contain my giggles. "Is that a hat?"

His eyes widen. "Are you serious? You have to ask?"

I try to look serious, but fail miserably. "I'm sorry. What was I thinking?"

He shrugs with a teasing smile. "It was my first attempt. I'm open to revisions."

This is the sweetest thing that any guy has ever done for me. I cover his hand with my own. "I absolutely love your designs. Thank you."

The look in his eyes tells me that if he were closer he'd kiss me.

"Let's get out of here." His voice is husky as he waves down our waitress.

I'm torn. I really like this guy but Reed has screwed with my head and my hormones. I really, really want to feel something with Brandon. I just need to give him a chance. "Okay."

After he pays, he helps me out of my chair and presses his hand to the small of my back, steering me toward the door.

"Would you like to go dancing?" Brandon asks.

Dancing seems safe. I suspect Brandon is capable of keeping his hands in publicly acceptable places. "Eager to show me your foxtrot?" I tease.

His eyebrows rise in mock admonition. "You joke now, but once you see the foxtrot unleashed, you'll be completely underwhelmed."

I laugh. "I'm preparing myself."

We banter lightheartedly on the drive over. Brandon is quick-witted and fun to talk to, but something is missing.

That damned Reed Pendergraft. This is all his fault. I plan to fix this tonight, one way or the other.

# Chapter Twelve

I'm cursed. I'm not sure what I've done in a prior life, but my karma sucks.

Tina is at the club with Reed.

Brandon doesn't notice as we find a table, and I consider telling him that I want to go somewhere else. But Reed sees me, watching as we walk through the crowd. My pride refuses to let him see how he affects me.

"Do you want a drink?" Brandon asks.

"God, yes." *Classy Caroline.* "Seven and Seven."

Brandon doesn't seem to notice my comment. I sit at the table and he makes his way to the bar.

We're overdressed for this place. Belvedere's is one of three clubs that Southern students tend to hang out at. The Voodoo Lounge, the club I went to with Dylan, features live music. Tina usually frequents another bar, Luna's, the one we dragged Scarlett to last winter. When Brandon mentioned Belvedere's, I figured I was safe, especially since it's a little more upscale. I figured wrong.

Not that I thought Reed would willingly subject himself to coming here, but then again, he was at the Voodoo Lounge. Why wouldn't he come here?

Perhaps because he's looked miserable both times.

Brandon returns with our drinks. His eyes are on me as he takes a sip of what looks like whiskey. "Have I mentioned how beautiful you look tonight?"

I grin and lift an eyebrow. "No, as a matter of fact, you haven't since you picked me up."

He slips closer to me and leans over to my ear. "You look beautiful."

His breath tickles my ear and I wait for heat to wash through my body, but nothing happens other than a mild excitement.

"Hey, there."

I recognize the voice before I look over at her. "Hi, Lexi."

She's parked herself in a chair at our table.

"Aren't you too young to be here?" I ask.

She grins. "These things can be easily taken care of."

"Fake ID, huh?"

She gives a half shrug with a smug look.

"I'm surprised your brother approves." I purposely leave Reed's name out of the conversation.

She shrugs again. Perhaps that explains his current crankiness. I'm not sure what explains his surliness the rest of the time.

Brandon watches our exchange with interest.

"Brandon, this is Lexi. Lexi, this is my date, Brandon." I stress the word *date*. Her obvious matchmaking yesterday with me and Reed needs to be discouraged.

Lexi turns toward Brandon and gives him a dazzling smile, and I feel like I'm in some cheesy movie.

Brandon's face lights up and he can't tear his eyes from her. "Hi."

They stare at each other for several seconds.

This is awkward.

As though Brandon can read my mind, he remembers I'm sitting here. "Uh, how do you know Lexi?"

"She's on the fashion show committee."

Brandon turns back to Lexi. "Are you a design student?"

Her eyelashes flutter and she shakes her head. "No, a business major."

He's even more intrigued. "How did a business major get on the committee?"

Lexi gives him an explanation about the foundation while I down my drink. Goddamn my luck with men.

"So you know Reed Pendergraft?" Brandon's eyes darken.

I lean forward, my coordination slightly off. I had half a bottle of wine at dinner and I just drank my Seven and Seven in less than five minutes. "Of course, she knows Reed." I look at Lexi raising my eyebrows and hoping she gets my point. "He's on the committee."

She seems to grasp that I don't want her to spill that he's her brother. Her eyebrows lift. "That Reed's a handful."

I choke on the last of my drink, and they both turn to me.

"Are you okay?" Lexi asks.

"Yeah, fine." I stand. "I think I'm going to run to the bathroom."

Lexi looks up with a questioning glance.

"You stay with Brandon. I'll be right back."

On my way to the restroom, I see Reed with Tina. His attention is on Tina, but he looks unhappy. Not that she seems to notice. She's laughing with her friends, all non-math students. Tina's not the usual math department student. She actually has a social life.

I still haven't figured out where Reed fits on the social scale. If the scale is one to ten, Scarlett rates about a three. Tina is an eleven.

Thankfully, it's early enough that the restroom doesn't have a line. I check my appearance. All still good, not that it matters. Brandon's completely taken with Lexi. I should be angry. I should be frustrated. Instead, I'm ambivalent, and I don't understand it at all. Brandon is everything I'm looking for, and I'm fixated on Reed.

I need another drink.

I stop at the bar and order another Seven and Seven when I feel him behind me. How can I know it's him before he even says a word? But I do. It's as though my body is tuned into his, a frequency that no one has ever come close to matching.

The bartender brings my drink, and I realize I don't have my purse. But Reed senses my conundrum and silently places a folded bill on the bar. The bartender takes the money and walks away as I take a sip, trying to hide my shaky hand.

Reed continues to stand behind me, and as much as I hate it, this man sends electrical currents racing through my body and wicked thoughts through my head. I feel his eyes looking over my shoulder, checking out my cleavage. I'm flushed and the hair on my arms stands on end. Every part of me aches, and it pisses me off that the thing it aches for is the asshat behind me.

I down my drink in several seconds, bang it on the bar then spin around to tell him off. But when I face him, the words stop on my tongue. The look in his eyes is primal, a stark contrast to his usual prim and proper self.

I have never wanted anything more, propriety be damned.

I grab a handful of his shirt and pull him down toward me. "You. Come with me."

His eyes widen, but I pull him down the hall to the back storeroom. I jerk the door open and drag him in with me then push him against the door as I close it. His shirt is fisted in my hand, and I maintain my grip, pulling him toward me, as my other hand reaches for the back of his head. I grab a handful of his hair to hold him in place as I press my mouth to his.

If I expected him to protest, I would have been wrong. I've released him from whatever has held him back. A low growl escapes into my mouth, and his tongue follows it. His arms wrap around my back and pull me to his chest, crushing my hand between us as he takes control.

His mouth is punishing as he claims mine. Simmering anger ignites my desire, a strange mixture of hate and lust. The concoction makes me so hot I want to strip off my clothes. And strip off his. I want to see what's under his shirt. I want to feel his skin under my fingertips.

And it pisses me off.

This isn't me. This isn't who I am, a sex-craved possessed woman. He's ruining everything.

His hands slide down my back, cupping my ass and pressing his pelvis firmly against me, so there's no doubt he wants me as much as I want him. I lift a leg and wrap it around his waist, pressing myself closer to the bulge in his jeans.

A low rumble vibrates his chest as I grab the bottom of his shirt and jerk it up, breaking contact with his mouth as I pull it over his head.

I lean back to examine the fruits of my labor, barely getting a glimpse of his broad chest and toned stomach, when one of his hands grabs the hair at the nape of my neck, tilting back my head, giving him full access to my mouth. His tongue searches my mouth, demanding my own to join with his.

His other hand glides over my ass to my leg, jerking the hem of my dress up so his fingertips brush the back of my thigh as they slide up and hook under the edge of my panties. He palms my butt cheek, pulling me closer. I press against him, desperate to fill this craving for him, pissed at him for turning me into this person I don't recognize.

His mouth tears from mine and he growls, "You drive me fucking crazy." He releases my hair then pushes my leg off his waist. I'm about to offer my protest when he slides my panties down over my hips in one fluid motion. They fall to my ankles and I step out of them as I reach for the front of his jeans, fumbling with the button. He groans and helps me but when he gets the button undone, I reach for his zipper, unzipping his pants, then reaching inside and stroking his erection. He groans and presses himself into my hand.

He finds the zipper at the back of my dress then tugs the straps off my shoulders, jerking the front of my dress down to expose my black strapless bra. Then suddenly, his mouth is on mine again, bruising as he claims me. His arm pins me to him while one hand finds my breast and slips under the cup of my bra. He fondles my nipple, making me gasp, but his mouth continues its onslaught as his fingers send a bolt of want straight to my pelvis.

"God, I want you," he mumbles against my lips as his hand leaves my breast. I'm about to complain when he slips his fingers between my legs, finding the spot that makes my knees buckle. His arm holds me up while his fingers continue their torture, and I moan. "Reed."

He's got me so worked up that I'm ready to beg him. He lifts me up and sets me on the edge of a table, tugging up my dress and exposing me. He pulls the front of my bra down so that every private part of me is exposed to him, but instead of shame or embarrassment the raw desire in his eyes makes me bold.

He pulls a foil square from his pocket, quickly slipping on a condom, then he kisses me roughly, his tongue plunging into my mouth as he enters me in one full stroke.

I cling to his neck and wrap my legs around his waist, as one of his arms circles around my back, holding me in place. He pulls back and enters again.

I lean my head back and groan. His mouth moves down my neck, licking as he slows to short strokes.

The ache deep inside me builds, begging for more.

His mouth lowers to my breast, licking and nipping until I moan. "*Reed.*" I press my hips into his, grinding into him.

The arm around my back pulls me up and his mouth moves to my neck. I cling to him as his pace quickens and the pressure in my pelvis builds. He's frantic as though he can't get deep enough and I match his need. My feet lock around his back and he lifts me off the table and moves to the side, pressing my back into the wall. He continues his punishing pace and I'm climbing to a level I've never reached before, teetering on the edge of oblivion. And then he plunges deeper and I break, losing all control and crying out. His mouth covers mine as he pushes deeper still and he groans loud and long into my mouth.

When he stops, he turns to set me on the table, still inside me. His hands cup my face as he looks into my eyes, filled with wonder and lust. The sight of his desire kindles the flame in my gut, and I'm ready to go another round, but the doorknob shakes. We both jerk to reality. We're in a storeroom in various states of undress. Alarm spreads across his face, and he blocks the door.

I scramble off the table pulling up the front of my dress as I search for my panties.

*Oh, God.* I can't find them.

I look up at Reed, but he's bent over, picking up his shirt off the floor and pulling it over his head.

*Shit.*

The door opens, and Reed pulls me against his chest, turning me away from the door and zipping my dress. He kisses me long and slow. I wonder why he's kissing me when we've been caught. The sex-crazed maniac he's turned me into craves him all over again.

The door opens and a guy grumbles. "Get a room."

Reed lifts his head and grins at the employee. "What do you think I'm doing? How about you leave so I can get lucky?"

I want to cry with gratitude. Reed's saving me from embarrassment.

"How about you do it somewhere else?" The guy holds the door open, waiting.

Reed keeps an arm around my back and escorts me out the door, then pushes me against the wall, kissing me again. When the employee leaves the storeroom and walks past us, Reed lifts his head, resolve replacing his lust.

"This was a mistake."

"*Excuse me?*" I've never experienced anything like I just had with him. And now he's calling it a mistake?

He takes a step back, the man who fucked me senseless retreating behind his wall of disdain. "Caroline, we're both here with *other people.*"

Oh, dear God. He's right.

How in the hell could I forget that?

What is this hold he has over me? It has to be chemistry or powerful pheromones. Voodoo. Only something unearthly would make me behave this way. Tears fill my eyes at the realization. I just did what every guy in high school thought I did. For three years, I've been so careful with my reputation, careful to not give anyone just cause to call me a slut. Look at me now.

"I have to go to the bathroom." I push past him toward the restroom door, but he grabs my arm and pulls me to his chest.

"Caroline."

I look up and the disgust on his face rips away my last shred of dignity.

Anger roars in my head. Anger at him but mostly anger at me. I'm a fucking idiot. "You got what you wanted, Reed. Congratulations. You just achieved what every guy in my high school and a good portion of the guys at Southern hoped to achieve: a quick fuck with Caroline Hunter. You're the lucky winner, but don't worry." Hate rushes through my blood and disgust because this close to him, I still want him. I still ache for him even after what he's done. I *am* a complete fucking idiot. "I won't make that *mistake* again."

I jerk out of his hold, and shove the bathroom door open and hide inside.

I can't stay here long. He's right. We're both here with someone else. And even as infatuated as Brandon was with Lexi, one of them is bound to notice I've been gone awhile.

I need to pull myself together. I can lose it when I get home, but not now.

I can't face Reed again and not crumble, and I'm scared Reed will be in the hall when I open the door, but he's gone. I'm equally relieved and devastated. What I expect from him at this point is beyond me.

I feign a half-smile when I reach the table. Brandon and Lexi are deep in conversation, and they look up, surprised to see me. If I had even half the feelings for Brandon that I feel with Reed, I'd fight for him. For the possibilities of what we could have. But every fucking relationship I've ever had doesn't even come close to what I just had with Reed. I want to burst into tears. Instead, I grimace. "I have a headache."

Concern washes over Brandon's face, but I hold my hand up in reassurance.

"It's only a small one, but I ran into a friend and she's offered to take me home."

"No." Brandon reaches for his jacket. "You're my date. I should take you home."

Disappointment and guilt flood Lexi's eyes.

At least one of us should be happy. Why is it always someone other than me? I pick up my purse and wrap and smile at Brandon. "You're a wonderful guy, but you don't deserve someone like me." No, he doesn't deserve a girlfriend who fucks another guy in a bar storeroom while on a date with him. "Thank you for dinner, but I've got a ride home, so stay with Lexi."

"Are you sure?" Lexi asks.

I give her a genuine smile. I like Lexi and I want her to be happy. She has a far better chance of that with Brandon than I do. "I'm positive. Have fun." I raise my eyebrows and tip my head toward Brandon.

She laughs. "Thank you, Caroline."

I turn to leave and walk out into the parking lot and pull my cell phone out of my purse. I hate to call Scarlett but she's the only one who I trust right now. The phone rings twice before Tucker answers. "Hey, Caroline. What's up?"

"I need to talk to Scarlett." I try to stop the tears welling in my eyes and a lump burns my throat.

"She had a headache and went to bed."

"Okay." I choke out. "I've got to go."

"Caroline. Wait." His tone has changed to hesitant. "What happened?"

Tucker is the last person I want to see, but I can't afford a cab and it's too far and too dangerous to walk. Especially in these shoes. "I need a ride."

"Where are you?" He sounds worried. "Was it the dickhead you went out with tonight? What the fuck did he do?"

I laugh through my tears. I inherited an enforcer when Scarlett got herself a boyfriend. "I'm at Belvedere's. I'm waiting outside."

"Go back inside. It's not safe for you to be waiting outside alone at this time of night."

"Tucker, it's only ten o'clock." Great. I fucked a guy in a storeroom and I have time to get home and watch the evening news. I choke back a sob. Look how efficient I am. "I'm fine."

But I'm the furthest thing from fine I've ever been. I just need to get to the safety of my home.

"I'm already on my way. But go inside if you feel threatened."

"Just get here. *Please.*" I hang up before I embarrass myself anymore. I've done that enough tonight to last a lifetime.

The air is crisp and my wrap barely covers me. I wrap my arms around myself in an attempt to keep warm and to stop my shaking. After about five minutes, Tucker's car pulls into the parking lot as Reed storms out of the building. He searches the parking lot, worry on his face when he turns to see me. He squeezes his eyes shut for several seconds then starts toward me as Tucker's car pulls up to the curb. I reach for the door handle.

"Caroline. *Wait!*" Reed shouts.

I shake my head, not trusting myself to speak. I climb into the car and lock the door.

Tucker's knuckles are white as he grips the steering wheel. "Do I need to get out and kick that fucker's ass?"

"No." I choke out. "Go."

As Tucker pulls out to the parking lot, Reed shouts, "*Caroline!*"

The sobs are building in my chest, and I'm not sure I can hold them in until I get home.

"That was Reed Pendergraft, wasn't it?" Tucker is seething with rage.

I nod. "Yeah."

"What did that son of a bitch do this time?"

I shake my head. "I'm fine." If I told Tucker what just happened, Reed and I would both be dead. I'd die of humiliation and Tucker would beat the ever-loving shit out of Reed.

"The fuck you are."

"Tucker, you have no idea how much what you're doing means to me right now." Tears stream down my face, taking pressure off the sobs begging for escape. "But I need to deal with this on my own."

"I'm taking you to our place."

"No. Scarlett's sick and I'm fine."

"Scarlett only has a headache. She would want you at our place."

I'm tempted, but a meltdown is rushing to the surface, and I don't want Scarlett and Tucker to witness that. "Tucker. I need to be alone."

"What if he shows up at your apartment? Does he know where you live?"

I don't dare tell him Reed's on a date with Tina. Oh shit. What if he tries to see me when he takes her home? But surely he won't. Oh, God. What if Tina finds out? No, Reed wouldn't be so stupid to tell her, and Brandon and Lexi have no clue. The only person who knows anything happened between Reed and me is Tucker.

"You have to promise you won't tell anyone anything happened between Reed and me."

He turns to me, his forehead wrinkling in suspicion. "Why?"

"Please. Just promise me."

"Caroline, I don't even know what happened."

"Tucker, *please.*"

"Okay."

"Not even Scarlett."

"Now I can't—"

"Tucker, I'm begging you." If he tells Scarlett he picked me up, she'll want to know why, and I'll have to tell the whole sordid tale. I'd rather keep this walk of shame between Tucker and me. "Please."

"Fine." He grunts, clearly unhappy about what I've asked him to do.

Tucker insists on walking up to my apartment with me and waiting for me to unlock the door. My hands are shaky, and he takes the keys and opens the door. "Are you sure you're okay?"

I nod, refusing to look at him.

"Caroline." He waits for me to look up at him. "I'm here for you. Consider me the big brother you never had. If some guy messes with you, you tell me, and I'll take care of it. Okay?"

I nod, tears flowing against my will. I have a big brother and he never once offered anything like this. "Thanks." I'm grateful for everything Tucker's done, but I don't know how long I can keep my sobs in check.

Tucker kisses my forehead. "I'm only a phone call away, Caroline. Use me. Let me kick that fucker's ass."

"And mess up his pretty face?"

"That's what he gets for screwing with my girlfriend's best friend."

Tucker's word choice hits too close to home. "Good night." I shut myself in the apartment, locking the door, sobs erupting before I make it to my room. I kick off my shoes and fall onto my bed, sobbing for what seems an eternity until I fall asleep.

# Chapter Thirteen

"You look like shit," Tina mumbles the next morning. She's sitting at the kitchen table with a textbook and a cup of coffee.

I pull a box of cereal out of the cabinet and find a bowl. "Gee, thanks."

"Bad date, huh? I saw your guy hanging out with some other chick at the club I was at."

"Yeah." I open the fridge to get out the milk and peer at her through the hair hanging in my face. She looks relatively happy, even if it has a surly edge. "How'd your date go?"

She groans. "He's a bore."

I think about what Reed and I did in the storeroom and boring is the last thing that comes to mind. "That's too bad." Pouring the milk in my bowl, I keep my back to her. "What are you doing up so early?"

"Reed brought me home before eleven o'clock. Can you fucking believe it? That's what I get for dating a guy in the math department." She looks up from her book. "Say, do you know why Tucker was here last night, sitting on the steps to our apartment?"

I nearly choke on my cereal as I spin around. "Tucker was here?"

"Yeah, totally random. Just sitting there. I asked him why he was there, and he said something about how he'd been out for a run and needed to rest, but his car was in the parking lot, and he was wearing jeans." She turns the page of her book. "I suspect it had something to do with Reed."

Blood rushes to my feet. "Why do you say that?"

"Because they had this weird vibe going. Tucker said something like 'You don't plan on going inside that apartment, do you?' and Reed said, 'I don't see how it's any of your business,' or something like that." Tina gets up from the table with her cup and heads for the coffeemaker. "Why would Tucker care who I go out with?"

"I don't know."

"Reed didn't come in, not that either of us wanted him to, even before Tucker said his piece. I think they talked after I came inside, though. I saw them in the parking lot."

"What?" I'm horrified. Did Tucker force Reed to tell him what happened?

"I wonder if it has to do with Scarlett." She puts a cup in the coffeemaker and pushes a button. "You know how protective he is of her." She shakes her head. "Who can figure those two out?"

My stomach is rolling, so I set my bowl in the sink and head to my bedroom. I lie on my back and stare at the ceiling. Maybe I can become a recluse and do all my classes online so I don't ever have to leave this apartment. It's bad enough I completely lost control and slutted it up, but what if Tucker knows what I did? And what does Reed think about me? Sure, he wanted me in the storeroom, but the look of disgust on his face afterward was enough to tell me what he really thought. Maybe that's his thing, to fuck girls in storerooms.

Of course, I'm completely dismissing the fact I dragged him back there. I instigated the entire thing. If anyone is to blame, it's me.

Tears prick my eyes but I force them to dry up. I had my cry and crying won't help anything. Okay, so Reed thinks I'm a slut. I've made it a point to make sure everyone else thinks otherwise. Even if he tells people what happened, who's going to believe it? We weren't at the club together. As far as I know, no one even knows we saw each other there. I'm freaking out over nothing.

But I'm not. I close my eyes and feel Reed's mouth on mine, his hands on my ass, his…. If I'm honest, my behavior isn't my only fear. My biggest fear is that I'll never experience that kind of primal, lusty sex again. And that is just as devastating to face as the fact I actually did it. Because I liked it. I liked it a lot.

Good girls don't behave that way.

I groan when I realize I'm going to have to face Reed on Monday. Will he give me the same look of disgust? Why did he come after me in the parking lot?

I'm horrified at what I did in the storeroom, but I'm frightened of my body's reaction even after he told me it was a mistake. The man has serious control over me, whether he realizes it or not, and that's dangerous.

I need to avoid Reed at all costs.

*** 

I decide to spend the rest of the weekend working on my designs. Once I push Reed from my head, as much as I possibly can, I focus on a theme for the collection. I need something narrower than *Everyday Living*. I think about what I wanted when I was Desiree's age—to look like all the other kids, to have name brands like Justice and Abercrombie.

What if there was a brand that made trendy clothes affordable? It wouldn't help kids like me when my dad was laid off for a year. But kids, whose parents have money for clothes—just not very much—could afford them.

The usual budget for each design student's collection is five hundred dollars, but the foundation has kicked in an additional amount. I have fifteen hundred dollars to make real clothes for these kids. Clothes they can keep when the show is over. I search eBay for some fabric bargains then realize I'm going to have to leave my house.

What are the chances I'll run into Reed at a fabric store?

I don't want to risk it. I call Scarlett. "What are you doing?"

"Studying."

"How's your headache?"

She pauses. "How did you know I had a headache?"

*Shit.* Tucker told me and I told him not to tell Scarlett. "Um, I called you last night. Tucker answered and told me you were asleep because of your headache."

"Do you happen to know where he went last night? I woke up and he was gone. When he got home, he wouldn't tell me where he'd been."

Guilt rushes through me like a tidal wave. "That's odd."

"I totally trust Tucker, and we never keep anything from one another. But I have to admit, I'm worried. He's used to partying and we both know I hate it." Her voice breaks. "What if he's tired of me, Caroline?"

I push down a groan. I can't let her think Tucker is going out without her, but I don't want to tell her my secret shame. But she's my best friend and I need to set her straight. "He was with me."

"You? I thought you were on a date."

"I was. But then I needed a ride home, and Tucker answered your phone and came and got me instead."

"Oh." She's quiet for a moment. "Where were you? He was gone for over an hour."

I sigh. "I promise you that Tucker picked me up and dropped me off. But Tina said he was sitting on our steps when she came home around eleven."

"Why?" She sounds confused, not that I blame her.

"I need to tell you all of this in person. I'll buy you lunch if you come to the fabric store with me."

Scarlett groans. She hates the fabric store. "Lunch is hard to pass up. I want Mexican."

"Done. I'll pick you up at eleven. We'll go to the fabric store before lunch."

When I get to her apartment, I climb out of the car and see Tucker running down the steps. I walk toward him and he stops, a fierce look on his face. "Reed won't bother you anymore."

My stomach drops. "What happened?"

"I waited around to make sure he didn't come looking for you. I was kind of surprised to see he was with Tina."

My face blushes. "What did he say?"

"Not much. I did most of the talking. I told him I didn't know what he'd done to you, but he had his two strikes and I guaran-damn-teed him I'd beat the shit out of him if he so much as talked to you again."

I'm both relieved and disappointed. I look up at Tucker, surprised by the anger in his eyes. "Thank you. You didn't have to do that."

"You and Scarlett had each other's backs before she moved out, and we all know that Tina's in her own little selfish world, which means you're on your own. It worries Scarlett sick. I meant it when I said I'm here for you, Caroline. You're like a sister to Scarlett, and she loves you more than her own family. That alone is good enough for me. If you're upset, Scarlett is upset. But not only that"—his voice lowers—"you're a sweet girl, Caroline, and the world is full of fuckers who only want to screw you and move on."

I look down, my humiliation resurfacing.

"What you do is your business, but if some asshole hurts you in the process, he's answering to me, got it?"

I nod, swallowing my tears of gratitude. When Tucker started showing up at our door last winter, I warned Scarlett that he was trouble and would hurt her. If someone had told me what he'd be doing for me now, I never would have believed it. I reach up and wrap an arm around his neck. "Thank you."

"Anytime." He squeezes me before pulling free. "Now I've got to get to the soccer field. Or a bunch of ten-year-olds will be without a coach."

He jogs to his car, and I see Scarlett coming down the stairs. Her gaze follows him as he gets in his car. "Good chat with Tucker?" There's no jealousy in her voice, only curiosity. She knows I'd swallow cyanide before I'd betray her.

"Yeah. For the record, I retract all objections to your dating him."

She laughs. "He is pretty great, isn't he?"

"Just don't tell him. His head is already big enough."

"True."

On the way to the store, Scarlett fills me in on her decision to stay at Southern for graduate school, purposely avoiding anything about my personal life. She knows me well enough to know I need to ease into this slowly.

We wander through the store, and Scarlett asks, "So are you looking for something for the fashion show?"

I tell her my idea for my collection. She not only thinks it's a great idea but has a few suggestions of her own. Now that she knows I'm making designs the kids from the center get to keep, she's more willing to help.

I finger a soft denim, distracted. I need to tell Scarlett, but I'm not even sure where to start. "My date was a failure."

She waits a second. "I figured that since Tucker came and got you."

"But it wasn't Brandon's fault. He was thoughtful and witty and funny. He's a pre-med student. He's everything I'm looking for."

"I'm sorry to hear that," she says in mock sympathy. "How awful."

She's joking, but tears fill my eyes.

"Hey, I was teasing."

"I know. That's why what I did is so awful."

She grabs my arm and pulls me to the wall filled with clearance fabrics. "What *you* did?"

I swallow the lump in my throat and look at the ceiling to regain control before I face her. What can I tell her? We've never been prone to share the details of our sex lives with one another, and I don't intend to start now. I lower my gaze. "I ran into Reed."

She shakes her head. "I'm confused."

"Scarlett." I lower my voice. "This week, Reed kissed me. When we were at the nonprofit with Lexi. I saw a photo of me when I was a little girl and I got upset and Reed stayed with me and then before I knew it, we were attacking each other in the hallway. Oh, Scarlett. This is such a mess." The words tumble out.

She studies me for several seconds. "Fabric shopping has to wait." Grabbing my arm, she heads to the door. "We need food to go with the margaritas we're about to drink."

After Scarlett takes my car keys, she drives to an authentic Mexican restaurant we like. It has zero atmosphere, but the food is great and it's cheap. The seating area is also usually filled with Hispanic men who won't pay attention to my pathetic tale. When we order our food, Scarlett makes sure they send our drinks out right away. Once they're on the table, she looks at me with a determined look in her eye. She's analytical

Scarlett, set on finding facts. "Start over. Way back to the second meeting with the committee."

After I tell her about the committee meeting and our field trip and our kiss, I tell her about Brandon asking me out and my reluctant agreement.

"That's not like you," she says as the waiter sets our food in front of us. "You don't turn down dates with cute guys who have great majors."

The way she says it sounds superficial, but then again, I suppose it is. "Reed was already messing with my head. Even before he kissed me."

"You've got it bad."

"It gets worse." I take a drink.

"Worse than you not being interested in what sounds like the most eligible bachelor at Southern University?"

I nod.

"Wow." She sits back in her seat. "That has to be bad." She's teasing me, but little does she know.

After I tell her about Brandon picking me up and Reed showing up and the standoff at our apartment, I tell her about dinner with Brandon and how wonderful it was. "But when he leaned close, Scarlett, there weren't fireworks or tingles."

She shakes her head. "That's not good, Caroline. I never felt it before Tucker, but once you've had the real thing, you can never go back to mediocre."

"I've had the real thing."

Confusion wrinkles her forehead. "You mean with your old boyfriend Justin?"

I slowly shake my head. "No, although I thought I did until I experienced the real thing."

She looks worried. "You mean your kiss with Reed?"

I take a deep breath. "Our kiss was unlike anything I've ever experienced, but no. Not the kiss." I look into her eyes.

"After dinner, we went to a club. Tina and Reed were there." I pause, letting everything I've said sink in.

To her credit, she keeps her shock to herself and remains matter-of-fact, collecting the data before she comes to her conclusion. "So you were both at the club, with other people?" Her eyebrows rise with the question in her voice.

I nod. "But Lexi sat down at our table and the connection she and Brandon had was like…."

"The connection you have with Reed."

I don't say anything.

"Something happened in that club to upset you. That's where Tucker picked you up."

"Yes. Something happened in the club."

She groans in frustration. "I'm not a mind reader, Caroline. What happened?"

"We had sex in the storage room." I blurt out before I can stop myself. I release a sardonic laugh. "Who would have guessed that Five-Date Caroline turned out to be a slut who would fuck a guy who hates her in a storage room?"

Her eyes harden. "I love you, Caroline, and it's because I love you that I'm saying this, but if you talk about yourself like that again, I *will* slap you. Got it?"

The way her jaw is set, I believe her. I nod.

"Okay." She closes her eyes then opens them. "I don't need the backroom details, please. But tell me what happened leading up to the storage room … incident."

"I saw him there, with Tina and he'd been watching me. I went to the bathroom then went to the bar to get another drink when I felt him behind me. And I was … horny." I take a deep breath. "But that doesn't describe it. I was so angry with him for treating me badly a few weeks ago. And I was pissed at his arrogant, bossy attitude during our committee meetings, but at the same time, I felt this overwhelming urge. It was like he had something that I needed so desperately that I'd do anything to get it."

"So then what happened?"

"I decided to go for it." I look down at my glass. "I downed my drink, grabbed his shirt, and pulled him to the back room. You can figure out the rest from there."

"He willingly went with you?"

"He was shocked at first, but once he realized what was happening, he was a willing and *eager* participant."

"But something bad happened."

My mouth drops open. "I already told you I had wild, sweaty sex in a storage room. I think that counts as bad."

Scarlett leans forward. "No, Caroline. It's not bad all on its own. Sure, it's a bit risky and true you don't know him very well, but lots of relationships start with chemistry. *Most* relationships start with chemistry. Tucker and I are different." She puts her hand over mine. "So when did it turn bad, because I'm guessing the sex in the storeroom part was pretty good."

I pull my hand out from under hers. "Scarlett!"

"What?" she asks in mock innocence. "You started this story telling me you'd had the best sex of your life."

"I did no such thing."

She lifts an eyebrow. "Okay, I'm paraphrasing, but you *know* that's what you were saying. So when did it go wrong?"

I close my eyes in embarrassment. "When we were … done … we honestly could have gone again, but someone tried to come in. So Reed blocked the door while I pulled my dress up and then he kissed me when the guy walked in, trying to make it look like we were back there making out."

"And…."

"Then the guy kicked us out, and Reed pushed me up against the wall and kissed me until the guy left. But when Reed pulled back, he told me what we'd done was a mistake." I bit my trembling bottom lip. "I asked him how he could say that. He looked at me with disgust and said because we were there with other people. I could handle what he said. It was how he said it." I shake my head. "Like what we'd done was filthy." I release a bitter laugh. "I suppose it was."

"Caroline," Scarlett's voice is harsh. "You stop that right now. What you did was not filthy. You were both consenting adults. You both have feelings for each other."

"Do we?" I ask. "We've barely had a civil conversation in the entire few weeks I've known him. No wonder he was disgusted with me. He thinks I'm a slut."

Her eyes narrow. "I told you—"

"No, Scarlett." My voice is hard. "Girls who fuck guys in a storage room who aren't their boyfriends are sluts."

Her face reddens. She's furious with me. Finally, she says, "We'll agree to disagree on that."

"So I congratulated him on achieving what no other man had ever done and went into the bathroom. When I came out, he was gone, so I told Brandon I had a headache, but I had a ride home, and that he deserved someone better than me. Then I called you."

"And Tucker picked you up."

"Reed came out of the club as I got in the car, calling my name. Tucker knew I was upset and put things together. He wanted to beat the shit out of Reed, but I stopped him. He must have stayed after he took me home to make sure Reed didn't come by and bother me."

Scarlett's lips lift into a sweet smile.

"Tucker's a great guy and you're lucky to have him." I take a drink of my margarita. "I wasn't going to tell you any of this, but I couldn't let you think that Tucker isn't happy with you. He's crazy about you."

"I can't believe you weren't going to tell me. You can't keep something like this to yourself."

"I'm humiliated, Scarlett. You and Reed are the only two people who know. I'm not sure what Tucker thinks, but I didn't tell him anything."

"It's going to be okay, Caroline. I promise."

"I have to face Reed on Monday at our meeting. I have no idea what I'm going to do."

She grabs my chin. "You're going to hold your head high, and if he treats you with the tiniest amount of disrespect, Tucker will beat the shit out of him."

I laugh, grateful for the millionth time that Scarlett is my friend. "Why, Scarlett, Goodwin. You're usually not pro-violence."

"I am where you are concerned." She stabs her enchilada. "We need to eat."

"There's something else."

She looks up in surprise.

"Non-Reed related." Scarlett's bound to be upset that I kept this next subject from her. "It's about my mother."

Scarlett puts her fork down. "You talked to your mother?" She knows we haven't talked since the day I left.

I nod and take a deep breath. "She called me."

She takes a moment before she asks, "What did she want?"

"She called to tell me she's dying."

"Caroline, I'm sorry. What is it?"

I shrug, still amazed at my indifference. What does that say about me? But I can't confess this to Scarlett. "She said it's lung cancer, and she doesn't have long."

"What did you say?"

"Nothing. I wasn't sure what to say."

She nods. She of all people knows my relationship with my parents. "Are you going to go see her?"

My eyes widen. "Why would I do that? They made their choice. They told me if I drove off to college, thinking I was better than my upbringing, not to come back. I've done what they told me to do, Scarlett."

"She reached out to you, Caroline."

I shake my head, refusing to cry.

"You think you're over this, but you're not. This is your chance for some closure."

I release an ugly laugh. "Funny, I don't see you running off to get closure with your mother."

What I've said is the ugliest thing I've ever said to her, but she doesn't bat an eye. "Maybe this is a wakeup call for both of us. Maybe we both need more resolution to our pasts. But you're about to run out of time. Don't do something you'll regret."

I almost say *Like have sex with Reed in a storeroom*? But the ugly truth is I don't regret that part. I regret what happened afterward.

"Just think about it, okay?"

But I can't think about it. My life is too messed up as it is. My mother is the proverbial last straw. She made her choice. Now she has to live with it. Or die with it.

# Chapter Fourteen

Reed's not at the committee meeting when I get there on Monday. I've worried myself sick all day. My heart races each time the door opens until everyone but Reed is seated.

"Reed won't be able to attend today." Lexi announces. "We're in really good shape, though, and Reed has sent notes of what he thinks we need to address."

We get through the list within thirty minutes and Lexi adjourns the meeting. "Caroline." She looks into my face. "Can I talk to you for a minute?"

I want to tell her no. I've spent the last half hour wondering where Reed is and why he's not here. Is it because of Tucker? But I ask myself why I care. Isn't it better this way?

Everyone else vacates the room while I stand and gather my items.

"Evelyn called and said she has a list of thirty-three children whose parents have agreed to let them take part in the fashion show."

"That's great," I say, trying to find some enthusiasm. I'm not sure why she couldn't announce this during the meeting.

"She said if you want to tell the other students to coordinate a time to come and take measurements, that would be great. But she told me that you had e-mailed and said you were using children for all of your designs, so she said you could come tomorrow afternoon if you like."

I nod. "Thanks. That'll work with my schedule." I start for the door.

"Caroline, wait."

I pause, my back to her.

She hesitates. "About Friday night."

I squeeze my eyes shut. Oh, God. Did Reed tell her something happened between us? "Lexi, I don't really want—"

"I wasn't trying to steal your date."

I breathe a sigh of relief. I turn around with a tired smile. "Lexi, please don't worry about it. Brandon is an awesome guy, but there was something missing. I just didn't feel it with him."

"Because you feel something for Reed."

I feel light-headed and press my back to the door. "Why do you say that?"

"I can see there's something between you two."

I'm not sure how to answer her. She's right, but I refuse to admit it and I refuse to deny it. I decide to risk my pride and ask the question I'm dying for an answer to. "Where's Reed today?"

She glances down then back up at me with a half-smile. "He's sick."

That's a lie, and we both know it.

What did I expect? I reach for the doorknob. "I was serious when I said I don't feel anything for Brandon. I hope he asks you out." I swallow. "Is there anything else? Because I'm seriously behind on my project."

She blinks. "Sure … no…."

I leave the room and hurry across campus to the design lab. I spent most of Saturday night and Sunday sketching and I have seven semi-completed designs. I groan, realizing I should have asked how many boys had volunteered. I can work on figuring the seven girls' designs and then determine the rest when I know who my models are.

I try again to push Reed from my mind, but it's impossible. My imagination runs wild with reasons why he didn't show up today and none of the conclusions are good. Part of my problem is that I'm not sure how I want this situation resolved. Do I want to date him? Doesn't that question alone make what we did even more despicable? But whenever I think about Friday night there's a tiny bit of guilt and the rest is molten desire.

The answer is that I do want to sleep with him. That alone isn't a basis for a relationship.

For now, I need to focus on the fashion show and providing outfits for ten children who need a bright spot in their life. Nothing else matters.

\*\*\*

The next afternoon the October rains move in, coming down in sheets. I've forgotten an umbrella so I stand at the door to the Human Environmental Services building and wait. But I'm running late already. I need to measure ten children by five o'clock. My appointment is scheduled at four and it's already three-fifty. Considering that it's a fifteen-minute drive with no rain, I'm in trouble.

I make a run for it, holding the canvas bag that holds my notebook and measuring tape over my head. It does little good at keeping me dry.

My clothes are soaked by the time I get in my car. My long gauzy skirt twists between my legs and my white blouse is plastered to my skin, revealing every detail of my lacy white bra. I toss the bag into the passenger seat and turn the ignition. Nothing. I try again and realize I left my headlights on when I drove in this morning.

Closing my eyes, I lean my forehead against the steering wheel and groan.

*My life sucks.*

There's no way my car is going anywhere until I get a jump, and I can't jump it until the rain lets up. I really need to measure the kids *today*. With the crazy tight schedule to get things done in time, I should have measured the kids last week and already had one design completed. I haven't even begun to make patterns. Using children for all my designs is great in theory. But since I have no idea how old the children are, let alone their clothing size, I'm behind. At least there are standard model sizes for women and you only have to make adjustments for the fitting.

I pull my phone out of my purse and call Lexi. "Hey, Lexi. This is Caroline. Can you call Evelyn and tell her I can't come today? My car is in the student parking lot and the battery is dead. Maybe I can make it tomorrow." My words are heavy with disappointment.

"Wait." She pauses. "The problem is your car, right?"

"Yeah...."

"I'm done with classes for the day. I'll just pick you up and take you. Then you can get their measurements today."

"I hate to bother you."

"Oh, it's not a bother at all. Besides, Evelyn said the girls were excited. You don't want to disappoint them."

I don't and I need to get started. I push my guilt over inconveniencing her away. "Okay."

"Great! I'll call Evelyn and tell her that you're running late because of the rain. I should be there in about fifteen to twenty minutes. What do you drive?"

"A blue Ford Focus." I'm embarrassed to tell her. It's a clunker. I give her directions.

"Okay, just sit tight in your car, and I'll pull up right behind you. When I stop, hop out and run into my car. It's the black Altima that we drove to the charity."

"Sounds great."

I spend the next fifteen minutes with my sketchbook. I have a couple of ideas for boys if any volunteered, but I also have an outfit in mind for Desiree. While the design theme is *Everyday Living*, I'm stepping out of the guidelines for her. Desiree wants to look like a princess and I'm going to make sure that happens.

A car pulls up behind mine and idles. I can't easily see through the rain, but it looks like Lexi's sedan. I grab my bag and run for the door, climbing in. "Thanks, Lexi. I don't—" I turn toward her and realize it's Reed.

Gasping in horror, I reach for the door handle. My worst nightmare has come true. I'm stuck in an enclosed space with Reed Pendergraft. My pulse races and my hormones spring to life, my body hyperaware of his and what he can do to me. What I *want* him to do to me.

"Caroline, wait." His hand grabs my arm and holds me in place.

The skin where he touches reacts, my hair standing on end, and all I want to do is throw myself into his arms. I force out my words. "I was waiting for Lexi."

"She came by to get the car keys, but I told her I'd take you." His words are clearly enunciated and seem carefully chosen.

I take a deep breath in a desperate attempt to calm my jolted nerves. "Don't you have a math lab now?" As soon as the words leave my mouth, I realize he'll know I've memorized his schedule. Just like a stalkerish jilted lover. *Great.*

But he doesn't seem to notice. "I got someone to cover it, so I have the afternoon free."

Scarlett works in the math lab, so I know how it works. There's no way he could have found someone that quickly. "You didn't have to do that." Defensiveness rises to the surface. "I can go take the measurements tomorrow."

"I wanted to come, Caroline." His voice is soft and pleading.

I turn to him in surprise. "Why?"

"We need to talk about what happened—"

I bolt for the door handle. "No! No we don't—"

His fingers tighten their hold. "Caroline, we do. We can't leave things the way we did Friday night."

I close my eyes and press my head against the seat. "I can't do this now, Reed. I can't risk getting upset before I go and measure these kids."

"It's okay. We can talk afterward."

I nod. I might agree, but I hope I can find some way to permanently delay our discussion.

Reed releases his grip and my arm screams in protest. Scarlett's right. I have it bad, which is why being this close to Reed and alone in the car is the worst idea ever. I'll just make a fool of myself again.

But I remind myself I'm a grown woman with a semi-functioning superego, even if my id tries to overrule. Self-control and I have been lifelong friends. I can't let it abandon me now. I fold my hands in my lap, twining my fingers as we ride in silence. The only sound is the Coldplay album playing on the car audio system and the thump-thump of the windshield wipers.

He's stiff in his seat. He looks nervous.

I cast a glance at him, but keep my body facing forward. "Tucker said he told you that he'd beat the crap out of you if you so much as talked to me. Tucker doesn't make idle threats. Are you willing to risk it?"

His mouth presses tight. "I'll take my chances."

The rain has let up slightly when we reach the tutoring center, but Reed has an umbrella. He's out of the car and holding it over my head when I get out.

My hair has begun to dry, but my clothes are still damp and stuck to my body. I glance down and see that my white blouse is still transparent, giving Reed a perfect view of my bra.

But he doesn't look down. In fact, he keeps his eyes averted. "I have a jacket in the trunk. I can pull it out if you want to wear it inside."

I don't want to take anything from him. I don't want him to be so nice to me. It's hard to be mad at him, and he deserves my anger. Still, I can't go inside flashing my bra to a group of kids. "Yeah, thanks."

He leads me to the covered front porch then runs back to the trunk, pulling out a khaki jacket. When he reaches me, he holds it up to help me put it on. *Reed, ever the gentleman. Until he looks at you in disgust after fucking you in a storage room.*

*Stop. Just get this over with.*

When we walk in, the excited squeals coming from down the hall make me smile despite my anxiety over my personal life. Once again, I need a reality check. There are bigger problems than my own.

Evelyn isn't in the tutoring annex, but the tutors are expecting us. One young woman looks familiar. I think she might have been in my French class in my sophomore year.

I extend my hand. "Hi, I'm Caroline Hunter, and this is Reed Pendergraft. We're both on the fashion show committee. I'm also a design student and I'm here to take measurements of some of the children."

The girl shakes my hand, then Reed's, her eyes lingering on him. She gives him a flirty smile. "I'm Bethany, and we've been expecting you. The kids are *very* excited."

A twinge of jealousy stirs in my head. I'm the one measuring the kids. Why is she talking to him? Because Reed Pendergraft is one sexy man, especially since I know what's under that blue dress shirt and I know what he can do with what's hidden beneath his gray dress pants.

"Are you okay?" Bethany asks. "You look a little flushed."

Great. Now I've been caught daydreaming about Reed's body. "I'm fine. It's a little warm in here."

"Do you want me to take your coat?" she asks reaching for it.

"No." If I stop thinking about Reed, I'll be fine, but that's hard to do when he's standing so close to me. "I'll keep it for now."

"Okay." She looks around the room. "Where would you like to do this?"

"We can do it anywhere. I'm measuring over their clothes so there won't be any modesty issues."

"Very good. We'll just take you to a classroom and bring the students to you. Evelyn has already assigned them to the design students." She leads us to Desiree's room, which is empty. "We thought this room would be easier because there's more space. Margery is getting the children now."

The girls pour into the room, giggling with excitement. Reed stands in the corner watching the children like they're hyenas about to attack.

I set my bag on the table and pull out my notebook, pen and tape measure. I'm excited to see two boys in the group, but I notice Desiree is missing.

"Where's Desiree?"

"She's sick today," one of the little girls answers.

I hide my disappointment. I'll just come back to measure her. It's not convenient, but I'll make it work.

I study the excited group, trying to figure out whom to start with. The girls are giggly, but the boys have begun to roughhouse. "Why don't we measure the boys first, then send them back to their rooms?"

Bethany laughs. "Great idea. You must have worked with kids before."

"Nah, I had a brother."

Bethany looks over her shoulder. "Mark, you're first." He approaches with a shy smile, refusing to look at me.

"Hi, Mark. I'm Caroline, and I'm going to take your measurements."

He nods, but he looks nervous.

"How old are you?"

"Nine." His eyes dart from me to Reed in the corner.

"It won't hurt at all, okay." I hold up the measuring tape. "See? This is all I'll use and then I'll write the measurements down."

Reed moves next me and pulls out a chair, sitting on the tiny seat. He looks like a giant in Lilliput. His dress pants, blue dress shirt and yellow tie make him look even more out of place. Several of the kids snicker.

Reed makes an exaggerated face to make them laugh and looks around in mock surprise. "What?"

I stare at him for a moment. With his gruff exterior, I never expected him to tolerate children, let alone entertain them. There's more to the guy than I expected.

Mark keeps his eyes on Reed.

"That's Reed. He's going to watch."

Reed reaches over and picks up the notebook and pen. "Reed is going to *help*."

I give him a questioning look. "You don't have to do that. Your responsibilities only include playing chauffeur."

"I want to help. I'll write down everything you tell me to. I promise I won't screw it up." He glances at Mark and grimaces. "I mean mess it up."

Mark continues to watch Reed and he's less fidgety and stiff. Reed's helped the boy relax.

I lean close to Reed. His scent fills my nose and goes straight to my head. If I was standing, my knees would go weak. Over his scent. I give myself a mental shake. *Get yourself together*. I avoid looking into his face as I point to the paper. "Okay, but write these vertically: shoulders, chest, waist, hips, torso, legs, shoulder to floor."

Reed writes them down without comment in tight, legible script. I was worried I'd have trouble deciphering his handwriting later, but it turns out Reed's handwriting is neater than mine.

I turn to Mark and spin him around so I can see his back. "Are you excited about the fashion show?"

He shrugs.

"You look more like a sports kind of guy." Reed says, tapping the pen on the notebook. "Do you play soccer?"

"Yeah," Mark answers as I measure his shoulders.

I tell Reed the measurement, then spin Mark to face me.

"Do you know Tucker Price?" Reed asks.

Mark's eyes light up as I slip the measuring tape around his back to measure his chest. "Everybody knows about Tucker Price."

Tucker was Southern's claim to fame—acclaimed soccer star who got recruited by the Chicago Fire his junior year. The entire town would show up for Southern's home games just to watch him play.

"Well, Caroline is good friends with Tucker."

Mark's mouth drops. "*You are?*"

I wink. "I am. In fact, I just saw him a couple of days ago."

His mouth forms a disapproving frown. "Why'd he quit the Chicago Fire?"

I wrap the tape around his waist. "Professional soccer is a lot of work and it wasn't fun for him anymore."

His eyes narrow as he considers my answer then his eyes light up. "Math's not fun. Can I quit it?"

I laugh. "Good try, but I should warn you about this guy"—I point to Reed with my thumb—"He's going to school to *teach* math. I think you might have insulted him."

Mark looks unimpressed as he turns to Reed. "What about you? Are you friends with Tucker Price?"

"As a matter of fact," Reed pauses, writing something in the margin. "I met him just the other day and he promised to let me get to know him even better." He gives Mark a smirk.

I watch Reed for several seconds. He fully expects Tucker to enforce some type of physical punishment. And yet he's here anyway. Why?

"Cool…." Mark's impressed with Reed's answer, oblivious to what he meant.

Reed snorts and shakes his head.

We finish Mark's measurements then Bethany sends over the next boy.

By the time I've measured seven kids, Reed and I have worked out a system. He writes down measurements, and I notice that he's adding notes about each child's age, personality and interests.

We finish measuring Brittany, a twelve-year-old girl who wants to be a model when she grows up, and the crazy thing is that she has the frame and face for it. "Brittany, could you wait a second?" I ask. "I want to draw a quick sketch."

I reach for the notebook as Reed hands it over, our fingers brushing and sending a jolt to my core. *No touching.*

But I quickly forget Reed as I study Brittany, sketching a skirt and fitted shirt with ruffles, matched with a pair of boots and a purse. She looks the drawing over when I'm done and squeals. "Is that what I'm wearing at the fashion show?"

I laugh. "I'm not sure yet, but you definitely have the figure of a model so I'd like to make sure you look like one when you strut down the runway. Let me see your runway walk."

She looks self-conscious as she walks across the room, bowing her head.

"You can do better than that," I tease, standing and handing the notebook to Reed. "If you want to be a model, I'm sure you've watched *America's Next Top Model*." My shirt has dried and the room is stuffy with so many bodies in a small space. I slide Reed's jacket off and lay it on the table.

"Yeah...."

"What would Tyra or Ms. J say about that walk? You need to look *fierce*." I lift my chin. "Head high, shoulders back, then walk with a strut, moving your hips, but not too much, crisscrossing your feet as you walk. Like this." I put my hands lightly on my hips and walk, a stern look on my face, and the girls giggle. I walk back across the room, demonstrating how to pivot. "Now you try it."

Brittany gives it a try but still looks embarrassed.

"It's easy," I say. "Even Reed can do it."

Reed's gaze is on me, his expression unreadable. It takes him a moment to realize what I've suggested. "*What?* No."

The girls cheer.

"Yes!"

"Come on, Reed."

"Do it."

Reed groans and gets out of his chair. His eyes narrow and he walks past me, looking into my face. "You *so* owe me."

My stomach tingles as I think about what I could do to pay him back. *Calm down, Caroline.*

He stands against the wall and looks down at the girls. "The only way I'll do this is if you girls do it with me."

They giggle and form a line, Brittany next to Reed. She looks up at him with adoring eyes, and it's obvious she's formed a crush on him. *Welcome to Team Reed.*

Reed flashes me a dazzling smile and my knees turn to Jell-O. Where has that smile been the entire time I've known him, but self-preservation tells me it's a good thing he keeps it to himself, or it wouldn't take any time for me to be naked underneath him, begging for him to take me, consequences be damned.

"Caroline?" Brittany asks.

I shake my head, realizing she's asked me a question. "What?"

"Should we start?"

"Yeah." I give them all instructions and Reed follows them as well. With his dress clothes and perfect face, he looks like a real model. He's a perfect package on the outside and I know what's under his shirt is perfect as well.

*Stop. Focus.*

"Okay, work it, girls." I wink at Reed. "And guy."

They walk across the room, and I'm stunned that Reed actually puts in an effort, but Brittany notices too and this walk is her best effort yet. They practice a few more times, but Reed comes and stands behind me to watch.

Reed's participation has boosted Brittany's confidence and after several passes, she starts to look like a real model.

"Keep practicing," I swing my gaze around the room. "All of you. And when I come back to do a final fitting, you can show me how well you've done."

"Will Reed come with you?" Brittany asks wistfully.

"Uh … I'm not sure Reed can—"

"Yes," Reed says. "I'll be with her."

I look over my shoulder at him, and the expression on his face takes my breath away. His gaze is full of something I haven't seen before. Respect.

I turn back to Brittany. "Well, I guess he'll be here."

Bethany returns and takes the girls back to their rooms, leaving the last two with Reed and me. I take their measurements, acutely aware of Reed's leg several inches from mine. I'm sure he wasn't this close before. He's scooted closer.

When the last girl leaves the room, Reed and I are alone, sitting in chairs designed for six year-old-sized butts, but neither one of us move.

This afternoon with him has proven to be dangerous. I've seen a playful, appealing side to him and now I don't just want him, I want *him*. The whole package. Every part of him.

This is ridiculous.

I stand. "I need to ask Evelyn when I can come back to measure Desiree."

He stares at my lips, then his gaze moves to my eyes. "It sounds like the rain has let up. We can walk over together."

I pick up my measuring tape and stuff it into my bag. Reed hands over the notebook and I scan his notes.

"Thanks for these." I point to the page. "This will be really helpful with personalizing their outfits."

Reed shrugs and looks a bit embarrassed. "I know how important this is to you. I just wanted to help."

I pick up his jacket and hand it to him. "Thanks for this."

The look on his face tells me he'd rather help take off my clothes instead of putting them on.

It takes every ounce of strength to not grab him and kiss him.

He moves to the door and stands next to it. "After you."

We thank the tutors on our way out the back door. The paver stone path is narrow so Reed stays behind me. We walk in silence, but when we approach the back door to the main office, Reed reaches around and opens the door.

Evelyn is on the phone in her office so we stand in the hallway and wait. Reed stares at the wall of photos, and my stomach balls into a knot. He's drawn to the photo of me, an eight-by-ten close-up, set among a half a dozen five-by-seven frames. It's meant to draw attention. The poor, little destitute girl. I know enough about these things to know parents had to sign a release for the organization to use my photo. I wonder if they were paid. I wonder if my mother spent the money on cigarettes. The cigarettes that are killing her now.

I haven't given much thought to her phone call. I have too many other issues to deal with. But part of me wonders if Scarlett is right. Maybe I need to see her just so I can say all the things left unspoken. When the fashion show is over, I'll go back for a weekend. I don't call it home. That place is no longer my home. I realize I no longer have a home. When Scarlett lived with me, our dorm room and then apartment were home. But she has a new home now, and the apartment with Tina doesn't feel like a place I belong. Isn't that what I fought for, what I ached for in high school, somewhere I belonged. Someone I belonged to?

Funny, three years later, I'm still alone.

Reed's eyes are hooded as he watches me stare at the photo. He's got a perfect poker face. Is he wondering why I'm looking at the photo? Or is he thinking about our first kiss?

I was right that day he kissed me. Reed and I are all fire and ice, passion and lust. I see a side to him that intrigues me more than sex, but whenever I'm next to him, I can't think straight. All I want to do is throw myself at him.

When did I become this person?

"I can see you now. Come on in." Evelyn stands in the doorway of her office. Reed and I both startle, as though we've have been caught in our own personal turmoil. Or maybe I'm projecting.

Reed sits next to me in the chair in front of the Evelyn's desk and rests his hand on my leg.

I restrain a gasp.

"I'm glad you came by, Caroline," Evelyn says, resting her forearms on the desk. "I wanted to thank you for including the children in the show and for being so concerned about their anonymity."

"No, thank you. Including them has inspired my entire collection." I'm trying to ignore the heat pouring through his hand and running straight to my crotch.

"Yes, that's what I gathered from your e-mail." She takes a breath and folds her hands. "I need to talk to you about Desiree."

I sit upright, uneasiness creeping down my spine. "Okay."

Reed notices my change in demeanor and moves his hand to his lap.

"Her parents are reluctant to let her participate."

I stave off my disappointment. I might be able to swing this around. "Did they say why?"

Evelyn shakes her head. "No, and when I pressed the issue, her mother was reluctant to give a reason." Evelyn notices my disappointment. "We've had plenty of volunteers to take her place, though."

I lean forward. "Do you think her parents would let me talk to them?"

Reed shifts in his seat as Evelyn's eyes widen. "I'm not sure what good it would do."

"Please. I promise to handle the situation respectfully. I'll tell them I understand their concerns, and I'd like to personally address them. Then if they're still uncomfortable letting Desiree take part, I'll respect their wishes."

Evelyn looks concerned. "I'm not sure they'll agree to it."

"I'll come with her," Reed says, resting his hand on the desk. "Tell them I'm a representative of the Monroe Foundation."

The two of us joining forces seems to sway her. "I'll try, but don't get your hopes up. Desiree's mother sounded adamant."

"That's all I can ask," I say, standing. "Thank you for trying."

Reed follows me out of the office, keeping a respectful distance.

"I'll be in touch," Evelyn calls after us.

When we get outside, Reed's arm wraps around my back. My breathing shallows. How can one touch drive me to such distraction? I concentrate on putting one foot in front of the other.

Reed opens the passenger car door and holds it open. I climb in and wait for him, sorting through my muddled thoughts. As Reed gets behind the wheel, the rain begins to fall again.

He pulls out of the parking lot and asks, "Why is it so important to you that Desiree take part in the show?"

His question catches me off guard. "Because it's important to her."

I expect him to question me more, but he lets it drop, concentrating on the road.

"Why did you say you would come with me to talk to her parents?"

He flashes me a soft smile. "Because it's important to *you*."

My breath freezes in my chest, burning my lungs. I'm not sure what to say to that. I'm not sure what's going on with us. He's turning into a park, determination on his face as though he's preparing for a fight.

I panic. "Where are you going?"

"We need to talk."

# Chapter Fifteen

My panic soars. "No, we don't."

"Yes, we do." His tone lets me know I'm not getting out of this until he's satisfied.

The sky darkens from the approaching storm so the park is empty. Reed pulls the car to a back lane and turns the engine off.

"We're not leaving until you hear me out."

"Then say what you have to say and let's go."

"Friday night was a mistake."

I cringe. I'm horrified and humiliated all over again. I berated myself enough this weekend to equal a flogging. I don't need Reed to do it too. "Why are you doing this? You made that clear Friday night."

"It was a mistake because we were with other people."

"Again—"

He leans over to me and places his fingertips over my mouth. "Will you just let me talk? And then you can skewer me all you want. Okay?"

I nod, my breathing shallow. My lips are on fire. His touch makes every part of my body ache.

"Contrary to what you seem to think of me, I don't routinely have sex in back rooms. And I've *never* had sex with someone while on a date with someone else. *That* was a mistake. Tina deserved better than that and so did Brandon."

He's right.

"*You* were not a mistake. Is that clear?"

I nod slowly in disbelief.

"You were definitely not a mistake." His voice is rich and heavy, but he pulls his fingers from my lips, and they feel naked.

He's still leaning over me, his eyes dark. "Why did you pull me into that room?"

My face flames. "Reed…."

"It's a simple question, Caroline."

I look down. "It's embarrassing."

He lifts my chin and looks into my eyes. "Then let me tell you why I went with you in that room, even though I was on a date: I wanted you. I've wanted you since the moment I saw you at Scarlett's party. Granted, I didn't handle the situation well. Then Lexi dragged me to that club, and I saw Dylan manhandling you. I was furious he was treating you that way when it was obvious you weren't interested. So against my better judgment, I intervened. Then when we danced, and I touched you"—he lifts his hand to my cheek—"I wanted you even more."

Reed leans closer. "I don't know what this is between us. I've never been this physically attracted to anyone, and I've never lost complete control like I did Friday night. You drive me insane, Caroline."

My breath is so shallow, I'm about to hyperventilate.

His hand slides down to my neck, his fingers brushing my pulse point. "Why did you pull me back to that room?"

A thousand reasons rush into my head. A thousand explanations, but it all boils down to the simplest of reasons. "I wanted you." My voice is low and heavy and almost a moan.

Reed's mouth lowers to mine, his hand on my neck, lifting my chin so his tongue can search deeper.

I lift my hands to his head, grabbing fistfuls of his hair and pulling him closer.

I need him closer.

His hand leaves my neck and reaches for the buttons of my blouse, unbuttoning them faster than I think possible given the fact his mouth is still plundering mine. When he reaches the last button, he spreads my blouse open, then turns me sideways and pushes my back against the passenger door.

He studies my chest then looks into my face, his eyes dark with lust. "God, you're beautiful." His hands skim up my waist, resting below the curve of my breasts.

I reach for his tie and unknot it, unbuttoning his shirt so I can see his chest.

He slides his hands onto my shoulders, slipping my bra straps down my arms until my sleeves impede his progress. He pushes my bra cups below the swell of my breasts and lowers his mouth to my chest.

I arch my back and cry out as his mouth finds my nipple. But he's twisted at an odd angle. He glides his seat back as far as it will go, then grabs my upper arms and pulls me over the console so I'm straddling his lap.

I lean over him, the raw hunger on his face driving my libido higher. I bite his lower lip, then run my tongue over it.

He groans and wraps his arms around my back, and pulls me against his chest as he takes control of the kiss. He lifts my skirt, so that he has full access to my legs and ass. "I like it when you wear skirts," he mumbles. "I can see your sexy legs, and it gives me easy access." His fingers loop around my panties and slide them down. I rise up on my knees and lift my legs as he pulls them off and tosses them onto the passenger seat.

I unfasten his jeans and tug them down over his hips.

The rain pounds the windows, blurring the outside world. Nothing else exists except for Reed and me in the confines of this car. The two of us and this primal need.

His hand slips between my legs and circles in small sweeps. I gasp as his fingers slide inside me, and he presses the palm of his hand into my mound and begins to move as his mouth takes my breast again.

I moan with frustration and need.

He lifts his head, and his free hand pulls my head down as he reaches up to kiss me. His kiss is wild and frenzied as I press myself into his hand. He leans his head back to look into my eyes. "I want you ready for me."

His words and the need in his eyes almost push me over the edge. "I'm ready for you now."

Reed reaches into his pocket and pulls out a condom, quickly putting it on. He looks into my eyes as he enters me, grabbing my hips and pulling me down on top of him. I lean my head back and gasp.

Reed sets the pace, starting slow so the pressure builds and builds until he's not keeping up with my body's demands. I lean over him and press my hands onto his shoulders, taking control. His head tilts back and stares into my face, a sheen of sweat covering his forehead. I grab his cheeks between my hands and kiss him, mimicking with my tongue what he's doing with his pelvis.

I'm close, sooner than I thought possible. I quicken my movements, a moan building low in my chest. Reed matches my pace, pushing me over the edge. I cry out, pressing hard against him, desperate to have him deeper.

He's close behind me, lifting my hips and pulling me against him at a frantic pace until he groans and pushes deeper one last time.

I lean my forehead against his. His eyes are closed as he recovers, then he lifts his lips to mine, kissing me gently.

We're still in our own sanctuary, the rain so heavy against the windows that there's no way anyone can see in.

He lifts me off and turns me so my legs drape over the console. My back is against the driver's door. My skirt is pulled up, my blouse spread wide. I'm exposed to him again, but the awe on his face abates any embarrassment I might feel.

His mouth lowers to mine and he turns my head toward him. His kiss is soft and gentle, but I feel my need for him growing again. I pull his head down, exploring his mouth with my tongue.

Reed groans into my mouth, his hand reaching between my legs. He has me writhing in his arms within minutes. His mouth leaves mine, finding the sensitive spot on my neck.

My breath is fast and shallow. "Reed." I plead. I'm not sure how long I'll last.

"Come for me, Caroline." His voice is husky against my neck, and his words tip me over the edge. I arch up into his hand and cry out as wave after wave washes over me until I'm limp in his arms.

I lie against him for several moments. The rain has let up and I can see the blurred outline of the trees around us. I look up into his face, surprised at the intensity of his gaze.

"What is this, Reed? What are we doing?"

His mouth lifts into a lopsided smile. "I can't believe no one's explained the birds and the bees to you."

I smirk and sit up, turning to face him. "We have this hot physical relationship, but what about the rest?"

His smile falters. "You've made your position on my career path clear." The Reed I first met is slipping back into place.

I close my eyes. Me and my stupid mouth. "Reed…."

"I don't expect you to settle for me and my paycheck. So I have a proposition."

I look up at him, skeptical. "What kind of proposition?"

"I take it you're not going out with Brandon again?"

I want to ask if he thought I'd be here if I was. But my behavior last Friday night stops me. "No."

He places his fingers between my breasts and brushes tender strokes between my cleavage. "We've admitted we're both attracted to one another, and we both find it difficult to control ourselves around each other."

I nod, unable to be as direct as Reed is.

"So what if we keep doing this until you find someone else?"

I stiffen and sit up. "You want me to be your booty call?"

His eyes widen. "No. No, that's not what I meant." He closes his eyes and groans.

"Then what *did* you mean?" I try to slide over to the passenger seat, but Reed holds me in place.

"Caroline, will you listen to me?" he asks in frustration.

I purse my lips.

His gaze softens. "I mean see each other, and of course this too. *This* is why we can't stay away from each other." His voice lowers. "But the next time we do *this*, I want it to be in a bed."

A thrill races through me at the thought of what we could do in bed.

"We're both consenting adults. We're both between partners. We're both *incredibly* attracted to one another. Why not?"

Maybe because I've never been a casual-sex kind of person. I still can't believe I did *this*. "I don't know."

"But it can be more than just sex. I'm looking for more than a booty call. We can try to be friends too."

It sounds so wrong the way he says it. Try to be friends? Shouldn't we already be friends? But he's right. This thing between us is carnal and unlike anything I've ever experienced. Can I really just walk away now that I've had a taste of it?

Reed fondles my breast, and I suck in my breath in surprise. He grins at my reaction. "The only drawback I can see is that we might not get much else done."

My eyes narrow in concern. "You're right, but I need to work on my collection. It's not even about the grade anymore. I'm doing it for the kids."

"Like Desiree?"

I drop my gaze. "Yeah."

"I'll make sure you work on your project. You know how bossy I can be."

I laugh. "So if I agree to this, you think this gives you permission to boss me around?"

"You'll like it when I boss you around in a bed."

Electricity runs straight through my body to my pelvis.

He pulls my mouth to his. "Say yes, Caroline. One word. *Yes.*"

His mouth works to convince me, and my body responds, wishing we were closer to a bed.

I'm not sure I have the power to resist this man. "Yes."

His grin turns playfully wicked. "You won't regret it."

But I'm already worried I will. I'm not sure my heart will survive this.

# Chapter Sixteen

The rain has all but stopped. I grab my panties and put them back on as I crawl back to my seat.

"I'll never be able to sit in this car again without thinking of you," he teases while cleaning himself up.

The first sign of embarrassment strikes. I look down and adjust my bra and begin to button my blouse.

"Caroline."

I turn toward him.

He lifts my chin. "We haven't done anything wrong. There's no reason to be embarrassed."

In the afterglow of our passion, uncertainty is slipping in.

"What are you doing tonight?" Reed asks.

"Working on my project."

"You have to eat. Let's get dinner and then I'll take you back to campus and jump your car. Lexi said your battery died."

Somehow I've forgotten about my car. This man messes with my head.

But I'm not ready to leave him yet and I want to try the *other* part of this arrangement. "Okay. But I hate Indian food."

His eyes widen. "How can you hate Indian food?"

I scrunch my nose. "Curry is disgusting."

He shakes his head in amazement. "Okay. How about Chinese? Then the continent of Asia won't feel slighted."

I laugh. Who knew Reed had a funny side? "Deal."

Reed starts the car then leans over and kisses me senseless. "To prove to you that this can be more than sex, I'm going to take you to dinner, walk you to your classroom, and then leave you. I can assure you that will probably be the hardest thing I've ever done, but I'll do it. For you."

I kiss him and smile against his lips.

He drives to the restaurant, and we have trouble finding something to talk about. I give evasive answers when he asks about my past.

*I grew up with both parents. I had an older brother. I lived in Shelbyville.* It's the most he gets from me, but he's just as evasive.

"You grew up in Boston?"

"Yes." His answer is short and terse.

In my flustered state of trying to fill the silence with conversation, I don't even think when I say, "I've never been to Boston. I've only left the state once. My sixth-grade class took a field trip to the Atlanta zoo." Why in the hell did I say that?

He looks at me like I've just grown gills. "How is it possible you've never left Tennessee?"

The way he asks makes me defensive. "I just told you that I *have* left the state. The last time I checked, Atlanta was in Georgia."

He shakes his head. "I mean, other than that."

The last thing I plan to tell him is that I couldn't afford to drive out of Shelbyville, let alone the state. I decide to play up my state pride. "Everything I could ever want is in Tennessee. Why would I want to leave it?"

"Then why are you trying to win a trip to New York with this fashion show?"

*Shit. Shit. Shit.*

"I thought I was asking you questions, not the other way around."

His scowl returns.

"I know your sister, Lexi. Do you have any other brothers and sisters?"

"No."

How are we supposed to have a conversation with one-word answers?

"So why did you major in math?"

This is the first time he's relaxed since I started questioning him. "I love the complexity of it. The need to pay attention to detail. One missed step, one misplaced decimal point, and the entire problem is wrong. Then you either start over again or backtrack and figure out what went wrong."

I cringe. "Oh, my God. That's exactly why I hate it."

His eyebrows rise. "You hate math? You could have fooled me when you helped Desiree with her homework."

"That was different. I can handle addition and subtraction. And even multiplication and simple division, but throw an algebra formula at me and I'll run screaming." I shift in my seat. "You said you were focusing on analysis of algorithms."

His eyes widen. "I'm impressed you remembered."

I smirk. "I'm not just a pretty face."

His gaze sweeps over me and ends at my eyes. He grins. "No, you're not."

"So why that focus?"

"When most boys were falling for girls in middle school, I fell for computers. I started teaching myself computer programming, and then I discovered Donald Knuth, the father of analysis of algorithms. He's been my idol ever since. That's why I wanted to go to Stanford." He stops talking, as though he's said something wrong.

"So why didn't you go to Stanford?"

He gives me a tight smile. "Because I came to Southern instead." The tone of his voice tells me this isn't up for further discussion.

When we get to the restaurant and order, I rest my arms on the table. "What are we going to tell people ... about us?"

His face is serious. "How about we tell them something completely crazy? Like we're going out." Then he winks.

"I'm serious, Reed. This was your idea."

He reaches across the table and takes my hand. "I'm serious too, Caroline."

Holding his hand makes me feel more connected to him than anything we've done up to this point. He's seen me in the most intimate moments of my life, but that was lust and sex. This is tenderness.

"So if we tell people we're going out, what makes this different than every other relationship in the world?"

"The fact you're with me until you find the man you're looking for."

I feel like I'm a deer caught in headlights.

He sees my expression and leans toward me. "No guilt. The night I met you, you told me I didn't stand a chance. I know this going in. I've seen the guys you date. High profile. High society. Old money. Dylan was an asshole, but I'm not sure what flaw you saw in Brandon. His money is deep-South old money. I would have thought that alone would interest you."

He makes me sound like a selfish, self-centered, gold-digging bitch. But then why wouldn't he think that? He's paraphrasing what I told him the night I met him.

I feel nauseated. "Why in the world do you want to be with me after knowing that about me?"

His jaw works and he glances at the door before turning back to me. His voice lowers. "Because sex with you is unlike anything I've ever experienced. And honestly, I think the connection we have is once-in-a-lifetime. If it means I only get to have you until you find what you're looking for, I'm good with that."

I'm still horrified that he'll settle for being with me until I find his replacement. He sees this too.

"Caroline, don't worry about me. I'm a guy and guys think with what's in their pants." He winks but something's missing. "We're both getting something out of it. Hot, unbelievably fantastic sex and we haven't even had a chance to take our time and enjoy it." His voice lowers. "And I already have several fantasies of you I need you to act out. How do you feel about a schoolgirl outfit?" He grins.

He's teasing. But is he telling the truth about the rest? Tucker says guys think with their dicks. Isn't Reed telling me the same thing? I should be humiliated and insulted, but Reed Pendergraft is a hot, sexy man trapped behind a tie and a stuffy degree. Most girls don't care about the degree and find the tie sexy. I do too, but I like the way he looks right now, with his tie off and the top button of his shirt undone. Then I think about his shirt spread open in the car.

"You were just picturing me naked, weren't you?" he asks.

I feel a blush rise to my cheeks.

"If it makes you feel better, I was thinking about you naked too. That's priority number one the next time we have sex. I want to see you completely naked. Wearing heels," he says. "The ones you wore Friday night. The black strappy things that poked me in the ass when you wrapped your legs around me. When I close my eyes, I can still imagine you pressed up against the wall with your legs around my waist. Your hair hung over your bare breasts and your lips were red and swollen from kissing me."

If it were possible to have an orgasm without being touched, I'm sure I'm worked up enough over his word picture for it to happen right now.

His smile is replaced by a look of molten desire. "God, I love the way you look when you're turned on."

How can I want to sleep with him already?

"We need a bed." I force out in a breathless rush. "Now."

He takes my hand and traces circles in my palm. "We'll have a bed. But not tonight. I promised to prove to you that I want you for more than sex. Dinner, then I'll take you to the design lab."

"What if I want it? Then you have to give it to me. Our arrangement was for sex. The rest is superfluous."

Some emotion flickers in his eyes before his wicked smile returns. "No sex tonight. Driving you crazy wanting me is a bonus. Then when we have sex—in a bed—it will be even better."

The way I feel right now makes me want to argue, but the waiter brings our food, and I'm surprised to find I'm starving. I eat most of my chicken lo mein.

"When I bring you to my apartment to fuck you, I'll make sure I have plenty of food to help you regain your strength."

I'm slightly shocked by his coarse language. I'm totally shocked it turns me on so much.

When we finish, Reed doesn't want to linger. "First, you need to get to work. If you don't get your work done, then you'll blame our arrangement and call it off. I'm not willing to risk that when we're just getting started." He stops next to his car, pressing my back against the passenger door and placing his hands on either side of me. "But mostly, if I stay with you much longer, I'll break my promise to not have sex tonight, and I hate broken promises." He kisses me, his lips tender and tentative until I wrap my arms around him to hold myself up. His tongue finds mine, searching and coaxing. I moan again. I have such little self-control with him, I'd probably lift my skirt right here in the parking lot.

And that scares the shit out of me.

Thankfully, Reed pulls back and opens the door. On the drive to campus, he asks questions about my project and my designs for the kids.

"Thanks for your help today."

"It was fun."

I laugh. "It was fun writing down measurements?"

"It was fun seeing you do what you love."

"And what's that? Strutting my stuff on the runway?"

He takes my hand and twines our fingers. "That was *definitely* fun. As you swung your hips, I kept thinking about how gifted those hips actually are."

"Reed! There were children in the room!"

"I didn't touch you, although I should get a medal for that. But we better hope none of them were mind readers or they might need therapy after the things I fantasized."

"And what did you fantasize?" I ask against my better judgment.

He grins, lifting his eyebrows. "Some things are better demonstrated than explained."

My imagination runs wild, and I feel flushed as he parks his car next to mine in the half-empty campus parking lot.

"Are you sure you can't break your promise?" I ask. "Just this once?"

He leans over, and his lips hover over mine. "Abstinence makes the heart grow fonder."

I laugh. "That is *not* how that platitude goes."

He pecks me on the lips with a chaste kiss. "Same difference." He gets out of the car and walks around to open my door. "If you give me your keys, I'll jump your car and bring them back to you."

"Reed, you don't have to do that."

He grins. "Isn't that one of the perks of having a temporary boyfriend? Having him do things like jump your car?"

I'd rather he jumped *me*, but I keep that to myself. "Someone forgot to put that in my last boyfriend's job description."

His mouth parts. "You're kidding me, right?"

"Nope." I say, digging my keys out of my purse.

I put them in Reed's outstretched hand but his fingers close around mine, and he pulls me against his chest. Irritation simmers behind his eyes. "Promise me that when you find a guy, you'll make sure he does that stuff for you."

I look up into his face, surprised at his insistence. "Reed, I'm perfectly capable of jumping my car. I've done it before."

"It's not a matter of being capable, Caroline. I never doubted you were capable. In fact, I suspect you're capable of a lot more than you give yourself credit for. But it doesn't mean you don't deserve to have a guy who does it for you." He releases his hold. "Do you need anything out of your car?"

"Uh ... no."

He takes my bag and starts to walk toward campus.

"You don't have to carry my bag."

He turns back to me, spreading his hands wide. "It falls under the category of *he should do it anyway*."

"Maybe I should have you interview potential boyfriends."

"I doubt you want that."

"Why?"

"Because I'll never find anyone I think is worthy of you." He snags my hand as we walk side by side, and I think about what he said.

If Reed really feels that way, then why isn't he fighting to keep me? Why is he so willing to let me go?

I consider that maybe he likes the idea of sex without strings. But the truth is he thinks I'll never consider him good enough for me.

The thought sickens me. Yet, if I'm truthful, I love what I feel with Reed but the thought of committing to someone who won't make a lot of money brings me close to a panic attack. I've got a mountain of student loans and Reed has to have even more if he really went to an Ivy League school. I won't make much money with this degree, idiot that I am for choosing it, and he won't make much either. How would we pay off our student loans and survive, let alone raise a family? Superficial or not, I can't let myself think about a long-term relationship with Reed Pendergraft.

I can have the best of both worlds. A guy who gives me incredibly hot sex but understands my need for financial security. So why does it feel so wrong?

When we reach the design lab, I stand outside the room. "This is it." I point to the rectangular window in the door with my thumb. "You can come in if you want, but there's not much to see. My designs are all on paper at this point."

"So what will you do now?"

"I'll pick one and work on it, coming up with a pattern and cutting out the fabric. If I can start sewing, all the better."

He tilts my head back and looks into my eyes. His hand caresses the spot where my neck meets my jaw, and my knees turn weak. How can he do that with one simple touch?

"Do you have my cell phone number with you?" he asks.

"What?" I can't concentrate, caught in this lusty haze.

"My number. Do you have it?" he repeats, but he looks like he's having trouble focusing too.

"I don't know."

"Get out your phone."

I come to my senses and pull my phone of my purse.

"Now put my number in and call me." He tells me his number and when I call, he answers, lowering his voice. "Caroline Hunter, if your car won't start when you leave, promise to call me."

"Okay."

He ends the call and puts the phone in his pocket. "But call me anyway, okay? Otherwise I'll worry your car didn't make it home."

"Why?"

He looks at me like I lost my mind. "I jumped your car. That makes me responsible for you getting home safely." His lips brush mine. "Promise."

He fights dirty. He knows he's my kryptonite, and he's using it to his advantage.

"I promise."

His lips barely touch mine, and he's driving me mad. "Get a lot of work done so I don't feel guilty when I keep you in bed for hours tomorrow."

"Hours?"

"We'll need at least that long for everything I want to do with you."

I stand on tiptoes to press my lips more firmly against his, but he lifts his head.

"First work. Then playing."

I shake my head with a laugh. "You know how to inspire a girl."

"I promised to be bossy. Now go get a lot of work done because I have big plans for you tomorrow."

Tomorrow can't get here soon enough.

# Chapter
# Seventeen

I push stray hairs from my face, exhausted, but happy with the progress I've made. It's later than I expected, but not only did I make a pattern for a skirt, top and vest, I cut the fabric and sewed most of the skirt.

When I'm halfway to my car, I realize Reed never brought back my keys. I lean my head back and groan. It's two o'clock in the morning. I'm going to wake him. But he made me promise to call him anyway. I hope he doesn't live too far off campus.

He answers on the first ring, and he sounds more awake than I feel.

"You still have my keys," I say, pausing mid-sentence to yawn.

"I'm still on campus. Are you still in the design lab?"

"No, I'm halfway to my car."

"It's two in the morning. Did you call security to walk with you?"

"No." I'm surprised by his protective tone. "It never occurred to me."

"Are you telling me that you routinely walk across campus in the middle of the night?" His voice is tight.

"I think you're overreacting."

"Tell that to the six women who were raped on Southern's campus last year." He sounds angry, but he also sounds breathless.

I stop in the middle of the sidewalk under a beam of light coming from a street lamp. "What are you talking about?"

"Are you telling me you never check the campus crime reports?"

"Why on earth would I?"

"To be *safe*?" He's furious now. "Where the hell are you?"

"I told you. Halfway across campus."

"Goddamn it, Caroline. I'm coming."

My anger soars. Who the hell does he think he is? "Well good for you." I hang up, but keep my phone in my hand in case I need it. Was he serious that there were six rapes on campus last year? Southern's always felt safe, cocooned from the outside world. Now Reed's ripped away that perception.

If there were really six rapes on campus, wouldn't I have heard about it?

Well, screw Reed Pendergraft. I start walking the rest of the way, imagining monsters lurking in the shadows. When I reach my car, I see Reed's Altima still parked next to mine. I don't think he left campus after he dropped me off. Why would he stay all this time waiting for me? What the hell has he been doing?

I sit on the hood of my car and watch as he stops jogging at the edge of the parking lot when he sees me. My anger has cooled by the time he reaches me, but the same can't be said for him.

"What the hell were you thinking?" He's still furious, perhaps even more so.

"I told you, it never occurred to me that something could happen and nothing did. Other than being verbally berated by an angry grad student."

"I'm serious, Caroline."

"So am I, Reed." I pull him toward me between my spread legs. "Do you know how sexy you are when you get all protective like that?"

Some of the tension leaves his shoulders.

"What are you still doing on campus?" I ask.

"Working. You're not the only one with projects. I have a midterm due next week."

I close my eyes. I really am a selfish bitch. It never occurred to me to ask about his own work. "Did you get a lot done?"

"Yeah, what about you?"

"More than I expected." I'm tired but when I kiss him, my exhaustion fades away. "Is it tomorrow yet?" I murmur against his lips.

His answer is the way he devours my mouth, kissing me like he hasn't seen me for six months instead of six hours.

"Come home with me," I say. "I have a bed. With a mattress and everything. Pillows too."

He stops and brushes the hair out of my eyes, staring into my face with a worried look. "Aren't you tired?"

"Not anymore. Although I'm not sure I'll last for hours."

"We can see how long you last."

I giggle. "Is that a challenge?"

"Take it as you like."

I slide off the hood, and down the front of Reed's body. He groans and holds me close.

"Did I mention I have a bed?" I ask.

He grabs my wrist and pulls me to the driver's door of my car. After he unlocks the door, he hands me the keys.

I narrow my eyes with playful suspicion. "Could keeping my keys be a ploy to try out my bed, Reed Pendergraft?"

He winks. "You caught me. I'm bed-less and beg you to give mercy to a mattress-challenged man."

I stand on tiptoe and press my lips to his. "Then tonight's your lucky night."

Before he can kiss me back, I dart away and slip into my car.

He grins ear to ear. "I'll follow you."

My car starts without a problem, and I've never been so eager in my life to get home, keeping Reed's headlights in my rearview mirror.

He's out of his car before I grab my bag and get out of mine. He takes my hand and practically drags me up the stairs to my apartment. After he takes my keys, he unlocks the door and pulls me inside, closing the door and pushing me against it.

"Unbutton your shirt," he says. He wasn't kidding about bossing me around.

I smile and take my time pushing the buttons through the holes.

The room is dark. The only light comes from a small lamp sitting on the kitchen counter.

When I finish my task, I wait while he studies my breasts.

"Where's your room?"

Good idea. Tina's not a light sleeper, but it would be awkward if she found us, especially since she was on a date with Reed less than a week ago.

I walk toward my room, and I'm surprised he doesn't reach for me. When we enter my room, I switch on the lamp on my bedside table as he closes the door.

"Take off your shirt and skirt."

I turn around to face him, sliding my shirt down my arms and letting it fall to the floor. Reed brings a confidence out of me that I've never felt in the bedroom before. I tried to strip for Justin once, but it ended with me feeling awkward. The way Reed watches me now, the last thing I feel like is awkward.

I hook my thumbs under the waistband of my skirt and slowly slip it over my hips, shimmying a little in the process when I remember he liked watching my hips during my model walk. Before the skirt hits the floor, he's pulled me into his arms, his mouth searching mine.

We both take off his clothes, a joint effort that ends up with Reed in his briefs and me in my lingerie.

He stares at my body for several seconds then kisses me again, with a tenderness we've never shared during sex before. He lowers me to the bed, and his hands skim my body, up my arms, then down my sides.

"Caroline, you're so beautiful."

I grin up at him. "You're gorgeous yourself."

He gives me a mock arrogant grin. "It must have been my model walk." Then he laughs, and my heart swells with something I don't recognize. Before I can stop to figure it out, he's pulling me up and removing my bra.

"I told you I want to see you naked in bed."

I offer a mock frown. "But alas, no heels."

His smile turns wicked. "That is *so* easily taken care of." He tugs off my panties and tosses them onto the floor then he kneels on the bed, not touching, only watching. "I want to be on top, watching your face as I fuck you."

I hold back a moan and heat pours through my body.

"You like it when I talk dirty to you, don't you?"

"Yes." The word is guttural and an octave lower than my usual voice. I should be embarrassed to admit this to him, but I'm not.

The erection in his briefs swells. "Where are your heels?"

I rise up on my elbows. "You weren't kidding."

"No."

This man turns me on in ways I never thought possible. "In my closet."

He opens the door and a few seconds later he turns around with the black heels I wore Friday night hanging from his fingers. "Put them on."

I've never worn heels in bed, but the act of sitting up and strapping them on while I'm naked as Reed watches is highly erotic.

"Now lie down," he says as he takes off his briefs.

I do as he says, taking in the sight of him completely naked. Heat spreads throughout my body, and I'm desperate for him to touch me. Not to mention I'm excited and nervous to see what he has planned next.

"You're so gorgeous, lying there naked, your hair spread out on your pillow. And your eyes ... you have the most beautiful eyes." He kneels at the foot of the bed, between my feet. "I've tasted the upper part of your body, but the lower half has been seriously neglected." He picks up one of my legs and rests the back of my ankle on his shoulder. "I plan to take care of that." His lips slide up my ankle as his places kisses up my calf, stopping in the hollow behind my knee.

He laughs when I squirm then he lowers my leg and lifts the other to his shoulder, repeating the same process. "Am I driving you crazy yet?" he asks, his mouth skimming up to my thigh, just above my knee.

"Yes."

He laughs softly as his mouth continues its ascent. He leaves one leg on his shoulder and spreads my other leg open then leans over to kiss the inside of my thigh. My breasts rise and fall with my quickened breaths.

"I've fantasized about this. You naked, wearing your heels, your eyes telling me how much you want me and the evidence of it between your legs so there's no doubt."

If he doesn't turn his attention to the place he just mentioned, I'm going to spontaneously combust.

As if reading my mind, his tongue finds the spot that drives me wild. I arch my back and gasp. Reed may be going to school for a graduate degree in math, but his real expertise lies in what he's doing now. The only comparison I have is Justin and his half-hearted attempts. Reed has just proven Justin had no idea what he was doing.

Reed lifts my hips and slips a finger inside me, then moments later, he inserts another while his mouth concentrates on its assigned task.

"Reed." I plead.

"It's okay." His tongue circles in its tortuous dance. "I want you to come this way."

I moan.

"*Oh, fuck*, I love to hear your little sounds." One of his hands slides up my stomach and over the swell of my breast, fondling my nipple.

I arch into him, the onslaught of sensations pushing me to dizzying heights, and I can barely keep up, but Reed pushes me higher and higher, until I can hardly breathe. And then the bottom falls away and I cry out his name again and again. And when I land, I'm surprised to find my hands fisted in his hair.

Raw hunger fills his eyes and this sight of him between my legs, watching me with such longing, causes my passion to build again.

My hands still in his hair, I pull his mouth to mine. The taste of myself on his tongue is shocking, but it turns me on even more. I wrap my legs around his waist.

"Oh God, Caroline. I have never wanted anyone like I want you."

His words turn me on too.

Reed has turned me into this wild, wicked woman and not only do I not care, I want more. I'm insatiable.

"Fuck me, Reed."

The muscles in his neck tense. "I have to get a condom." He sounds impatient.

I lock my ankles at the small of his back. My heels press into the soft flesh of his ass.

He sucks in a breath as his eyes close.

"Do you still like my heels?" I whisper huskily.

"God, yes," he groans. "I want to be in you *now*." He tries to get up, but I tighten my legs around him.

"I've had sex with four guys, and all but one wore a condom. The one who didn't was an ass, but he didn't cheat on me. I'm clean, and I'm on the pill." I pull his head down and take his earlobe in my mouth, biting the soft flesh. "You always wear a condom, don't you?"

"Yes." His breath warms my cheek.

"I want to be your first without one. I want you to have lots of firsts with me, just like almost everything we do is a first for me." My mouth moves to his neck and his pulse throbs against my lips as his erection throbs against my core. "Fuck me."

He groans and rises on his forearms, his gaze on mine as he slowly slides into me. His eyes roll back as his head leans back. "Caroline." He pushes deeper until he's all the way in. "*Fuck*," he growls.

I lift my pelvis so he can slide deeper. He grabs my hips, his fingers digging in to hold me where he wants me as he begins to move. "You feel so good."

The pressure builds again, and Reed pushes me higher with every thrust.

"Fuck me, Reed." I arch my back. "Fuck me harder."

He groans and obeys.

I'm not the only one who likes dirty talk.

I'm so close but I hang on, letting the pressure build, and when I don't think I can hold on any more I let go, flying apart into a million pieces.

I'm vaguely aware when he growls. It starts low then builds. His fingers dig into my hips, pulling me closer, as he tries to get deeper. When he comes, he releases a primal groan then collapses on top of me. I unlock my ankles, and he slides to my side, slipping his arm under my back then rolling to his back, my head resting on his chest.

"I swear to God, you're going to be the death of me," he murmurs against my temple.

"Are you complaining?" I yawn.

"God, no." His hand cups my cheek and lifts my face so he can see me. Instead of the usual lust in his eyes, there's tenderness instead. He brushes stray hairs from my cheek. "The next time you walk to your car again at campus in the middle of the night, promise me you'll call the campus police to escort you."

"That again?" I close my eyes with a sigh. I'd forgotten about our previous disagreement.

"If you promise me, the next time we have sex, I'll make sure it's even better than tonight."

"I don't think that's possible." But every time with Reed has been better than the last. Maybe it is possible. "Good call on the bed," I murmur, my eyelids so heavy I can barely keep them open. I need to take off my heels, but I can't find the energy.

"Say *you were right, Reed.*"

"God, you're so bossy."

"Say it. I want to hear you say it."

I'm too tired to fight him. "You were right, Reed."

He kisses my temple again, and the last thing I hear before I drift off to sleep is Reed whispering, "Yes, I am." But he doesn't seem happy about it.

# Chapter Eighteen

I wake in a tangle of sheets and limbs. I'm not wearing my heels. Reed must have taken them off.

His arm lies across my chest. I turn to watch him sleep, and I wonder again how I could have so easily dismissed him the night I met him. Granted, I was intent on getting a date with Dylan, and Reed was a bit awkward, but Reed has to be the most attractive man I've ever known. Or is he more attractive because of what we've experienced together?

His eyes flutter open, and he grins before they close again. "Good morning." He pulls me tight to his chest. "I had the most *amazing* night."

"Really?" I tease.

"Not only did I get the most beautiful woman in the world to strip for me and lie naked wearing her heels, but she begged me to fuck her." He groans, and I feel his erection against my thigh.

I laugh, but I feel a stir deep in my abdomen. "As difficult as it is for me to be the voice of reason, we both have classes we need to get ready for."

One of his eyelids slits open. "And you know about my class, how?"

"You handed out copies of your schedule. I memorized it in case you threw a pop quiz and then executed anyone who scored less than eighty percent."

He laughs against my hair. "So maybe I was a bit intense…."

"You think?"

He rolls me to my back and rises on an elbow. "It's all your fault, you know."

"Mine? How?"

"You drove me crazy. It was either be a fucking prick or beg you to give me a chance." He laughs. "I would have begged you if it came to that, but listening to you beg me is so much better."

It's my turn to moan. "As much as I want to spend the entire day with you, we both need to get up."

Reed leans over to check the time on my bedside clock, then drops his face into his pillow with a groan of protest. "No." He grinds his head into the pillow as he shakes. "Somehow I don't think my Algebra 101 students will appreciate the sacrifice I'm making for them."

"You're probably right, but I have an environmental impact class I can't miss." I swing my legs over the side of the bed, then give him a saucy look over my shoulder. "Want to take a shower with me?"

He lowers his mouth to my shoulder. "Now here's a neglected part."

"Focus, Reed."

"It's quite difficult to focus with you purposely distracting me. You are *very* naughty." I know from the way he says it that he's not talking about this morning.

I start to stand but he pulls me back down. I turn to him, laughing. "Shower or no?"

His smile falls. "I need to get home and check on Lexi."

I try not to react to his news. "So Lexi *does* live with you?"

His eyes narrow. "What does it matter?"

"She's a sophomore in college, yet she can't seem to do anything without her big brother. That's just...." I search for a non-insulting word.

"Weird?" His tone is dry, and the shutter over his eyes—

the signal that announces that cold, unyielding Reed Pendergraft is open and ready for business—falls into place. He sits up, his playfulness gone.

Damn my mouth. Why did I start down this path? But now that I've frolicked headlong into it, I decide to press on. I owe it to Lexi. "Don't you think she should have a real college experience that doesn't include living with her brother and having him chaperone her every move?"

Anger flickers in his eyes. "Let it go, Caroline. You don't know what you're talking about."

He slides off the bed and picks up his clothes, angrily stuffing his legs into his underwear and jeans.

"You can't smother her forever."

"Let it go, Caroline."

But for some reason, I can't. I'm like a dog with a bone, and I refuse to give it up, even when I know it's suicide. "Have you ever asked Lexi what she wanted?"

Reed pulls his shirt over his head, his face red. "Caroline, let's not forget this isn't a real relationship. We're doing this until your Prince Charming shows up on his white horse. Based on those limiting parameters, I think it nullifies any say you have in my affairs with my family." Cold Reed is back, the man I've encountered in a host of places. But I never thought I'd find him in my bedroom.

"If I'm so disgusting, what are you doing here? You can't find anyone else to talk dirty to?"

His face softens, and he closes his eyes with a groan. "No, Caroline. God, no." He grabs my arms and drags me against his chest. His arms wrap around my back and hold me in place. "Please don't say that. This isn't dirty, and I don't want to be with anyone else. I don't think of you in any way but with respect and adoration."

I try to pull back, but his arms hold tight.

"I'm just protective of my sister."

"I guess we'll have to agree to disagree."

"Have dinner with me tonight."

I grin against his shirt, but my earlier happiness has faded, leaving an empty ache in my chest. "I don't know if I'll have time."

He sighs, gripping my arms and taking a step back. "You're giving me the brushoff."

"No. I'm being truthful. I've got so much to do and so little time."

"We have a committee meeting this afternoon. You can tell me if you think you can make it then." His eyes have lost their earlier sparkle.

I want to cry, and I'm not even sure why. I feel like I'm losing him, but then again, the plan is that he's temporary. He's never been mine to lose. The ache in my chest expands and steals my breath.

"Reed?"

His hand lifts to my cheek. "Um?"

"Will you kiss me before you go?"

He smiles, but it doesn't reach his eyes. "As if I could physically leave you without kissing and fondling you again." His mouth lowers to mine, and his hands cup my butt, pressing my pelvis into his. "If I were getting a doctorate in physics, I'd concentrate my studies on the unexplained and unprecedented phenomena of the pull you have on me. Is it gravitational? Electromagnetic? Is it some new force science has yet to discover? Perhaps I should change my doctorate. I'm sure I could get a Nobel Peace Prize out of it."

I grin against his lips, grateful some of his playfulness has returned. "Maybe you could be an overachiever and go for both."

He kisses me softly then leans his forehead to mine. "I think I'll see how my current attempt at overachieving goes." His presses another soft kiss to my bottom lip and drops his hold on me. "I'll see you this afternoon."

I'd follow him out the door, but I'm completely naked. I've had this entire conversation with him without a stitch of clothing on and I never gave it any thought. What has this man done to me?

After I take a shower, I throw on my robe and pad out to the kitchen to make a cup of coffee.

Tina's standing in front of the sink, eating a bowl of cereal. She sees me, sets the bowl down, and claps, a cheesy grin on her face. "Bravo." She holds her hand up to high-five me, but I ignore it. "That was one *hell* of a good time you had last night."

*Shit.* I squeeze my eyes closed. I'm going to die. "Sorry."

"Oh, hell no. Don't ever be sorry for great sex. Is it that Brandon guy? I thought you decided not to go out with him anymore." She picks up her cereal and shovels in a spoonful.

"No, it's not Brandon."

"So? Who is it?" Her words are muffled by her mouthful of food. "Do I know him?"

I turn my back to her and change the cup in the coffeemaker. "Yeah, you do." I press the button to make a cup of coffee, then turn to face her. "It's Reed. Reed Pendergraft."

She blinks. "Wait. The Reed Pendergraft in the math department? The boring guy who took me home before eleven o'clock on a Friday night?"

The Reed in my bedroom was anything but boring. "Yes, the Reed you went out with."

A wicked grin lights up her face. "Maybe I need to give Mr. Pendergraft another chance."

I'm surprised at the possessiveness that shoots through me. "I think he's currently taken."

She holds her fingers up like claws and scratches them at me with a wicked grin. "Look at you. Pulling out your claws over a math professor." She laughs. "Who would have thought it?" she says as she sets her bowl in the sink.

My back stiffens. "What does that mean?"

She scrunches her face in disbelief. "Come on, Caroline. Everyone knows the guys you date have to meet certain *criteria*. Reed definitely doesn't make the mark."

"What criteria?"

Laughing she shakes her head in disbelief. "Are you serious?" Tina rests her butt against the counter and crosses her arms. "Major. They have to have a major with a huge potential salary. Then there's their current financial situation. Coming from families with established money is a big plus. And of course, looks." She lifts an eyebrow. "I don't blame you on that one. You're gorgeous. You deserve to marry a gorgeous man."

Nausea rolls in my stomach. "Anything else?"

She twists her mouth to the side in thought. "Only that you're a Virgin Mary in the bedroom. Although what I heard last night disproves that."

"Wait. What do you mean I'm a Virgin Mary? Who says that?"

She squints at me like I've lost my mind. "That's your reputation, Caroline. Guys see it as a challenge to, one, see if you'll even go on a date with them. And two, see how far they'll get. Rumor has it they can't get to third base until after the fourth date. You're known as the Ice Princess of Southern."

I close my eyes in horror. "I think I've heard enough."

"Good to have evidence that you aren't the cold fish most guys think you are." She rinses out her bowl and puts it in the dishwasher. "When you're done with him, let me know. I might try to get him to go a round or two. Color me intrigued."

I go back to my room, leaving my coffee in the kitchen. If I try to drink it, I'm sure I'll vomit.

Is that why Reed made this proposal? He knew my criteria, and this is his way of getting in my pants? Is that why he's agreed to make this temporary, thinking he'd get a shot at Ice Princess Caroline?

Scarlett and Tucker were fuel for the gossip mill because Tucker was a soccer star with a bad-boy reputation. He changed when he started dating Scarlett. But I'm not like Tucker. I'm a nobody. I faced more than my share of ugly gossip in high school. I thought I had escaped rumors at college. Stupid me. Gossip is everywhere.

I call Scarlett on the way to school, still feeling ill. "Did you know there were rumors about me at Southern?"

"Uh…" she pauses. "In any particular topic?"

"There's more than one?" I wail.

"Caroline, stop. I was teasing. No, I haven't heard anything, but you know the only people I hang out with are math people and Tucker. That's who you need to talk to. Tucker knows all the gossip while I don't care."

I latch onto something she's said. "So you mean the math students don't hear the gossip? What about Tina? She knows some of the gossip."

Scarlett snorts. "Tina is an anomaly. I can't speak for everyone, but the probability is that people in the math department aren't privy to gossip. Nor interested."

So maybe Reed hasn't heard it.

She pauses and her voice takes on a suspicious tone. "This is about Reed, isn't it?"

I remain silent.

"Spill."

I tell her about my car not starting, and Reed driving me to the center and how wonderful he was with the kids. "He wanted to talk about last Friday night."

"I should hope so."

"He told me that I'd read things wrong. He was disgusted with himself because we were there with other people."

"Do you believe him?"

"He seemed genuine." I clear my throat. "There's something else." I can't bring myself to tell her our arrangement. It sounds superficial and dirty.

"And...."

Simple is best. "We've agreed to try to date."

She's silent.

"Why aren't you saying anything?"

"Why are you wasting your time with him? You know he's not your type."

"You mean poor."

"I prefer to think of it as financially challenged," Scarlett says.

"You of all people should understand my reasoning."

"There's more to life than money."

I laugh and it's ugly and raw. "Tell that to eight-year-old me. The one who's immortalized on the wall of pictures at the Middle Tennessee Children's Charity. The little girl who went to bed crying because her stomach burned with hunger. The girl whose clothes came from the charity and were so worn and faded, they had to be fifth- or sixth-hand, not second. Or the twelve-year-old girl who only had one pair of shoes. A worn pair of sneakers with holes and the soles falling off. I wore them all fucking year, Scarlett." I choke on the lump in my throat. "You tell the girl whose life was a living hell all because she didn't have money. You tell *that* girl money isn't important."

"Caroline." Scarlett's soft voice soothes my pain at my remembrance.

"So even you think I'm a gold-digging, frigid bitch?"

"Did Reed say that?" She sounds livid.

"No." I smirk. "Ironically, he's the one person who didn't."

"Does he know about your past?"

I blink and remain silent for several seconds. "You know the answer to that."

I can hear her disappointment in her silence.

"How's your mom?"

"I have no idea."

"Don't blow this, Caroline."

"Enough with the lectures, Scarlett. I've gotta go."

"Okay." She sounds worried. "But I hate for us to hang up this way."

I sigh. "We're good. I'm pulling into the west parking lot now so I need to focus on getting a parking spot."

"Okay."

I hang up before she finishes the word.

I call Tucker next and immediately ask, "What are the rumors going around campus about me?"

Tucker's voice raises two octaves. "*Hello, Tucker this is Caroline. How are you? Good, I have a question.*" His voice returns to normal. "That's how it's done."

"And yet we still get back to the same question. What are the rumors going around about me?"

"Caroline."

"I'm a big girl and I'm about to go into class so I don't have time for the tiptoe bullshit. I want to know now."

He pauses. "The fluffy version or the straight version?"

So Tina was right. There really *are* rumors about me. "Give it to me straight."

"You're at Southern for your M.R.S. degree."

"I see." The sad truth is the rumors are right.

"Most guys see it as a personal challenge to get you to bed." He lets that one soak in. "That's why I put the fear of God into Reed Friday night. In case that was his reason for sniffing around."

"Thanks." I hang up and walk across campus toward my Environmental Sustainability for Designers class. I want to trust Reed, I really do. But I need to hear it from his own mouth. If he really got me into bed as a challenge, wouldn't he get laid and move on? But then why would he? The sex is great. Why not stick around and enjoy it? I've handed him a commitment-free relationship on a silver platter. Isn't that what most guys dream of? And all set up by my own rules.

It's difficult to concentrate on my class, and I consider calling Reed and confronting him but when my class is over, I pull out my phone and find a text:

*Did your car start this morning? I should have stuck around to make sure you got to campus okay.*

That doesn't sound like a guy looking for a quick lay. For now, I decide to take him at his word until he proves me otherwise.

*It started fine. Thank you. For everything.*

*My pleasure.*

I laugh at his last text, sure it has more than one meaning.

My next class isn't until this afternoon so I grab a coffee and a bagel from the student center and head to the design lab. I can get a good three hours in before I have to stop for class, then I can get another hour in before the committee meeting. I'm going to practically be living in the lab for the next two weeks.

I get the skirt constructed and realize I'm in huge trouble. The dressmaker forms are adult women sizes.

"Caroline, you've got to go," one of my classmates calls out. "Don't you have a committee meeting at four?"

I glance up at the clock on the wall. It's 4:02. "Shit."

I grab my bag and toss in a few items, but leave my fabric and pieces at my worktable. "I don't have time to pick this up. I'll be back in an hour."

"Go. I'll watch it."

I hurry across campus and walk into the conference room in the dean's office at 4:10. Everyone looks up at me as I walk in. I half expect Reed to give me a stern admonishment, but that was the old Reed. New Reed looks up with a soft smile and says, "We were just finishing the marketing report."

Everyone's eyes widen and they look from Reed to me then back at Reed as though he's grown a third eye on his forehead. It's obvious to everyone this is uncharacteristic of Dictator Pendergraft.

They've skipped my report so they come back to me, even though I don't have much to tell. The company in charge of setting up the runway has been hired and confirmed. The theater department has agreed to help with lighting and all the design students now have child models.

When everyone reports on their duties, Reed looks happy. "We're in good shape. How about we skip a meeting on Friday and discuss anything that comes up in a group e-mail?"

No one complains. The last thing anyone wants to do is spend late Friday afternoon at a committee meeting. The glance Reed slips my direction tells me he has other ideas of how to fill the time.

After the meeting is adjourned, everyone files out, but I take my time putting my legal pad back in my bag. Reed hangs back as well, but so does Lexi. When the last person walks out, Lexi's face lights up. "Where were you last night, Reed?"

Reed's head shoots up. "I told you I stayed all night in the math department and came home to shower."

She sucks in her lips and looks back and forth at us as she tilts her head. "Hmm." She doesn't believe it for a minute. She directs her attention to me. "Did Reed take you to the center to measure the children?"

"Of course," I say. I feel like I'm being interrogated. Then I realize I am.

"And did he behave himself?"

My face burns with a blush. "He was a perfect gentleman." I don't know what Reed has told her about us. Perhaps he doesn't want her to know, since this is temporary.

Reed walks over to me and wraps an arm around my back. His hand rests on my hip, so there's no doubt we're together. "We went to dinner when we finished up."

Thank God he doesn't tell Lexi *what* we finished up before dinner.

Her eyes light up. "Dinner that lasted all night?" Her eyebrows rise playfully.

Reed's fingers dig into my hip and I fight the urge to let my body melt into his. I really need to work on self-control with him. "I jumped her car but stuck around the math department working until she called asking for her keys. So I followed her home to make sure she didn't have any trouble."

"I bet you did. You're such a gentleman, Reed," she teases.

But the truth is that Reed *is* a gentleman. I'm sure he would have followed me home even if I'd told him no to sex.

She lifts up her hands. "What you two do is your business. But I couldn't be happier for you. I love Caroline." She winks at Reed. "I think she's perfect for you."

When she picks up her bag, I ask, "Did Brandon call you?" Reed's arm stiffens against my back.

Her smile fades. "No."

"He still might."

She shrugs and leaves the room.

"Don't do that." Reed says in a low voice.

I take a step away from him to watch his face. "Do what?"

"Meddle in Lexi's life."

I put my hands on my hips. "What are you talking about? I asked her a question."

"You're encouraging her to go out with Brandon McKenzie."

"Well, why not? He's a nice guy."

Reed is livid. "He had a DUI two summers ago. His father is rumored to have multiple affairs. The apple often doesn't fall far from the tree."

My eyes fly open. "Oh, my God. You did an Internet search on him? Why?" Did Reed even know that Brandon was interested in Lexi?

Ice water floods his eyes. "I had my reasons."

I shake my head. "I don't have time to discuss this right now. I have to get back to the lab before someone moves my things."

"So that means you won't go to dinner with me?"

My chest squeezes with regret. Despite how badly this conversation is going, I still want to be with him. But I'm also beginning to panic. "I have to work. I would have said no, even if we hadn't had this disagreement."

He gives me a curt nod. "I see."

Does he? I don't think so, but I'm not sure how to convince him otherwise. I take a step toward him, lifting my arms around his neck. "Telling you no to dinner has to be the hardest thing I've done today."

I press my mouth against his, intending to only get a taste to get me through the evening. But at the touch of my lips, Reed wraps his arms around my back. Pulling me tight against his chest, he takes control, showing me how much he wants to see me.

"You wore a dress," he murmurs. "I love it when you wear a dress."

"I know. I wore it for you." His hand creeps down my thigh, gripping the fabric and pulling it up a few inches. "Reed, someone could walk in."

Reed lifts his head, and grins. "I'm very tempted to see this through, but I want you to get some work done."

"You're turning me down?"

"No, I'm postponing. What I have planned is better than a quick round on a table."

"You have something planned?"

He grins. "No, but I kind of like a bed now that we've tried it. I think it went rather well."

"Definitely, no complaints here."

He kisses me again and drops my skirt, then picks up my bag and his. "How about I walk you across campus? If I can't have dinner with you, at least I'll get to spend a little more time with you."

"I'd like that."

He leads me out of the office. The sun is out but the air is crisp. When we get outside, Reed takes my hand in his.

I'm surprised by how much I like this nonsexual connection to him. For the first time in a long time, I feel comfortable with someone. Like I'm not watching my every move. "I love fall."

He looks down at me. "Why?"

"I don't know." I shrug. "The cool air, the changing leaves. The holidays are just around the corner."

"You like the holidays?"

"It's more the idea of it."

He stops and turns to me. "What's the idea of it?"

"You know … family. Traditions."

"You mean presents?"

When I was kid, of course I wanted presents. But Christmases were always sparse. It was hard going to school and hearing the kids talking about their PS2s and iPods. But it was more than that. Since we had so little money, my parents tried to downplay the entire holiday. There was no Christmas tree once I hit middle school. No stockings, no Christmas dinner. Scarlett teased me the first year in our dorm when I bought a small Christmas tree, but only lightheartedly. She knew what Christmas was like at my house. The second year she helped me decorate. Last year she surprised me with a live six-foot Douglas fir tree. I cried like a baby for ten minutes. I can't bear to think of Christmas without her this year. Alone.

I clear my throat and shake my head. "No, not the presents really. More the idea of being surrounded by love."

His mouth parts as though he's surprised by my answer. "Are you close to your family?"

What was I thinking telling him that? I tug on his hand and start walking. "No." My tone tells him the subject is off-limits. "What's your favorite season?"

"Summer, definitely summer," he says. "I like being on the water. There's nothing like the wind and the waves and the sun on your face."

I glance up at his smile. "Do you have a boat?"

He blinks. "Yeah. My parents do."

"Are there lakes in Massachusetts?"

"There's an ocean."

It's my turn to be surprised. I hadn't thought of that. "And did you like Christmases at your house?"

He pauses, then looks at me with a soft smile. "I like the idea of it, too."

We walk for several seconds in silence. I'm surprised how much I've shared with him. I always keep my answers superficial. Is it possible to share the intimate things we have and not find my heart exposed?

"How much work do you have today?" he asks as he opens the door to my building.

I close my eyes and sigh. "A lot."

"Can I see you later?"

I smile at him. "I hope so." We start up the stairs to the second floor. "What do you have planned tonight?"

"I have plenty of work to keep me busy." He stops outside the design room door. "I'll call you later, okay? To check on you."

"I'd like that."

He hesitates and for the first time since I've known him, he looks uncertain. "I really want to kiss you goodbye, but there's other people around. Are you okay with that?"

I've never been a big public display person, but when I think about it, I've always worried what people thought of me. I just found out most of the campus thinks I'm frigid. Seeing me kiss Reed will make them think again. But I'm surprised to realize when I'm with Reed, I don't care what people think.

I give him a sweet smile. Other than Scarlett and Tucker, he's one of the few people who actually cares about my feelings or what I want. "I think we should have a rule that we always kiss goodbye."

He wraps his arms around my back and pulls me close. "I like that rule."

I'm amazed I'm so familiar with his body already. How easily I mold into him. I rest my hands on his chest and stand on tiptoes, pressing my mouth to his.

He kisses me back, a lazy kiss full of promise and affection, and I lose myself in it. How is it in the two years I was with Justin, I never felt anything remotely close to this?

With a sigh, he lifts his head and kisses my forehead. "You're my addiction, Caroline Hunter. The more I see you,"—he leans into my ear and lowers his voice—"the more I taste you—"

I shiver.

"—the more I want you." He drops his hold and steps back. "I'll call you later," he says as he walks away.

I've never felt so lonely in my life.

# Chapter Nineteen

Hours later, I'm working alone in the design lab. I'm finishing the shirt for the first outfit, and I'm frustrated as hell. The dress forms are too big, and I can't make them any smaller. Even if I could get the waist and hips the right size, the fact that the form has breasts will throw off the draping.

The only thing I know to do is go back to the center and try them on the children. But that will take multiple fittings per child. I don't have the luxury of time for that, not to mention the inconvenience to the center.

My phone rings, pulling me out of my thoughts and a smile lifts my mouth. I can only think of a handful of people who could be on the other end, and I have a feeling who it is since it's after eight and he hasn't called yet. I drop a pair of scissors on the floor as I reach for the phone.

"Hey," I say as I squat down to pick them up.

"Hello, Carol Ann."

My breath strangles in my throat at the sound of my mother's voice, and I drop to my knees.

"I'm going through my affairs and I'm wonderin' if you want your Grandma Muriel's locket. You always liked it when you were little."

The locket can't be worth more than a couple of dollars. "Doesn't Aunt Minnie want it? She's your sister."

"Nah, she don't give two figs about it."

I close my eyes. One of the few memories I have of my grandmother is of her wearing the locket. I was always fascinated with a tiny lock of hair she kept inside it. When I asked her where it came from, she said she'd cut it off the head of her stillborn baby boy. Now I see how morbid it is, but back then I was fascinated. "Um, yeah." I'm surprised I really do.

"Is there anything else you want?"

Every conscious thought flees from my head. The only thing I can think of lies heavy on my tongue. *I want you to love me.* Instead, I swallow the words and force out, "No."

She breaks into a coughing spell that lasts for several seconds. When she stops, her breath is wheezy. "Well, if you think of something … you can call."

"Yeah."

She hangs up and I lean my head against the table leg next to me. Tears burn my eyes. *I will not cry. I will not cry.* She made her choice, and it wasn't me.

"Caroline?"

I lift my gaze to Reed standing the doorway. Worry covers his face, and I'm sure he's wondering why I'm so upset and kneeling on the floor.

He's over to me within seconds and reaches down to take my hand. "What happened?"

I shake my head as I stand and lean into his chest, the phone still clutched in my hand. He holds me close as I cry softly into his shirt.

Why didn't she pick me? She made it out as though it were my choice. No one on either side of Mom or Dad's family's had ever been to college, and she didn't see any reason why we should start now. Either I stay home or I go off to college.

*"You make your choice right now, Miss Too-Big-For-Yer-Britches."*

But I'd made it years before, back before I even knew how the world worked. I knew I'd never settle for the life she had. Broke and bitter. What kind of mother wanted her child to live that way? No right-minded person would ever believe someone's parents forbade them to go to college.

Reed rubs my back and smoothes my hair and after a minute I try to pull away, but he holds me close.

"What happened?"

I don't answer.

"*Caroline.*" I hear the pleading in his voice. Asking me to let him in.

Part of me desperately wants to tell him, which shocks me. I've never been tempted to tell anyone, not even my old boyfriend. But I can't. I'm ashamed. What would Reed, who attended an Ivy League school and is studying for his doctorate, think about a girl whose parents are red-necked hicks who didn't even graduate high school? What I have with Reed might be temporary, but I'm not willing to lose him yet.

I lean back to look at him, wiping my tears. "I'm just overwhelmed about the project." I force a smile. "What are you doing here?"

He stares at me for several moments, his eyes narrowed. He doesn't believe me, and he's trying to decide whether to press the issue. Then his scrutiny falls away, and his mouth lifts into a soft smile even if his disappointment lingers. "I wanted to see if you've eaten."

I close my eyes. I'd give anything to leave with him right now, and part of me wonders who I'm kidding. Why am I putting all this effort into a doomed project? Three and a half years of student loans, and my future all boils down to a fashion show.

My mother was right. I'm destined to fail.

But I'll be damned if I don't go down kicking.

"I can't leave, Reed."

"I know. I asked if you've eaten."

"No. I haven't had time to get anything."

His grin widens. "I had a feeling you'd say that." He puts a brown bag on the table. "I brought us dinner."

I'm overwhelmed by this man. I look into his face. "Thank you."

He kisses my forehead. "How much longer do you think you'll be?"

I take a deep breath. "I don't know. I've got a huge problem." I tell him about the dressmaker forms. "My entire collection is for children, and observing the drape of the garments as I make them is important. The only thing I know to do is keep running back and forth to the center for fittings."

"So how do you solve this?"

I shake my head. "I don't know how to solve this. I need a children's size dress form and the department doesn't have one."

"But they make them?"

"Well, yeah...."

"Don't worry, Caroline. We'll figure it out."

I'm not sure how he can say that. He obviously doesn't know how funding works here.

"Sit down and eat with me and tell me about what's laying on that table." He's pointing to my first design.

"God, you're bossy."

"I know." He flashes his ornery grin. "Eat with me."

He's brought deli sandwiches and chips, along with cookies. I tell him about my first design and why I created it the way I did, and he watches me intently, asking questions. "You don't have to do that," I say.

"What?"

"Pretend you're interested. It's okay if you're not. Most people find fashion design superficial."

"Do you love this?"

"What? Designing?" I ask.

"Yes."

"Well, yeah. Of course."

"Why? And not some bullshit answer like you gave Lexi in the car. Why do you really like it?"

I stare into his brown eyes, wondering where this man came from. In two years, Justin never once asked why I loved what I did. "Because clothes have power."

His eyes twitch but otherwise he doesn't react.

"Take a person, like me." I stand, surprised at my boldness. Surprised I'm opening my heart, even if he doesn't realize it. "What do you see?"

"The most gorgeous woman I've ever known."

I put my hands on my hips. "Reed."

He shrugs. "You asked what I saw."

"What would most people see?"

"The most gorgeous—"

"Reed!"

"Okay, I see a young professional. I'd say college student, but most schlep around in jeans and T-shirts and you're wearing a dress."

"Good. So you think I look like a professional because of my dress, but if I was on campus in jeans and a T-shirt, you'd take me for a college student. Clothes made the difference. If I'm wearing a ball gown and I'm attending a high society social event, what do you see then?"

"A socialite."

"Put me in skanky clothes and you see a prostitute or a slut. Clothes not only affect people's views of us, they also affect our view of ourselves."

He studies me. "What do you see when you look in the mirror, Caroline?"

I'm surprised at how perceptive he is. "That's not fair."

"It's perfectly fair."

"What do you see when you look at yourself?" I ask, sure he'll dodge my question.

But he looks me in the eyes, his gaze unwavering. "I see a man determined to get an education."

"Is that all?"

"He's loyal and loving and protective of the people he cares about."

"All from your clothes?" I ask.

"No. I see the last part in my eyes."

I move toward him. I see it too, and it scares me. "Are you saying that clothes don't matter?"

He shakes his head. "No, definitely not. Clothes are very important. I'd never dream of going into a meeting in jeans and a T-shirt, but even if I did, it wouldn't change who I am inside." He takes my hand and leads me to the window. The sun has set so the window acts as a mirror. "Your dress makes you stunning and maybe it gives you confidence, but at some point the confidence has to come from in here." He taps my temple. "And then it will come out here." He points to my eye.

I stare at our reflection. He's a head taller than me when I'm wearing flats. His arm is draped over my shoulder. I turn toward him, wanting to see the real him, not a fuzzy reflection.

"That's why you want the kids to take part in the show and you're trying so hard to give them each something they'll love. You want them to see themselves differently."

"Yes."

"And what part of that is superficial?"

His question stumps me.

"What about Desiree? Why is she so important?"

"Because she is."

Reed sighs.

"I can't spill all my secrets all at once," I tease. "Then I'll lose my intrigue and you'll move on."

"Lose your intrigue? Not a chance." He laughs. "So what are you going to do next?"

I run a hand over my head as I survey my workspace. "Since I can't work on the shirt until I fit it on something, I guess I'll make a pattern for the next design."

"Mind if I stick around and do my own work?" He points to his bag. "I brought it with me."

I like the idea of him staying with me. "I'd love it if you did."

"Good." He picks up his bag and pulls out his laptop. "I'm here to make sure you don't walk out to your car alone."

"So you're like my bodyguard?" I tease.

He winks. "Can I guard your naked body?"

I place a kiss on his mouth. "I think that can be arranged."

"Then consider me hired."

I work another couple of hours making patterns for the next design. When I finish, it's too late to start anything else.

Reed sits in one chair, and his legs are stretched out on another. His laptop rests on his thighs. A pair of dark-rimmed glasses perch on his nose. Whatever he's been working on for the last hour has captured his attention. I've been stealing glimpses of him, and he's hardly moved from his position.

"What's got you so fascinated?" I ask.

He blinks and looks up over his glasses. "What?"

God, he's sexy. "You look very intent on what you're doing. What is it?"

He grabs the laptop with one hand and stretches with the other. "I'm working on a program. What are you up to?"

"I'm done for the day."

His feet drop to the floor and he clicks a few buttons on his laptop before closing it. "Well, let's get out of here."

I pack up my things and put them in the backroom then grab my purse, flipping the lights off on the way out the door.

"If I wasn't here, would you be walking out alone?"

I roll my eyes. "Reed...."

"Caroline, it's not safe to walk alone. You promised me you wouldn't."

I hold up a hand. "I don't remember agreeing, but I do have a hazy recollection of a sexy man promising me great sex if I did."

"Not just great sex. Better sex than you've ever had before."

"That's quite the boast. What do I have to do? Sign an oath in blood?"

"No, just give me your word." He shrugs. "Along with a verbal oath."

I pull him to a halt, in the fading light of a street lamp twenty feet away. "Then what are we waiting for? Let's do it here." I lift up my hand. "I, Caroline Hunter, do solemnly swear." I pause. "What's next?"

"To never walk alone at night."

"*Anywhere?*"

"You can walk out your front door, but wandering across campus? No."

"Reed."

"Did I mention how incredible it was going to be?"

I tilt my head. "This oath is null and void if your performance doesn't live up."

He leans his head back and laughs. "I'll agree to that because I have no doubt I will *rock your world*." He finishes in a goofy voice.

I burst out laughing. "Rock my world?"

His lips press in mock annoyance. "I don't know if you've heard, but I'm a nerdy math guy. We're not hip to the lingo."

"Hip to the lingo?" I put my fingers over his lips. "Stop, just stop, before you embarrass yourself anymore."

"So promise then," he says under my fingers.

"Fine." I take my hand off his mouth and hold it upright. "I, Caroline Hunter, do solemnly swear to never walk alone at night, unless I can help it. This oath is negated if Reed Pendergraft doesn't deliver the best sex of my life within the next twelve hours." I start to put down my hand then raise it again. "So help me God." I flash a smile. "Happy now?"

"You have no idea."

"Good, because I'm sure I'm going straight to hell for invoking God and mentioning hot sex within a sentence of each other."

Reed laughs and pulls me close. "Then I guess I'm going with you." He takes my hand and leads me to the parking lot. "Let's get going. I only have eleven hours to deliver."

It takes him less than one.

# Chapter Twenty

Reed spends the night again, but gets up and leaves around seven. I don't mention Lexi and he doesn't either, but we do make plans to eat lunch together. I have to wonder if this is a good idea. We've only known each other a short amount of time, yet we're already spending so much time together. But when I consider telling him I need more space, my heart aches. I can't do it.

My government class isn't until ten, and I have a test I'm not prepared for. The time I should have been studying was spent working on my designs or with Reed. I spend the morning studying, then rush to campus to take the exam. When I walk out, I'm hopeful I got an A, but confident I at least got a B.

I don't meet Reed until noon so I walk to the design lab to see about reserving a workstation for later in the day. I'm surprised to find the design students in an excited huddle.

Megan is on the periphery of the group so I approach her. "What's going on? Why is everyone so excited?"

"The department just got a delivery. Twenty dressmaker forms. All in child sizes."

I gasp. "What?"

"They were delivered this morning. From the Monroe Foundation."

"But ... how...?"

"I don't know, but it's definitely a godsend."

I stand on my tiptoes to look over the huddle and see multiple boxes in the middle of the workroom.

Reed.

I hurry across campus to the math department. I know he has a class now, but it should let out soon. Less than a minute after I reach the second floor, a door opens and a small group streams out. Including the man I'm looking for. "Reed!"

His eyes widen in shock, then he grins. "What are you doing here? I thought we were meeting in a half an hour."

"I'm here to ask you a question."

"And it couldn't wait?" His smile falters and he crosses his arms. "Okay."

"Do you have any idea how the Monroe Foundation knew we need child-sized dressmaker forms?

He pauses. "Well, the Monroe Foundation is sponsoring the show, and they *were* the ones to mandate that two outfits per designer be designed for children."

"I don't understand how you did it."

"I didn't—"

I put my fingertips over his mouth. "How did they find out?"

He kisses my fingers, then pulls my hand down. "I told them."

I shake my head. "But how did you know how to get a hold of them? When did you even do it? I didn't tell you that I had an issue until last night."

"I'm their representative and I report to someone at the foundation after our committee meetings. I sent my contact an e-mail while you were working last night."

"And they sent the dressmaker forms today? How could they get here so quickly? FedEx doesn't even work that fast."

Reed shrugs then takes my hand, heading for the staircase. "Don't overthink it. It's the Monroe Foundation, which is funded by Monroe Industries. They have their hands in all kinds of pies. I'm sure getting a bunch of dressmaker forms here this quickly was no big deal. Especially when their reputation is on the line. Remember, the show reflects on them."

I hadn't thought of it that way. "Thank you."

He leans down and kisses me. "Anything for you."

\*\*\*

Over the next few weeks, Reed and I spend time together every day. He comes to the workroom almost every weekday night and brings dinner for the both of us. Then he stays and does his own work while I work on my designs. He's actually interested in what I'm doing, and wants to know why I've paired certain fabrics or why I've added trim or picked a button size. His questions make me think more about what I'm doing, and the designs turn out better because of his curiosity.

When I'm done for the night, Reed follows me home and stays until six or seven, then he gets up and goes home to shower and change.

We often meet for lunch, sometimes coffee, and then again in the evening.

On the weekends, I slip in some time out of the studio. We've gone to two movies and out to dinner. But he still leaves early in the morning, to get back to Lexi, I presume. I stopped asking after the first few mornings.

I can't help wondering if this is a good idea. Our arrangement is meant to be temporary, until someone else comes along. But when I think about Reed not being in my life, I feel like someone has sucked the air from my lungs. I can't imagine life without him.

And that is a very bad thing.

Reed walks in the workroom carrying a pizza, and the girls catcall.

"There's Caroline's man."

"When you're done with him, I want a piece of that boy."

Reed flashes them a smile.

I set down the pins I'm using to hem a jacket for my eighth design. "Back off, girls, I'm not done with him yet." I take step toward him. "Hey, you."

"Hey, yourself." He sets the pizza box down on my chair and pulls me into a hug, giving me a sweet kiss.

"How did your test go?"

He sighs and pulls me onto his lap. "I think it went well."

"You spend too much time in here with me, Reed. You should study somewhere else."

He shakes his head. "I study other places. I have plenty of time to study. Trust me. I like hanging out here with you."

I like it too, but I don't want his grades to be affected by it.

I get up and hand Reed a slice, then grab one for myself and sit in a chair next to him. "You got my favorite. Sausage and mushroom. Thank you." I give him a kiss before I take a bite. "It was your turn to pick. How will you live without your black olives?"

"Somehow, I'll survive." He laughs. "I decided you needed a reward for working so hard."

"And here I thought your body was my reward." I tease.

"That's a given." He takes a bite and grins. "Have you thought about how we'll fill our time when you're done with the show? When we no longer get to spend hours upon hours sitting in this room."

I shake my head with a sigh. "It seems like a distant dream."

Reed shifts in his chair, and he doesn't look at me. "We've only really known each other since you've been consumed with this project. And we met at a party. What did you used to do for fun before…?"

"All *this* fun?" I ask.

"Yeah."

"I don't know." I shrug. "I went to parties to meet guys, but mostly I stayed home with Scarlett after I broke up with Justin. We'd watch movies and eat Ben & Jerry's." I nudge his shoulder. "We've had a long-term love affair. They usually hang out with me when I watch *Gossip Girl*."

His eyebrows rise. "*Gossip Girl?*"

I grin and lower my voice, teasing. "My dirty little secret."

Reed takes another bite and remains serious. "I know we met at Scarlett's party, but you should know that I'm not a partying type of guy."

"Um, that's not too hard to figure out, Reed." I cross my legs in my chair. "That's why I was shocked to find out you asked Tina out on a date."

Reed holds up his hand, still holding his slice of pizza. "In my defense, I didn't really know her that well, and I was trying to nurse my battle scars from you."

"Battle scars? You were the one who almost kissed me, just to make me look like a fool."

He looks surprised. "It was not my intention to make you look like a fool. I never intended to kiss you at all. But once you got under my skin...."

"I was like a case of scabies?" I giggle.

He shakes his head and rolls his eyes with a chuckle. "No."

"Well, if it makes you feel any better, I think Tina is regretting cutting you loose so quickly."

Reed's eyebrows scrunch. "What? Why do you think that?"

"She told me herself she wants to give you another go. She's heard us in my room."

He grins. "I guess we're not exactly quiet."

I wonder if that's why we never go to his apartment. Maybe he's worried Lexi will hear us. "Well, she's quite impressed with your skills, and she wants a chance at you when I find someone else."

Reed sets his pizza on the box. "Are you planning to find someone else?"

I hadn't thought about how it sounded. Now I feel like a bitch. I squint my eyes closed for second, but I can't look at him when I open them. "That was the arrangement, right? We dated until we found someone else." But as I say the words, I realize I don't want anyone else.

Reed's quiet for so long, I finally look up at his expressionless face. "Have you found someone else?" he asks.

*There's only you* stays on my tongue as it hits me.

I love him.

I've fallen in love with Reed Pendergraft, a debt-laden grad student who will never get out from underneath all of his student loans. How could this happen?

"Caroline. Have you found someone else?"

I jump out of my chair as panic races through my blood. I can't catch my breath, and I bolt for the door.

"Caroline." Reed heads me off before I can leave. "Have you found someone else?" He enunciates the words slowly.

I shake my head. "I need to get some air."

I run down the stairs and outside into the cold October evening, breathing in deep lungfuls of air.

*I love Reed Pendergraft.*

I should be happy. Aren't you supposed to be happy when you fall in love? So why am I panicking?

Because I'll always be poor.

This is okay. I'll have Reed. That's enough, isn't it? But my parents probably said the same thing when they got married. What if we end up like them? What if our kids have to go without?

I hiccup a sob. Maybe I can salvage this. Maybe I can make this work.

Reed comes out the door, his face still expressionless. He puts my jacket around my shoulders and waits next to me, his body ramrod stiff. "Talk to me, Caroline. You at least owe me that."

The wind gusts, and I swipe at a stray hair blowing in my face. "Did you go to an Ivy League school?"

"*What?*"

I turn to look at him. "Scarlett said she thinks you went to an Ivy League school. Did you?"

Reed's anger ignites. "Are you fucking kidding me? Are you comparing our pedigrees?"

"Reed!" I need an answer and he's not cooperating. "Did you go to an Ivy League school?"

Disgust covers his face. "I went to Harvard. Is that Ivy League enough for you?"

Harvard? Oh, God. That had to cost a fortune. "Did you get scholarships?"

He shakes his head. "I'm a smart guy, Caroline, but no. I didn't go to Harvard on scholarships."

Tears well in my eyes. How much debt would that be? How many hundreds of thousands of dollars? And he's only begun his post-graduate work.

"What's going on, Caroline?"

This can still work. I have to find a way to make this work.

"Caroline," he pleads.

"I...." I should tell him everything. Tell him about my past, about going hungry, and the humiliation I faced. Confess I never want my own children to go through what I went through. I should tell him that I love him. I love him more than I thought possible. Tell him that I'm terrified. I'm panicking. I'm desperate to make this work so I don't lose him. But nothing comes out. Only my terror.

"I realize we were only supposed to be temporary." Reed's voice is heavy with emotion. "But I deserve better than this." He turns around and goes back inside the building.

I should go after him, but I'm still frozen with fear.

I can't lose him. I'll do it. I'll tell him my deepest fears, and if he leaves me, at least I'll know I tried everything in my power to make it work.

I shiver in the cold and wait for him to return so I can tell him everything. But he must have used the back door because he never comes out.

# Chapter
# Twenty-One

Two days later, I still haven't heard from Reed. I've called him three times, and he won't pick up, despite my pathetic voicemails begging him to call me back.

I'm miserable.

This hurts worse than when Justin broke up with me. I'm not sure I'll survive the crushing pain that makes it difficult to breath. I want to curl up on the sofa and watch *Gossip Girl* and pretend I never met Reed. That I never fell in love with him.

They say it's better to have loved and lost than never love at all. Whoever made that shit up obviously never loved Reed Pendergraft.

But I can't wallow in my misery. I've completed all nine designs, and I'm taking the outfits for a fitting this afternoon. Since I haven't heard back from Evelyn, I've finally accepted that Desiree's parents aren't going to let her participate. I've designed an outfit for her, all I need is the measurements. But that design is for Desiree. Now I have to come up with something entirely new. But if Desiree can't do it, I'm not sure my heart can accept someone else taking her place. The alternative is a failed grade and no chance at the design job in New York. After losing Reed, I should try my damnedest to get as far away from him as possible, but I can't find the motivation. I'm hoping I'll find it at the center today.

On my way to the workroom, I stop at the coffee shop on campus and order a cup of coffee when I hear, "Caroline?"

I turn in shock, recognizing the voice. It's Justin. I haven't talked to him in a year. Since our breakup.

"How are you?" he asks, shifting his weight. He looks like he thinks talking to me might not have been a good idea.

"I'm good," I lie. "I hear you're engaged."

He squirms and looks away. "Yeah."

"I'm happy for you, Justin." I'm surprised I actually mean it.

His grin is tentative. "Thanks."

"Can I ask you a question?" The barista hands me my coffee, and I step to the side to face him.

His eyes shift before he says, "Sure, I guess."

"Why did you break up with me?"

Justin looks around the room, scoping out the exits.

I give him a soft smile. "Relax. I'm totally over you. Consider this a fact-finding mission."

He relaxes a bit. "When we were together, I felt like I never really knew you."

I shake my head in disbelief. "How can you say that?" When I see him get defensive, I hold up my hands. "No, I'm not attacking you. I'm trying to understand."

The barista calls Justin's name and he steps over to get the cup. I'm sure he's going to bolt for the back door, but he comes back. "Do you want to sit down? I have a couple of minutes, if you really want to know."

We sit at a table for two, and I set my bag on the floor at my feet and wait.

"When we first started going out, you were like this pretty girl with this mysterious persona. You let out little pieces of yourself, one bit at a time, and I kept thinking if I hung in there long enough, I'd find out the mystery. I'd discover the real Caroline Hunter." Justin's face reddens. "I realized I loved the illusion of you. I never really knew you at all."

The blood rushes from my head. "I see." And I do.

He runs a hand through his hair. "We were kids when we first started dating. Hell, we were eighteen and barely graduated from high school. We didn't know what we wanted."

I nod, unsure what to say. Finally, I choke out, "Thanks."

"I wish you the best of luck." He stands. "I really mean that, Caroline."

"Thanks. I wish you the best of luck too. Truly."

He bends over and kisses my cheek. "I'm glad we had this talk. It's good to get some closure. I ended it pretty shitty."

"Yeah, well, water under the bridge and all."

Justin walks away, and all I feel is numb. No wonder Reed won't call me back. He probably feels the same way and doesn't think I'm worth the effort.

I look up at the front entrance, as though my eyes are drawn by some unknown force and see Reed standing outside the glass door. His eyes follow Justin as he walks out the back door. Reed turns around and walks away.

I grab my bag and hurry after him, but a group of students pouring through the entrance slows me down. When I get outside, Reed's already disappeared into a crowd.

Maybe it's for the best. Reed deserves so much better than me.

But my heart still splinters into a million jagged pieces.

I call Scarlett, even though I know she's in the math lab.

"Caroline?" I hear her worried tone.

"He left me, Scarlett," I choke out, swallowing the sobs building in my chest.

"Wait. Slow down. Reed?"

I find a bench and sit. My legs are too shaky to make it to any spot offering privacy, and I'm in too much agony to care if I make a spectacle of myself. "Yes. He won't talk to me."

"No wonder he's been such an ass. This must have happened a couple of days ago, huh?"

"Yes."

"What happened?"

"I don't know." But I do. I'm just ashamed to admit it.

"I wish I could get away to talk to you, but I can't. I'm sorry."

I shake my head and wipe my eyes. "No, I'm okay."

"No, you're not."

I release a tight laugh. "No, I'm not, but I've been through this before and I survived." But loving Reed and loving Justin are two entirely different things. I'm not sure I'll survive this loss.

"I'll call you when I get done here. Maybe I can bring you your two favorite men."

"At least Ben and Jerry don't care if they make my hips wider. They love me anyway." I choke on the last words.

"Oh, Caroline." Scarlett's voice is tight with tears.

"I've got to go." I hang up the phone and smash down my sobs. There's no time to wallow. It's time to grow up, suck it up, and move on. Nine kids are counting on me, *me*. The only person who's ever counted on me is myself and I've screwed that one up. What makes me think I can come through for these kids?

I've sure as hell failed Desiree.

I head to a bathroom and try to salvage my face. I have to go to the center for the kids' fitting and I don't want to go looking like this. I touch up my makeup, and when I'm satisfied I've done the best I can, I head to the workroom to get my pieces.

It takes several trips to get them to my car, and I can't help thinking that if Reed were still with me he'd help me with this. Funny how I got so used to him being in my life in such a short time. But then again, my broken heart doesn't feel that amused.

When I get to the center, I'm surprised to see Reed's car in the parking lot. My chest constricts, and I become lightheaded.

Reed is here.

Why?

I get out and grab several hangers and walk into the tutoring center, preparing myself to face Reed. Instead, Lexi meets me at the door.

I blink. "Lexi. What are you doing here?" I try to keep the disappointment out of my voice.

"I thought you might need some help." She pulls me into a hug that lasts for several seconds.

She knows.

I take a deep breath and try to push away my disappointment with it.

"Are you okay?" she asks, searching my eyes.

"Yeah. Of course."

She squints, obviously not believing me.

I force a smile and a brightness into my voice. "Let's get started."

Lexi helps me bring in the rest of the clothes. We carry them to the classroom we used last time. I remember Reed sitting next to me. Reed doing his model walk. Reed talking to the kids.

I'm not sure I can do this.

But the girls are excited to try on their clothes, squealing when they see the piles. They have no idea what I've made for them.

"Where's Reed?" one of the girl's asks.

"Yeah! Where's Reed?"

Lexi gives me an apologetic look, then turns back to the girls. "Reed is here. He just can't come see you right now."

Reed *is* here.

I feel like I've been kicked in the gut. I pull out a chair and sit.

Lexi squats in front of me. "Do want me to have the first girl change?"

I take a breath, trying to get myself together, then stand. This is my project. Fuck Reed.

I have the clothes sorted, according to child, so I hand the first outfit to one of the girls and ask Lexi to have the boys sent in too.

She stares at me for a moment. "Are you sure you're okay?"

My shoulders stiffen. "I'm fine. I have a job to do, and I'm going to do it."

Lexi helps me keep the kids organized. She also has a good eye for design and loves what I've come up with.

"Caroline, these are beautiful but also practical."

"But most importantly, they're affordable."

Actually, the most important part is that the kids love them. For the first time in days, I feel a semblance of happiness. Even if it's fleeting.

After they've put their outfits for the show on, Lexi and I have them practice their walks. Brittany, the twelve-year-old aspiring model, has been practicing. When I'm satisfied, I hand them a paper with instructions on when and where to come to the show.

Lexi watches the kids leave the room. "There are only designs for nine kids. What are you doing for the tenth child?" Lexi pauses. "Oh. That's why Reed is talking to Evelyn."

My mouth drops. "He's talking to Evelyn about Desiree?"

"Yeah."

My mouth goes dry. "Why is he doing that?"

"Do you really not know?"

I shake my head.

"For two incredibly smart people, you are both so dense." She turns around and walks out of the room. "Come on."

We carry the clothes out to the car and walk to the main office. Dread drags my feet, making them so heavy I can hardly climb the steps. I want to see Reed. I'm scared to see Reed. Reed looking at me with disgust will kill me.

But when I walk in, there's no disgust on his face. Only sadness and regret. He's standing inside the door, as though he's been waiting for me, although I'm sure that's wishful thinking on my part. He doesn't speak, just stands to the side as Lexi and I walk past him.

I follow Lexi into Evelyn's office and we sit on the chairs, but I'm on autopilot. It's taking every ounce of self-control not to get up and throw myself at Reed and beg him to forgive me. He's here, and he'll have to physically run from me to get away. This might be my only chance to tell him how sorry I am. But now isn't the time.

Evelyn sits back in her chair. "Reed is a very stubborn and persuasive man. He's convinced Desiree's parents to talk to you. There's no guarantee they will let her be in the show, but they'll speak to you." She tilts her head toward the corner. "And Reed."

My heart leaps into my throat. I nod, unable to speak.

"All I ask is that you be respectful of their wishes. While Reed is representing the Monroe Foundation, you will be representing the charity."

The enormity of this responsibility isn't lost on me. "I'll do my best to not let you down."

She nods with a smile, then looks from Lexi to Reed. "I need to speak with Caroline privately for a moment."

My heart hammers against my ribs. I feel like I've been called to the principal's office, but for the life of me, I can't figure out what I could have done.

Reed leaves the room without a second glance, but Lexi raises her eyebrows in curiosity. I give her a half-shrug.

When they leave, Lexi closes the door, and I'm alone with Evelyn.

She smiles reassuringly. "The look on your face tells me you think you've done something wrong. I can assure you that that is not the case. In fact, it's the opposite."

My heartbeat slows a fraction.

"Involving the children in the fashion show has filled them with more excitement than any of us imagined. Not only that they are in the show, although some are very excited about that. It's the fact they are getting one-of-a-kind clothes designed just for them. So many of these children face so many hardships, this is a bright spot for them. Thank you for giving them that."

I twist my hands in my lap, embarrassed. "You're welcome. I wanted to make them happy."

"I know. We all have noticed."

I wait, wondering if there's more.

"The Monroe Foundation has learned of your efforts and not only are they impressed, but they wish to offer you a job after you graduate. It would be in conjunction with our organization. You would be in charge of the clothing program for children in need. Instead of giving them gently used clothing, you would be in charge of procuring new clothing."

I blink as I try to comprehend what she's saying. "I would make clothing for all the children?"

"No, I think that would be an impossible task for one person. But we have connections to children in need and Monroe Industries has the resources to alleviate need. You would be the liaison."

I release a breath and grip the arm of the chair. "I don't know what to say."

"I hope you'll say you'll think about it. You have the enthusiasm and fire to help improve the children's lives. That's what is going to make up for the anemic paychecks." She mentions a salary and my hopes drop.

I try not to show my disappointment. I knew it was too good to be true. "Thank you. I'll consider it."

"The foundation would like your answer by the end of the show. If you decline, they believe in the program enough that they'll find a new liaison."

"Yes, I understand. Thank you."

When I leave the room, Reed is waiting in the hall, staring at my photo. He glances up at me with an expressionless face. "We can go see Desiree's parents in an hour. Lexi had to get back to campus for a study group, so if it's all right, I'll ride with you to her parents. And if you could give me a ride back to campus, I'd appreciate it."

I nod, fighting my tears. "Of course. Reed, can we—"

Reed turns away and a sharp pain fills my chest. "We're expected at six. We still have an hour to fill."

"The kids were disappointed you weren't there. We could go over so they can see you."

He nods and opens the door, waiting for me to exit. If he really thinks I've found someone else, he has to hate me, yet he's still polite. It makes me want to cry even more. "Go ahead. I'll be there in a moment."

When he walks outside, I turn to the photo on the wall. I need every weapon I have at my disposal. I lift it off the nail and stick it in my bag, even if I feel like I'm going to throw up.

Reed waits for me on the sidewalk, and we walk in silence. I want to talk to him, to apologize, but it's obvious he doesn't want to listen. He's riding in my car. After we meet with Desiree's parents, he'll be forced to listen to my apology.

The children are excited to see Reed, and he gives them a genuine smile. Reed plays with them for the next half hour while I sit at a table, considering Evelyn's offer—the Monroe Foundation's offer. I could make a real difference in these kids' lives. Can I really pass that up? But Evelyn mentioned a salary that is barely over the yearly tuition I pay to go to Southern. How long will it take me to pay off my loans? Every time I seriously consider accepting, a panic attack brews in the background.

I sit on a chair and pull out my sketchbook, looking over the design I've made for Desiree. I've picked this thing to death, and I hope it will help Desiree's parents change their minds.

I glance up and find Reed staring at me, longing on his face. I suspect it would be easy to convince him I'm sorry, but I now wonder if that's fair. I still don't know if I can live with nothing, even if I'm certain I'll never find anyone as wonderful as Reed.

Does that make me weak or does it make me strong?

If I love him, I'll stop hurting him. I owe him that.

# Chapter
# Twenty-Two

The ride to Desiree's house is tense. Reed sits in the passenger seat giving me directions, while it's my turn to drive with white knuckles. Neither of us speak and the silence is awkward.

We pull up to the rundown house as the sun has begun to set. The porch light remains unlit but a light shines through the large living room window of the mid-century ranch house.

Reed opens the door and starts to get out but stops when he realizes I'm still gripping the steering wheel. He stares straight ahead. "You can do this, Caroline. If anyone can convince them, you can."

"How can you say that?"

"Because you believe in your project."

"You mean my collection?"

"No, your work with the kids."

I can't believe this man. He thinks I've found someone to replace him yet he's still supporting me. "Why do you want to help me?"

His head turns toward me. "Because I still believe in you. What's happened between us hasn't changed that." He opens the door. "Now let's go help a little girl."

I grab my bag and open the door. Reed stands at the edge of the broken concrete driveway. I ache to slip my hand in his. I'm surprised at how much I miss the little physical connections more than the sex. His fingers twined with mine. His hand around my back, his fingers resting on the curve of my hip. When he kisses me on the forehead.

I miss him.

But he was never mine.

We stand at the front door and knock. I'm about to jump out of my skin with nerves, but Reed who knows me so well, presses his hand to the small of my back, filling me with reassurance.

The door opens and light floods out through the crack, backlighting the man in the doorway.

"Are you the people from the tutoring center?" His tone is gruff, and it's clear he sees us as an intrusion.

I'm about to answer, but Reed intervenes. "Mr. Diehl? I'm Reed Pendergraft from the Monroe Foundation. We spoke on the phone. This is Ms. Hunter. She's a student at Southern and has been instrumental with involving the children in the show."

Irritation prickles the back of my neck. I can't believe he took over when this is my project. I also can't believe he's introduced me as *Ms. Hunter*. What is this? The 1950s?

Mr. Diehl scowls. "My wife and I agreed to meet with you, but we're only giving you ten minutes."

"Fair enough," Reed says.

Mr. Diehl turns around and leaves the door open, his invitation to follow him in. He waves to a sofa with sagging cushions. Cigarette burns dot the upholstery and the beige walls are stained brown with nicotine. The carpet fibers are matted and smashed. The décor is stuck in decades past and put together piecemeal, most likely with family castoffs and thrift store finds.

I feel like I've stepped back into my childhood home.

Reed and I sit on the sofa and wait until Mrs. Diehl steps out of the kitchen. Two little heads stretch around the corner to investigate, but Mr. Diehl hollers, "Get back in the kitchen!" and they disappear.

When Desiree's mother approaches, Reed stands and offers her his hand. "Mrs. Diehl, I'm Reed Pendergraft. Thank you for taking your valuable time to meet with us."

She takes his hand and timidly shakes it.

I stand with him, offering my hand as well. When I start to speak, Reed interrupts. "And this is Ms. Hunter."

I shake her hand then shoot Reed a glare as we sit, then start talking before Reed can take over again. "As Reed said, I'm a student at Southern. We work together on the fashion show to raise money for both the design department as well as the nonprofit tutoring center that Desiree attends."

"That's what we were told," Mr. Diehl says.

"Desiree is actually the one who inspired me to involve the children. I was touring the center as a committee member and had a chance to talk to Desiree. I helped her with her subtraction and I told her that subtraction is important to my work. She started asking about what I did and that's when I came up with this idea of including the children." I see Desiree's head poke around the corner and I smile at her. "Desiree is a beautiful little girl and I want her to have this opportunity. Being part of a fashion show can be wonderfully empowering, as strange as that might sound."

Mr. Diehl leans forward, his fingers digging into the worn recliner. "Put foolish nonsense in her head, is what it will do."

Desiree's mother gives me a sad smile. "I don't want her gettin' her hopes up. If she's part of something like that, she'll get her head in the clouds and think she can have a life like that, full of glamorous clothes and fancy cars."

I'm not sure what kind of fashion show they think we're having, but I understand their perception. "First of all, our show will be nothing like you see on television. We'll be much more low-key and make it as unstressful for the children as possible."

Mr. Diehl screws up his mouth. "Uh-uh. Nope."

I hesitate, knowing I'm stepping on shaky ground as I reach into my bag and pull out my sketchbook, flipping open the pages to my design for Desiree. I hand it over to Mrs. Diehl. She's the weakest link, but I doubt she has the decision-making ability.

She takes it with trembling hands. "What's this?"

"The outfit I've designed for Desiree."

Mrs. Diehl stretches her fingertips to the page, studying the design.

I hold my breath. I've spent a lot of time and put a huge part of my heart into the short pink ballerina skirt layered over bedazzled black leggings. The shirt is a long-sleeved black T-shirt, with airbrushed letters that say "Princess Power" and covered with a bedazzled pink jacket.

Desiree's mother covers her mouth with her hand and looks like she's about to cry. "It's so pretty."

"When I told Desiree I was studying fashion design, she asked if I could make her a dress that made her look like a princess. I took the concept and turned it into something practical. Something she can wear to school, but will still make her feel special. When the fashion show is over, the outfit is hers to keep."

Her father snorts. "So she's got one fancy outfit and a bunch of hand-me-downs. You put those clothes on that girl, and she'll get all high and mighty and think she can move up the social ladder."

I fight to control my temper. It's as though I've been transported back in time to my own childhood. I'll be damned if I let them tear down this child like my parents did to me.

"Why is feeling pretty wrong?" I ask, my voice tight. "How is having one nice outfit going to harm her?"

Reed tenses beside me.

"Because she'll want more!" her father shouts.

Reed places his hand on my leg, and although it could be a warning to me, somehow I know it's a protective reaction.

"And what's wrong with wanting more?" I ask, softening my tone. "Wanting more is what gives us hope. It's what makes us get out of bed every day. Wanting more is what has inspired many people to do great things. All because they wanted more."

"Wanting more only leads to disappointment," her father spits out. "This ain't no fairytale, missy. You think you're something coming in here and danglin' your fashion show and your pretty clothes, but you don't know nothin' about our life."

"I know all about your life."

He snorts and begins to laugh. "Ho boy. Do you now?"

Reed's face reddens. "I'll ask you to talk to her respectfully." His authority reverberates throughout the room and Mr. Diehl pauses.

"Reed." I warn under my breath, then I pull the photo out of my bag. I'm horrified to tell them this in front of Reed, but Desiree is more important than my pride.

I hold the photo upright on my lap. "This photo hangs in the hallway at Middle Tennessee Children's Charity. This is just one of many children the organization has helped."

Mr. Diehl's anger returns. "So what?"

"This photo is me."

He and Mrs. Diehl look stunned.

"I grew up in Shelbyville. My parents didn't even have a house. We lived in an old mobile home that leaked when it rained and was so drafty in the winter I had to wear two layers of clothes. But look at me now. I'm going to graduate from college this year and get a job doing what I love. I dreamed of more and my dreams are coming true. There's no harm in wanting more. Sometimes it's what we need to make us work harder."

Mr. Diehl's face is expressionless, but his wife has tears in her eyes. "We don't want her to get hurt. We want her to accept her life and not get her hopes crushed."

"But she's not destined to live without money. She can do well in school and get scholarships to college. Or she can get student loans like I did. But please, please don't tell her she can't have more. Because she can."

Mrs. Diehl strokes the design. "Yes," she says. "Yes, she can do the show."

"Verna," her husband warns.

"No, Fred. This girl is right. We think we're protecting her, when we're really holding her back."

He grumbles, shaking his head. "That ain't—"

His wife's shoulders stiffen. "I said she's doin' it."

He curses under his breath. "Fine. She can do it."

Desiree comes running out of the kitchen. "I can?"

Her mother nods and pulls her into a hug, and her father clears his throat. "Don't be lettin' those fancy clothes go to your head."

"Yes, sir." Her head bobs.

Mr. Diehl's eyes turn glassy, and he pushes himself out of his chair. "You've interrupted my dinner." He disappears into the kitchen.

After I take Desiree's measurements, I tell her I'll have something for her to try on tomorrow, but I might not have it all done until Saturday at the show. After I give Mrs. Diehl the paper with the instructions for Saturday, Reed and I move to the door. Before we walk out, Mrs. Diehl places her hand on my arm.

"We really do love Desiree. I can see how you might judge us, but we were only doing what we thought was best for her."

"I know." I squeeze her hand.

When Reed and I get in the car, I drive away from the house, waiting for his reaction to my news. I'm not sure what I expect, but I don't expect *nothing*. He sits in his seat, staring out the side window.

After we've driven for several minutes, I finally snap. Reed has heard my secret, my great shame. Is he that disgusted with me that he can't even acknowledge it? "I guess you just found out how lucky you are, huh?" I laugh, but it's ugly.

Reed's anger fills the car. "What the hell are you talking about?"

"You thought you escaped the gold-digging Caroline Hunter. What you didn't realize is that you escaped the white-trash Carol Ann."

His breath comes in short bursts. "Pull the car over."

"So you can ridicule me? No, thank you."

"*Goddamn it, Caroline.* Pull this fucking car over now."

I turn on my blinker, looking for a place to park, shocked I'm obeying. The first place I find is the park Reed took me to, the day we came to our arrangement.

There's no way in hell I'm going there.

Reed senses my reluctance and his voice softens. "Caroline, I just want to talk. Pull over." He's still angry, but he doesn't act like he's about to explode.

I drive to the back of the park, stopping in an empty parking lot. Once I've put the car in park, Reed reaches over and turns off the engine, then throws the keys into the backseat.

It takes me a half-second too long to react. "Wait! What are you doing?"

"We're not going anywhere until we've talked this out."

I press my back into the seat. "Go ahead. Tell me how disgusted you are."

"*Are you serious?*" he asks, his anger building again. "Do you really think I'm so shallow that your background could make me walk away from you? Do you even fucking know me at all?"

I gasp, turning toward him.

"Do you have any idea how insulting it is that you think your past would disgust me?"

I close my eyes and lean back into the seat. "No, I honestly didn't look at it that way."

"Would you have ever told me?"

I look out the front window. "I don't know."

"Does your new boyfriend know?" Bitterness fills his words. "Did you keep it from me because we were temporary?"

"No, Reed." Tears clog my throat. "I don't tell anyone."

He pauses. "What about Justin? Didn't you date for two years?"

"Yeah, and no. I didn't tell him."

He shakes his head. "That's fucked up, Caroline."

"I know."

"What did you tell him about your past? Did you lie?"

"No, I didn't tell him anything."

"He didn't ask?"

"Of course he did, but I told him it wasn't important. After a while he finally let it drop." I rest my hand on the steering wheel, sniffing back tears. "But I ran into him today at the coffee shop and asked him what went wrong with us." I laugh and cry at the same time. "I was so fucked up we had to sit down so he could tell me."

Reed tenses. "That wasn't your new boyfriend?"

"I don't have a new boyfriend, Reed."

"But...." He runs a hand over his head. "But you said...."

I turn toward him. "No, Reed, I never said I had one. You only assumed." I swallow the lump in my throat, and my words come out broken. "There's only you."

He's pulling me to him, and his mouth finds mine before I realize what's happening. I wrap my arms around his shoulders, worried he'll change his mind. I cry as he kisses me, and he pulls away, wiping my tears. "Don't cry, Caroline. I'm sorry. I'm an idiot."

I press my mouth to his. I've lived without him for days and now that I've had a taste of him, I crave more.

I reach for his shirt, but he grabs my hand. "No. Let's go home."

# Chapter
# Twenty-Three

H ome. I've only thought of two places as home. The first was when I lived with Scarlett, the second is in Reed's arms. "You mean my place?"

He kisses me long and slow. "No, mine."

"What about Lexi? Isn't that why we never go to your apartment?"

"She has a study group tonight. She won't be there." His hand cradles my cheek. "You have no idea how much I've missed you. Words are inadequate."

"Then show me."

He kisses me again, more ardent. His hands slip under my shirt and he fondles my breast. With a groan, he pulls away and practically dives over the seat. "Throwing these keys back here seemed like a great idea at the time."

I laugh and get out, opening the back door and bending over to search the floor.

"Why don't you have a bigger car? We wouldn't have to wait," he teases.

"I thought you were fond of beds now."

He twists his head so he's facing me and kisses me. "We can mix it up from time to time, but tonight we need a bed."

I find the keys jammed between the seat cushions and I lift them triumphantly. Reed gets out of the car and meets me at the passenger door, taking the keys from my hand. "I'm driving."

"You don't like my driving?"

"You drive like my grandmother."

"Maybe that's because my brakes are going out."

His playfulness disappears. "Why haven't you gotten them fixed?"

"I can't afford to, Reed." I sigh. "You know my deep dark secret. I'm poor. I have nothing."

"No, you have me."

But is it enough? I can't think about the logistics of us right now. I only know I need this man. I'm miserable without him.

He narrows his eyes. "I'm still driving."

I could put up a fight, but it wouldn't be worth the effort and would only delay getting to his apartment. "Okay."

He's careful driving toward the campus. When he pulls into the parking lot on the grounds of his apartment, I take in a breath. This is one of the nicer complexes in town. "How can you afford to live here?"

He hesitates. "My parents pay for it. Since Lexi and I share the apartment, it's cheaper this way than two separate places."

"Your parents pay for your apartment?"

He kisses me, effectively shutting down my questions. "Do you know what I'm going to do to you?"

"No," I'm breathless and feel the familiar ache burning low in my abdomen. I once again marvel at the hold he has on me.

"Come inside and find out." He's out of the car and opening my door, pulling me into his embrace. "I'm going to strip you naked." He kisses my neck, then trails his tongue to my ear. "And then I'm going to kiss you everywhere."

"Everywhere in your apartment?" I tease, but I'm finding it difficult to concentrate.

"There's an idea." He sounds surprised. "Maybe next time."

He threads his fingers through mine and takes me to the outside door, pressing a security code to get into the building. Once we're inside, we stop in front of an elevator.

"Oh, fancy," I tease. "You have a security system *and* an elevator."

His arm encircles my back, tugging me close to his body. He leans into my ear. "I can think of all kinds of fun things to do inside an elevator."

I grab the front of his shirt and look up into his eyes, wondering how I went from so miserable to so happy in such a short time.

The doors open and he pushes me backward inside until my back is against the wall. "Let me show you one of them."

I draw in a breath as he unfastens my pants. "Reed, the doors aren't even closed."

"No one can see. I'm blocking their view." But when the door closes, his hand slides down inside my panties. "Fuck, Caroline. You're so wet already." He growls before his mouth covers mine, his tongue demanding attention.

The elevator doors start to open and Reed withdraws his hand and grins. "I need to move to a taller building. That wasn't nearly enough time. Not to mention I'd have much easier access if you'd worn a dress."

"I didn't know we'd be doing … this."

Reed kisses me again. "Always assume we'll be doing this." He takes my hand and leads me down a hall. He stops at an apartment near the end, fumbling in his pocket for his keys. Spinning me around, he presses my back against the door, kissing me thoroughly as he unlocks the door. He pushes me inside, his mouth still on mine.

The door closes behind him, and he enters a code into a keypad, turning off an alarm. Then he pulls me to him again, fumbling with my waistband, pushing my pants and my panties to my ankles. I kick off my shoes, then step out of my clothes as Reed lifts my sweater up and over my head. My bra soon falls to the floor, and I'm completely naked.

"This hardly seems fair." I cock my head with a grin. "You have too many clothes on."

I take a step toward him, but he shakes his head. "No."

"No?"

He places his hands on my shoulders and pushes me backward again, until I'm backed up to a wooden kitchen chair. "Sit," he murmurs, lowering me to the seat, moving my butt to the edge and spreading my legs so I'm exposed. "Now reach behind you and grab the spindles."

I do as he says, but I'm anxious about what he has planned.

He stares at me for several seconds, his pupils dilating. "God, you're gorgeous." Then he steps back several feet and unknots his tie, watching me as he slides it off his neck.

"Should I be nervous?"

His hand stops on the top button of his shirt, his eyes becoming serious. "Do you think I'd ever hurt you?"

"No." He'd hurt himself before he'd ever hurt me.

"I just want to watch you while I take my clothes off. Do you know how sexy you are?"

I start to reach up for him, but he shakes his head. "No, I want you like you were."

Giving him a saucy grin, I grab the back of the chair. He leans over to kiss me, playing with my breast before he stands and watches me again.

I'm panting and throbbing. This seems to be the effect he wanted, because he smiles as he unbuttons his shirt.

"I've missed your body." He tugs his shirt out of his pants and lets it slide down his arms and to the floor.

"It was only two days."

"It was an eternity."

"I've missed you too." Time without Reed felt endless.

"What do you want me to do to you, Caroline?"

I gasp, suddenly embarrassed. Maybe it's the position he has me in. I feel vulnerable and exposed. "You know."

"I want to hear you say it." His voice is low and sexy.

I look up into his eyes as he unbuckles his belt. "I want you to kiss me."

He leans over me and takes my lower lip between his, nipping then licking it with his tongue. "Like that?"

"Yes." It seems like such an inadequate response for what he does to me.

He unfastens his pants and drops them, stepping out of his shoes in the process. His erection is obvious through his briefs, and I keep my gaze there.

"What else do you want?"

"I want you to fuck me, Reed."

He tugs off his underwear then kneels before me. "Oh, I will, my sweet Caroline. But not yet." His mouth lowers to one breast while his hand fondles the other.

I start to reach for him, but he lifts his head.

"No. I want you like you were."

I look into his eyes. "I want to touch you."

He grins. "You will, but I get to touch you first."

His mouth resumes its torture and I squirm, leaning my head back. "Reed."

"Patience." His mouth moves to my cleavage, licking and kissing as his lips begin to move down to my stomach.

A dull ache spreads as his tongue trails over my abdomen, moving lower and lower. Agonizingly close to where I want him, yet light years away.

His mouth glides down my leg and to the inside of my thigh, inching higher and higher but not high enough. And just when I think he'll drive me mad, his tongue finds the place that's begging for attention.

I arch my back and moan, lifting off the chair, but Reed pushes me down, renewing his efforts. My stomach tightens, and I'm close to an orgasm. "Reed…."

I try to hold on, to wait for him and as if he realizes this, his tongue tries something different, pushing me over the edge. I cry out as wave after wave washes over me.

Reed moves his mouth up my stomach as I recover. "I've missed the taste of you."

I open my eyes. "My turn." I stand and turn him around and make him sit on the chair, positioning him like he had me, except moving his back to the back of the chair. The sight of him this way turns me on more than I expected.

I lean over and kiss him, making sure the only part of me that touches him is my mouth. His arm moves, then he groans.

I lift my head and chuckle. "It's not easy not being able to touch, is it?"

His eyes are hooded. "You're already driving me crazy."

I grin. "And I've only just begun."

I kiss the corner of his mouth, licking his bottom lip but moving away when he tries to kiss me. He growls, and I laugh.

I straddle his legs, resting my thighs closer to his knees. I lower my mouth to his neck, licking and sucking as I make my way down to his chest, which rises and falls rapidly. Rising up, I grab the back of his head and bring his mouth to my breast.

"I want to be in you," he grunts.

"Not yet."

"*Caroline.*"

"Patience." I slide off his lap and lower between his legs, pulling his hips closer to the edge of the chair. I lower my mouth to his erection and lick in one long stroke.

Reed squirms and I press down on his thighs and continue my torture before taking him in my mouth. Reed lasts ten seconds before he's jerking me up.

I protest. "You can't touch—"

He pulls my mouth to his, his hands in my hair.

I lean back and grin at him. "No, you're not supposed to touch me."

"Until when?"

"Until you come."

A guttural sound comes from his throat.

"Do you trust me?" I whisper.

He's trying to catch his breath. "Yes."

I grab his hand and guide him to the sofa. Then I straddle his thighs and look into his eyes. "No touching."

He nods, his eyes focused on mine.

Placing my hands on his shoulders, I lower myself onto him and begin to move. He bucks his hips, pushing deeper into me.

"Tell me what you want me to do," I say. "Tell me how to move."

He begins to give me directions, and I feel myself building again, but I concentrate on Reed and his nonverbal cues as well as his verbal ones. I want to make him feel as good as he makes me feel. I want to show him how much I love him. I want to give him something for everything he's done for me, but I have nothing. The only thing I know to give him is myself.

I lower my mouth to his as I ride him, and I can tell he's frustrated. I move my mouth to his ear. "You can touch me."

With a grunt, he grabs my waist and lifts me, turning me so my back is on the sofa. His fingers dig into my hips and he takes control. I'm climbing again, amazed I can be this close already. That this man makes me feel things I never thought possible.

I look up into his face as I'm nearing the edge. The love and adoration in his eyes sends my flying. I cling to him as I fall, and he's right behind me. He collapses on top of me, catching his breath. Then he turns to his side, wrapping his arms around my back and holding me to his chest.

"I never want to lose you again," he murmurs.

His chest vibrates with his words, and I snuggle closer. "I don't want to lose you either."

"Stay the night with me."

I'm tempted. I want nothing more than to stay in this man's arms for the rest of my life, but Desiree is counting on me. "I can't. I have to get back to work."

He groans.

"Remember that field trip we took to Desiree's? That will be all for nothing if I don't finish her outfit in time."

"You have to sleep sometime."

"Not until very, very late."

He pushes up on his elbow. "I'll come with you."

I shake my head. "Remember how many people were in the design studio when you were there a few nights ago? There's twice as many now since we're this close to the show. Plus the juniors have a big project due. We won't have any privacy."

"I miss you, Caroline."

I kiss him softly. "I miss you too."

"You need to eat. Let me feed you first."

I lean back to study him. "You cook?"

A mischievous grin lifts the corners of his mouth. "Do I know how to *cook*?" He puts a goofy emphasis on the last word.

"In the kitchen." I laugh, shaking my head. "How can a man as sexy as you be so socially awkward?"

He pins me to the sofa. "Socially awkward?"

I rise up and kiss him on the lips. "Good thing I love you, anyway."

Reed freezes, his smile fading. "Did you just say you love me?"

Oh, God. I've known for two days that I love him. The knowledge has sunk into every pore, every cell in my body. Loving Reed has infused with my DNA, becoming part of who I am. But he didn't know that yet.

He's expressionless as he waits for my answer. I hate when he puts up this defensive shield. I have no idea if he's worried he heard me wrong or if he doesn't feel the same way. What if my declaration scares him away?

"I didn't … I mean … I…." I push up against him, panic racing through my head, kicking in my fight-or-flight response. But he holds me down.

"Caroline, I love you too."

I stop fighting. "You do?"

He looks at me like I've lost my mind. "I've never been a love-at-first-sight kind of person, but the night I met you, I knew you were the one."

I cringe. "But I was so awful to you. Why would you think that?"

He brushes a stray hair off my face. "There's just something about you, Caroline Hunter. You make the simplest things infinitesimally better. You captivate me."

"Thanks for not giving up on me," I whisper.

"Thanks for taking a chance on me."

He kisses me for several minutes. Sweet, leisurely kisses. I love our passion, but I love this side of us too. I love that we're more than hot sex.

"I need to feed you, woman." He gets up and pulls me to my feet.

I leer at him. "Did you just call me *woman*?"

"Would you rather I call you sweetie?"

"God, no."

"What can I call you?"

I give him a soft smile. "Yours."

He kisses me again, and we could do this all night, but I have work to do. "What time is Lexi coming home?"

Reed looks at the clock. "*Shit*. Anytime now."

I chuckle. "Maybe we should get dressed before she walks in."

I pick up my clothes and head to the bathroom to clean up and get dressed. Once I'm ready to go back out, I check myself in the mirror, surprised at the reflection. I look so happy. I can't remember ever being this happy. Why am I so worried it will all fall apart?

When I go out, Lexi is sitting on a bar stool, talking to Reed. He's cutting onions and peppers with a butcher knife on a wooden cutting board.

I stop when I see him. "Wow. You really *do* cook?"

Lexi turns to me and breaks out into a huge grin. "You have no idea. He's amazing."

Reed laughs, looking down at the vegetables. "No need to sell it, Lexi. Caroline's going to be around a lot from now on."

"Really?" She squeals and flies off the stool, hugging me so tight I can hardly breathe. "I knew it! You two are perfect for each other!"

I break free and sit on the spare stool. "I'm glad two of the three of us saw it."

"You just had to see what a great guy Reed is."

She's right. Reed is amazing. But it still doesn't negate the fact he's going to have student loans out the wazoo. His loans alone could pay for a comfortable home for a family of six. Add mine to the mix, and I suddenly feel nauseous. I know in my gut this will all work out. I just need the rest of me to catch up.

I stand. "I'm going to take a rain check on dinner. I need to get to work."

Lexi and Reed look as if I announced that I plan to kill a puppy.

"But it won't take long for Reed to make dinner. His spaghetti sauce is to die for," Lexi protests.

"I know." I grimace. "I'm just really nervous about getting Desiree's outfit done in time." And that part's true. It's just more than that.

Reed watches me with a guarded look. He moves to the sink and washes his hands. "I want to drive you to campus. I don't want you driving with your brakes in such bad shape."

I shake my head. "Reed, don't. I'll drive myself."

"Are you serious?" His eyes narrow as his voice rises. "You tell me you love me and *finally* let me tell you how much you mean to me, then you think I'll let you drive away in a car that's a *fucking time bomb*?"

Lexi backs up in her stool, looking back and forth from Reed to me.

"Let me tell you something, Mr. Bossy Pants." I jab him in the chest. "Just because you deem it so, doesn't *make* it so. Do I want to drive a car with bad brakes? No. But what part of *I don't have the money* do you not understand?"

His expression turns hard. "I can loan you the money."

"Where are *you* going to get the money? You've got hundreds of thousands of dollars in student loans, and you're only beginning your postgraduate work."

Lexi begins to cough.

Reed shoots her a glare before turning back to me. "I'll find a way."

"The hell you will. You already think I'm a gold-digger. I'm not going to feed *that* fire."

"God damn it, Caroline. I do *not* think you're a gold-digger."

I put my hand on my hip in disbelief. "How can you say that? Just two days ago, you walked away from me because you thought I found a guy who had more money than you."

"I was a fucking idiot!"

"Just like you're being now!" I turn around and head for the door. "I've got to go."

He grabs my arm and pulls me to his chest. His voice softens. "Don't go this way."

My anger ebbs, and I melt into him. "I don't want to."

He cradles my head. "I'm just worried about you. *Please* let me drive you. I'll go crazy worrying about you if you drive."

"But then I won't have a way to get home."

"I'll pick you up."

"Reed ... it won't be until late, maybe three or four."

"Caroline, I don't care." He lifts my chin and looks into my eyes. "That's what love is. Protecting and taking care of the people you love. *Please*, let me do this."

I sigh. "Okay."

"But you have to eat something."

I shake my head. "You're relentless. Don't get used to getting your own way."

He winks. "I wouldn't dream of it."

I grin. He's a terrible liar.

# Chapter Twenty-Four

The next afternoon, I'm working in the studio and pleased with my progress. I've finished everything for Desiree's outfit except for the jacket and the trim on the skirt. But it's close enough to completion that I can have her try it on. My only problem is that Reed has effectively impounded my car. While I appreciate his concern, and agree it's dangerous to drive, it's extremely inconvenient.

Around lunch time, he calls to check on me.

"Funny you should call," I grumble. "I'm stuck here carless, and I need to go back to the center for a fitting with Desiree."

He's silent for a moment. "I can't get away to take you."

"Reed, I have to go." I sit down on my chair, staring at the pink jacket on the dressmaker form.

"I know. What about Lexi? She's free, and I'm sure she'd love to take you. She likes you."

I sigh, staring at the jacket. Something is missing on it. "I like her too."

"Is there a time you need to be there by?"

I walk behind the form, trying to figure out what's lacking. "Between three-thirty and four-thirty."

"I'll have Lexi come by."

Around three-fifteen, Lexi shows up in the doorway, checking out the room. She's picked a bad day to see it for the first time. Students are stressed with their approaching deadline, and patience is thin. Not that Lexi seems to notice. She wanders from station to station checking out everyone's designs. When she reaches me, she examines the jacket. Everything is attached now. It only needs to be bedazzled and have some decorative stitching done.

She puts her hands on her hips. "This is your best one yet."

I grin, surprised how important Lexi's opinion is to me. "Thanks." I gather the four pieces and follow Lexi to the parking lot. "Thanks for taking me. Reed is being so stubborn."

"He loves you. The thing you have to know about Reed is that he doesn't do anything halfheartedly. Once he decides to do something, he's all in." She grins at me. "And *all in* with Reed means he plays mother hen. You might as well just give in and accept it now."

"Like you and Reed living together," I say. "And the way he's so careful about what you do. He's so overprotective."

Lexi presses her key fob and her car chirps. "Sometimes I need the chirp to tell me where the car is."

Did she really get distracted from answering or did she purposely avoid answering?

Once we're on the road, I decide to renew my efforts. "You and Reed seem close."

She beams. "You have no idea. He may be four years older, but he's always taken his role as big brother seriously. He had most of the boys in my middle school terrified to talk to me. I was never so glad for him to go off to college when I started high school."

"When he went to Harvard?"

She casts a glance in my direction and smiles. "Do you think it will rain tomorrow? If it rains, it's liable to keep people from coming to the show."

Lexi just changed the subject again. I'm sure of it. Why?

"Did you go to Harvard with Reed?"

She shifts in her seat. "No."

"So where did you go?"

"A small college out east. I'm sure you never heard of it."

"Try me. I might."

She doesn't answer.

"Did Reed live with you last year?"

"No."

"So this is your first year living together? Why did you change colleges your sophomore year?"

She draws in a deep breath. "Caroline, you really need to talk to Reed about this."

"I need to talk to Reed about where you went to college?" I ask, incredulous.

Her gaze swings to me. "Please. I want to tell you everything, but I can't."

Dizziness washes through my head. What are they hiding from me? I'm done with Reed's secret past. Tonight he's telling me everything, whether he likes it or not.

Lexi clears her throat. "Brandon asked me out."

Her abrupt change of topic takes me a couple of seconds to take in. "Really? That's great!"

"I told him I'd go out with him, but I haven't told Reed. He'll have a fit."

"Lexi, you're an adult now. You're eighteen. You can decide who you go out with. I realize you and Reed are close, but this is beyond ridiculous." Just how controlling *is* Reed?

She turns to me, her eyes pleading. "Will you help me? I want to go out with Brandon, but Reed is liable to figure out something's going on if I don't come home until late. Do you think you could get Reed to go to your place? Then he'll never know I went out. Now that he sees you two as more permanent, he's going to want you around our apartment all the time."

I scrunch my nose. "I don't know, Lexi. Reed will have a fit with me for covering. I don't want to lie to him." We already have enough issues we're still working on. Most importantly, his secrets.

"I know, but he's so scared of losing you that he'll be more understanding if you're a part of it."

I don't understand why an eighteen-year-old girl needs permission to date. For that reason alone, I decide to help her, but she's brought up a question. "Why is Reed so scared he's going to lose me?"

"Uh...." Lexi pulls into the parking lot. "You know. Because you've had a rocky start."

I don't believe her, but she refuses to tell me more. "What if he won't go to my place? You said yourself now that I've been to your apartment, Reed will want to spend more time there. He's bound to notice you haven't come home."

"Then you can distract him. I've seen you two together. That shouldn't be too hard."

My face reddens. It's weird to think about Lexi knowing Reed and I have sex. And not only knowing, but using it to her advantage.

"So will you help me?"

Against my better judgment, I nod. I have a sick feeling that I'll regret this later.

The children are excited to see us when we go in, Desiree most of all. As I watch her practice her walk with her outfit on, I'm grateful Desiree's parents changed their minds. But I also ponder their reasoning for holding her back. They thought letting Desiree get a glimpse of something else, a life she might not ever have would hurt her.

Was that the reason for some of the things my parents did? Did my mother think I had aimed too high with my dreams? Was she worried I'd come crashing down to earth? When I look at my parents' behavior through this new lens, my perception changes.

For the first time in three years, I want to talk to my mom and dad, but I'm running out of time. Scarlett's right. After the fashion show is over, I need to visit my mother before she dies. Maybe Reed will agree to go with me. He deserves to meet my family and see the world I came from. And I find myself surprised that I want my parents to meet Reed.

*\*\**

Hours later, I put the last jewel on Desiree's jacket. I'm exhausted, but I'm also incredibly proud. "That's it."

I did it.

Reed glances up from his laptop, taking off his reading glasses. It seems fitting that he sees the last piece finished, since he's been such a big part of the creation of the designs. "I am so proud of you, Caroline. I couldn't be more proud if I'd created them myself."

I lean over and give him a kiss. "Thank you. Although after all of your questions and observations, I suspect you could create your own line now." I hang the jacket on the form and look over the completed outfit, trimming several stray threads. "Yep, I'm really done."

"So now what?"

"I put all the pieces on my hanging rack, along with my accessories so it will be ready for tomorrow." I hang Desiree's outfit on the rack, which already holds all the other designs, and roll it to the back room. Most of the other racks are still out in the workroom, waiting for the students to finish their designs. Quite a few of them have all-nighters ahead of them.

Yawning, I pick up my workstation. "I'm exhausted. I want to go home and go to bed."

"Come to my place," Reed says, packing up his bag. "I'll cook you dinner."

"Reed, it's almost nine o'clock. You don't have to do that."

"I want to." He takes my hand in his. "Let's get out of here before you fall asleep standing up."

During the drive to Reed's apartment, I realize I'm supposed to be coercing Reed to go to my place for Lexi. But I'm too tired to make up an excuse to stay at my apartment. Maybe I can convince Reed to come to bed with me, and he'll never notice Lexi getting in late.

But it reminds me that we have bigger issues to address. Reed accused me of hiding my past, but his is an even a bigger mystery. I decide to start with something that's been bothering me all day. "Reed, when I told Desiree's parents about my past, why didn't you seem surprised?"

He hesitates. "Because I knew."

"What do you mean you knew?"

"The photo on the wall."

"So you guessed?"

"No. I found out. That first day when you saw it and got upset, I wondered why. So I asked if anyone knew the names of the kids on the wall. I got the list and found your name."

"When did you find out?"

"Before your date with Brandon."

I feel sick. He must think I'm a fool, worrying about my past when he knew all about it. "You've known all this time, and you never said anything? Why?"

He looks at me like I've lost my mind. "Because I wanted you to trust me enough to tell me yourself."

"So you hired a private investigator to dig up my past," I joke.

He sighs. "It didn't take a private investigator."

I sit upright. "Wait. You investigated me?"

A scowl covers his face. "Come on, Caroline. Are you telling me that you didn't look me up online?"

"No." Although I've been tempted.

His mouth opens then he swallows. "Why not?"

"I wanted to trust you."

He has the grace to look guilty.

If we're going to commit to this relationship, I need to tell him everything. I need to confess my insecurities and worries, then I need him to tell me his past. "Reed, I have to tell you something important."

Panic covers his face. "Wait. I don't want to have this conversation in the car," he says, turning into the apartment parking lot.

"It's not—"

"Caroline," he pleads. "Just wait."

I'm not sure what he thinks I'm going to say, but his panic scares me.

My car is sitting directly under a street lamp. I wonder when I'll have the money to fix it. Now that the fashion show is almost over, I can get another part-time job to replace the one I had before the beginning of this crazy semester. With the Christmas shopping season just around the corner, I'm sure I can get a retail job.

Reed leads me upstairs to his apartment, but tonight is different than the night before. When we get in his apartment, he takes my coat. "I'm going to get a drink. Do you want one?"

"Um, sure. What are you having?"

"Whiskey." He pulls a bottle out of his kitchen cabinet.

Now he's freaking me out. I've only seen him drink twice and both times were at a bar.

He pours a glass and looks up at me.

"No." I shake my head. "Reed, I need you to listen to me."

He takes a sip and waits.

"The reason I've dated guys who met certain criteria—the things I told you the night I met you—was because after living the childhood I did, I swore I'd never live like that again. That I'd sure never put my kids through that. That's why I didn't want to get attached to you. I didn't think you'd make very much money on a college professor's salary."

"It's very rare to find a college professor so underpaid they're forced into homelessness, Caroline."

I shake my head, embarrassed. "I know. It's just the fear is so inbred in me, that the thought of even coming close to living like that again, sends me into a full-fledged panic. It's irrational, I know that, but knowing it and accepting it are two different things. I'm still working on it, so I need you to be patient with me."

"Okay," he says, but he's acting weird.

"So in an appeal to your patience, I need to know how much you owe in student loans."

He looks at me like I've asked him to speak Japanese.

"Your student loans from Harvard."

He sags against the counter. He looks sick. "That's why you were asking about Harvard and scholarships a few nights ago."

"When you asked me if there was anyone else, I knew that I didn't *want* anyone else. I only want you. But you have that massive debt. It took me a few minutes to calm down and figure it out. But you never came back, and then you never returned my calls."

"Figure what out?"

"That I love you enough not to care if you have a mountain of debt. As long as I have you, I have everything I need. I'm still worried about kids, but after seeing how protective you are of Lexi and me, I know you'd never let your children suffer like I did."

"Oh, Caroline." He puts his drink down and loops his arms around my waist. "Do you have any idea how much it means that you trust me this much?"

I lift my face and kiss him, glad I've told him. Relieved he knows my fears.

He grabs my face and leans my head back. "I love you."

"I love you too." But my stomach knots at the worry on his face. Why does he look so scared?

"Caroline, I don't have any student loans."

I shake my head. "But you told me you didn't have scholarships."

His face hardens. "I didn't."

"Reed, I don't understand. If you went to Harvard…." My voice trails off.

I wait for him to continue, but he doesn't. That's all he shares.

My anger flares. "Are you serious? You tell me that you didn't need loans to go to Harvard, and you don't volunteer anything else?"

"Caroline…."

"So you're not going to tell me?"

He heaves a breath. "I will, but I want to wait until Lexi comes home. We should tell you together."

"I tell you about my past, and you give me a flippant *I already know*—"

"I would hardly call it flippant—"

"And then when I ask about your past, you still blow me off?"

"Caroline, I'm only asking you to wait."

The hell with waiting. "Where's your laptop?"

"*What?*"

"Give me your fucking laptop. If you're not going to tell me I'll just do an Internet search. You were surprised I hadn't done one. You obviously expected me to, so why don't I take care of that right now?"

He looks like he's about to protest, but he takes the computer out of his bag and sets it on the kitchen counter, entering his password on the startup screen.

When it boots up I search *Reed Pendergraft*.

The search results turn up a few posts about Reed at Harvard and Reed at Southern. There are no images. Nothing from his past. Just enough to give him a web presence but not enough to answer any questions.

I search *Lexi Pendergraft* and I get less on her. Just her page at Southern, nothing about the other college she attended or about her high school. It's as though she were dropped here at Southern with no past at all.

Look how well that worked for me.

Reed pours more whiskey.

*How bad is this?*

What are they hiding? My imagination runs wild. Are they criminals? Right. Criminals who go to college and live in a nice apartment?

Maybe they're in the witness protection program.

Then I latch on to another idea.

Reed doesn't have student loans. He lives in a nice apartment.

Reed is a representative of the Monroe Foundation.

I type *Reed Monroe* into the search box.

The page fills with multiple results for Reed Monroe, images even. Reed's face appears on the screen.

The top result says: *"Reed Monroe, heir to Monroe Industries, was seen at the Monroe Foundation Annual Fundraiser Ball with socialite Amelia Mitchell."* When I click, I see Reed in a tux standing next to a gorgeous woman, who is wearing a formal gown that had to cost thousands upon thousands of dollars.

Half the images are photos of Reed with Amelia.

He's the heir to Monroe Industries, yet he's here at Southern pretending to be someone else. He's used to dating rich, beautiful socialites. So why is he with *me*?

But most importantly, he says he loves me, but he's never made one attempt to tell me. He's known about my past, but waited for me to trust him enough to tell him on my own.

Reed doesn't trust me.

Or he had no intention of ever telling me.

I'm going to be sick.

I get off the barstool and head for the bathroom, Reed following behind. But I shut and lock the door, sitting on the side of the bathtub next to the toilet.

"Caroline, are you okay?"

"Go away!"

I want to cry, but I won't give him the satisfaction.

I sit on the side of the tub, trying to sort through the mess in my head. "Is she your girlfriend?" I call out.

"Who?" Reed answers from the other side of the door.

"Amelia."

"Oh, Caroline." I hear the defeat in his voice, and my heart plummets.

"So she is?" My voice breaks.

"Can we please have this conversation without a door between us?"

My nausea has passed so I get up and open the door.

Reed stands on the other side, looking like he's about to cry.

I run my hand over my head. "So many questions are racing through my head, I don't even know where to start."

"I'm sorry," he whispers.

"Was this a game? Fool Caroline? Are there points involved? Do you score more for screwing me in the storeroom the first time?"

"Stop right now!" He shouts. "Don't take what we have and—"

"And what? *What we have?* What do we have? I understand that you didn't tell me at first because you thought I was a gold-digger. But you said you knew better." My voice breaks, tears streaming down my face. "You said you loved me. But how can you love me and not tell me who you really are? Doesn't it make it all a lie?"

He reaches for me, but I back away. "I wanted to, Caroline. I did. But it's more complicated than it seems. It's not my secret to tell."

I take a deep breath. "Is it Lexi's? Because funny, she told me this afternoon that it was up to you to tell."

His eyes are wild. "When Lexi gets home, we'll both tell you everything. I promise. Please, just wait."

I release a bitter laugh. "Then you'll be waiting a long time. Lexi won't be home until late."

His face changes. "What are you talking about? Where is she?"

"She's on a date."

His face contorts into rage. "On a date? Who the hell is she on a date with?"

"Brandon McKenzie, not that it's any of your business."

"Do you have any idea what you've done?"

"She's eighteen years old, Reed. She should be dating."

Reed goes to his computer and enters an Internet address. After he enters more information, he releases a heavy breath. "Thank God, she has her cell phone on. It looks like they're at Belvedere's, the club we...."

I let his reference go, latching onto a bigger issue. "Did you really just track her cell phone?"

He grabs his coat. "Yes. Now I have to go get her."

"You are *not* going to go get her!"

His face reddens with fury. "If anything happens to her, I'm holding you personally responsible."

I shake my head in disbelief. "She's on a date!"

He points his finger at me. "This isn't any of your business, Caroline! I told you to stay out of Lexi's life!"

"I suppose I'm not good enough to be friends with your sister?"

"*God damn it, Caroline, that's not what I said!*" His voice vibrates the walls. "We'll finish this discussion when I get back with Lexi." He's out the door and slamming it closed before I can answer.

With Reed gone, my anger remains, but it lowers to a simmer. How can I think I've found everything I'm looking for only to find it's all a lie?

My phone rings and I consider not answering it. I don't want to argue with Reed right now. But when I look at the number, I see it's not Reed.

"Hello?" I answer, scared of what's on the other line.

"Carol Ann," my father's voice whispers in my ear. "It's your mother."

# Chapter Twenty-Five

No, *please don't let it be too late.*

"She's in the hospital. In the ICU. The doctors say she doesn't have much longer. Maybe a day. Maybe less."

I try to catch my breath.

"She's asking for ya, girly."

I start crying when my father uses my nickname.

"Will you come see her?"

"Yes," I sniff and try to get myself together. "I'll be there in a few hours."

"Carol Ann." My father's voice breaks. "I love you."

"I love you too." I hang up, crying.

How am I going to get there?

My car's in the parking lot, but Reed still has my keys, I move into the kitchen, pulling out drawers and doors. When I don't find them, I go back to his room, remembering sleeping with him the night before.

Before I found out it was all a lie.

I don't have time to think about Reed. I can only handle one life crisis at a time.

I pull open his dresser drawers, cringing at the invasion of privacy, even more so since I know he was hiding so much from me. The keys are in his sock drawer. I grab them and my jacket and bag, racing down the stairs instead of waiting for the elevator.

My car isn't parked where I left it, and sure enough, when I stop at the edge of the parking lot, I can tell the brakes are new. Part of me is furious he replaced them after I told him not to. The other part of me is grateful it's one less thing I have to worry about.

I grab my phone out of my purse and call Scarlett.

"Ready for your big day tomorrow?" she asks, her voice bright with excitement.

"Scarlett, I'm not going to the fashion show."

"What are you talking about? You've worked your ass off for over a month. Why wouldn't you go?"

"My dad called. Mom's in the hospital. They don't think she'll make it another day."

"Oh, Caroline, I'm so sorry."

I take several hiccupped breaths, trying to hold back my tears. "I'm on my way now."

"Is Reed with you?"

"No. We had a fight."

"I thought you two made up."

"We did." I hiccup again. "But it was all a lie."

"What are you talking about? What was a lie?" I hear the alarm in her voice.

"His name isn't Reed Pendergraft. He's not who he says he is."

"Who the hell is he?"

As weird as it seems, Reed wants to keep his and Lexi's identity a secret, and I won't be the one to betray them. "He's just not...." I swallow the lump in my throat as new tears stream down my face. "I think it's over." I cry for several seconds.

"Oh, Caroline, I'm so sorry."

"I can't worry about Reed right now. I have to get to my mom."

"Let me go with you."

"I'm already headed out of town."

"I don't want you driving by yourself. At least take my car. Your brakes are bad."

"Not anymore. Reed fixed them."

"Why would he fix your brakes if everything between you two was a lie?"

"I don't know, Scarlett." My chest heaves with several sobs. "But I'm not over-exaggerating. His name isn't Reed Pendergraft. He's not who he said he was. He lied to me."

"Okay, Caroline, you're too upset to drive. Come back and let me take you."

"No." I take a deep breath, trying to get control. "I need you to help me."

"Anything."

"If I'm not there at the show, those ten kids won't get to be in the show. They're looking forward to it and I can't let them down. Can you—"

"Anything but that."

"Scarlett, listen to me. The hard work is already done. Just make sure they get the right outfits. Their names are on them. There'll be some hair and makeup people there. Tell them I just want a natural look. Except for Brittany. Tell them to make her more dramatic."

"I can't do this, Caroline. I don't know anything about fashion shows. I'm going to screw it up."

"No you won't. You'll be fine. Besides, even if you screw something up, it's better than not doing it at all. I promised those kids. I can't let them down. I just can't."

"Okay. I'll do it."

"Thank you." My tears break loose again. "Listen, my phone is going to die sometime in the next hour or two. I haven't charged it all day, and I don't have my charger. So if you don't hear from me for a while, you know why."

"Be careful. You're driving those back roads at night. You know some of those curves—"

"I'll be careful. I love you, Scarlett."

"I love you too."

I hang up and cry soul-wrenching sobs for several minutes, but when I think I'm cried out, more tears find their way to the surface.

How could my world fall apart so entirely in one night?

Thirty minutes after I leave, my phone rings. Reed's name comes up on the caller ID, but I press ignore. I can't deal with him right now.

But Reed's a persistent guy, calling at least ten times over the course of an hour. I'm almost grateful when my phone finally dies, at least I would be, if I weren't traveling over one hundred miles on two-lane highways in the backwoods of Tennessee in the middle of the night.

I arrive at the hospital well after midnight. The main entrance is closed, so I go through the emergency entrance and ask directions to the ICU.

My stomach is a mess—a combination of butterflies at seeing my parents after so long and nausea over the reason I'm here.

When I approach the waiting room, I spot my father sitting hunched over in a chair. His hands are clasped, and his foot taps at a rapid staccato.

He's nervous.

"Dad?"

He looks up, and I restrain a gasp. I've been gone only three years, but he looks at least ten years older. His once brown hair has turned mostly gray, and his face is covered in wrinkles. Dad was never a strong man, but now he looks completely broken.

I thought I was cried out, but seeing him so distraught starts another round.

"Carol Ann." He reaches for me, pulling me into a hug and burying his face into my shoulder. "You came." He sobs chest-heaving cries that drench my shirt.

We stand holding each other for several minutes. I remember Dad holding me when I was devastated after my brother cut my doll's hair off. Dad cradled me on his lap in his recliner, his arms holding me in a loving embrace. My mother told him I was nine years old, too old to be sitting in my daddy's lap. Daddy usually caved to my mother's demands, but that one day he held me firm. "My girly's never too big for her daddy to hug her."

Dad takes a step back and wipes the back of his sleeve across his face. "Thanks for coming."

"Yeah." I feel like a bitch that my dad has to thank me for coming to my mother's deathbed. But then, we've never been normal. "Is Stevie here?"

Dad clears his throat. "Uh, no. He couldn't get back from L.A. He said something about not being able to get out of some recording studio time."

I nod. We both know it's a lie.

"The nurse said when you got here to have you go to the desk. If they're not doing a procedure, they're going to let you go back."

"Okay." Icy dread washes through me. I know I'm here to see her, but I'm not sure what to expect, both from her and what's going on around her.

I shuffle to the desk. "Hi, I'm Caroline Hunter. My mother, Kathy Hunter, is here."

The nurse's aide smiles up at me. "We've been expecting you. Let me get her nurse to take you back."

I look over my shoulder. "Are you coming, Dad?"

He sniffs. "No, she wants to talk to you alone."

I'm swamped with lightheadedness, and I realize I've hardly eaten in the last twelve to eighteen hours. But I'm also freaking out about what my mother has to say to me, that she wants to say to me alone.

The double doors open, and a woman pokes her head through the opening. "Ms. Hunter? You can come on back."

I cast a glance back to Dad before I go through the double doors.

The nurse is a head shorter than me, and she talks softly so I have to lean toward her to hear her.

"Now, your mother is hooked up to a lot of machines, so it might be overwhelming, and a little intense for you if you're afraid of hospitals."

I nod. I am.

"She has IVs and monitors. And she's wearing an oxygen mask. Your mother is having a difficult time breathing, which makes it hard for her to talk." The nurse stops and turns to me. "She's quite adamant that she speaks to you. She's been agitated for hours. So she might get overly excited trying to talk, so just help her calm down and have her take her time."

"Okay."

I'm scared. I've never been more scared in my life, and I'm second-guessing my decision to not have Scarlett come with me. I miss Reed and can't help thinking how supportive my Reed would be, the Reed I know. But Reed isn't here, and I realize I need to do this on my own.

It's time to face the demons of my past.

The nurse opens the glass door to my mother's room and looks up at me. "Your mother is quite proud of you, you know."

My eyes widen.

"She's talked about you to everyone who will listen. Her beautiful daughter who could be a model herself, but instead designs clothes for them. She says you're the first on either side of the family to get a college education. She thinks the world of you."

I blink at the tears flooding my eyes, the blood rushing from my head in shock. Why could she never tell me these things herself?

I swallow the bitterness lodged in my throat as I walk in. A hospital bed sits in the center of the room, surrounded by machines and multiple lines leading to the huddle in the middle of the bed.

My mother.

If Dad looked older and broken, my mother looks ancient and shattered. While she wasn't obese when I was a kid, she always packed more weight than was healthy on her frame. But now she's thin, her skin sinking into her cheeks and the bones of her arms.

When did my parents get so old?

Her eyes are closed, but her chest rises and falls in an exaggerated movement. The mask on her face releases a hiss from the steady stream of oxygen.

I take two steps toward her, and her eyes flutter open. She blinks and tries to focus.

"Carol Ann?"

I realize I'm holding my breath, and I let it out in a whoosh. "Hey, Mom."

"You came." Tears fill her eyes, and her chin trembles.

A lump clogs my throat. In the twenty-one years I've been on this earth, I've never seen my mother cry. Not even when her own mother died ten years ago. "I came."

Her shaky hand lifts off the bed and extends toward me, and I take another step toward her. She grabs my wrist, and more tears stream down her face.

I'm frozen with fear, not of the apparatus around her now, but the fact I have no idea what to say.

Her hand still circles my wrist, so I move closer until my legs are touching the side of the bed. I place my other hand over hers.

"Carol Ann...." She breaks into a coughing spell and it takes her several minutes to recover.

I pull up a chair and sit next to her. "I'm not going anywhere."

I hold her hand, careful of her IV, and try to remember the last physical contact I had with her. I come up with nothing.

When she stops coughing, she pulls her mask off her face. "I have a lot I want to tell you but not much time."

"Mom, don't say that."

Her face screws up in disgust. This is the first time since I walked in the room that I recognize the woman who raised me. "I haven't sugarcoated nothin' in my life, and I'm not about to start now. It don't take a genius to realize I'm dying, and I ain't got much time."

I try to hide my smile.

She replaces the mask and takes several deep breaths before she takes it off again. "That's what I want to see. Your smile. Not your pity."

I look up, embarrassed. "I didn't—"

"I'm dying, Carol Ann. It's a fact none of us can change. Ignoring the Grim Reaper in the corner won't make him go away."

I bite my lower lip to stop it from trembling. "I'm sorry."

She looks up at the ceiling and exhales, producing a wet cough that makes me nauseated. "No need to be sorry. I've lived a good life. My time is done."

Does she really think she's lived a good life?

As though reading my mind, she turns her head to face me, breathing in deep from the oxygen mask before removing it. "I know what you're thinking. Just because my life doesn't meet your standards, don't mean it wasn't good for me."

I close my eyes. "Mom, I never meant leaving for college to be a criticism of you or your life."

"Bullshit," she barks out and starts coughing. She replaces the mask for a minute before she removes it. "You judged our life. And by many people's standards, we didn't have it good. But it was good enough for me." Her eyes narrow. "Don't you judge me for that."

I shake my head as tears flow down my face. "I'm sorry."

"Nah," she chuckles and I wonder if her mood swings are from narcotics. "I was hard on you, girl. You were soft. You cried a lot. You cared what other people thought of you, and it made you miserable." She replaces her mask and takes several breaths. "I wanted you to accept who you were and not worry about what others thought of you." She shakes her head. "I just did a piss poor job of it."

My mouth hangs open. "Mom, I had no idea."

Her eyes squint. "I told you I did a piss poor job of it."

I laugh despite my tears.

"You're a beautiful girl, Carol Ann. Maybe too pretty for your own good. Too pretty for the likes of your father and me. We could never give you what you wanted so I didn't even try." She shrugs. "I suppose I should have made more of an effort."

I watch her, in shock. I never thought she gave my feelings or what I wanted any thought. Sure, she made little effort, but it's nice to hear her acknowledged it.

"You were always such a stubborn thing." Tears fill her eyes. "I remember back when you were three or four, I said you couldn't go out and play with that Scarlett girl from down the lane until you'd taken your plate to the sink. You sat at the table for three hours until Scarlett came inside, begging you to do it so you could play. And then I suspect Scarlett did it for you." She laughs, then begins to cough. When she stops coughing, tears stream down her face, she looks me in the eye. "It took me nearly eighteen years to accept that you wanted a different life than your father and me. It took me that long to accept that that was okay. I know I wasn't the best mother to you and your brother, and somewhere deep down, I knew that being a mother meant sacrificing for your kids, even if I hadn't done much sacrificing.

"Some people think I shoulda never told you to choose—your father and me or college. But you were dead set on going. I always worried you'd get there and think it was too hard, and you'd come back home—to a life you hated. I had to know how bad you wanted it. I think you needed me to help *you* find out how bad you wanted it." She looks into my eyes with an intensity I've never seen. "You see, I never hated my life. I didn't love it either. It just was. But you were set on more. And I'd done a piss poor job of helping you get it."

Her chin trembles, and she grabs my hand. "I've only done a handful of things I'm proud of. One of them is giving birth to you. The other is the day I set you free. When I made you choose, I took your security blanket away. Even if it meant I'd probably lose you forever. When you went to college, it was sink or swim, and I knew you were too goddamned stubborn to sink."

I start crying, my shoulders shaking with my sobs. "I didn't know." I can't see her through my tears. "I'm sorry, Mom. I didn't know."

She pats my hand. "You weren't *supposed* to know. Not this soon." Her words come in rasps, and after she replaces the mask, it takes her longer than before. "When I found out I was dying, I had to tell you. I didn't want you to think I didn't love you." She lifts my chin and stares into my eyes. "I'm proud of you."

I struggle to catch my breath.

"You're a beautiful, strong woman, and you deserve the life you want, Caroline." She pauses, giving me a moment to digest that she's called me by my full first name and not the nickname she knows I hate. "Fight for the life you want."

I nod.

She pats my face. "That's my good girl." She closes her eyes, and I'm scared she's passed away, but her monitors are still beeping and flashing.

After several minutes, the nurse comes in behind me and rests her hand on my shoulder. "She's sleeping. It looks like she's said what she was desperate to tell you and wore herself out. If you want to stay with her for a little bit, you're welcome to."

"Thank you," I say, not bothering to hide my tears.

"Now that she's made her peace, it probably won't be long now."

I nod.

I watch my mother sleep, still stunned by her revelation. How could I know that my greatest heartache was her greatest gift? She's right. Back in my sophomore year, I'd struggled with a couple of classes and had moments when I considered dropping out, but the fact I had nowhere to go ensured I stayed. Would I have stayed if I thought I could come home? I'd like to think I would, but now I'm not so sure.

I'm exhausted, but I'm not ready to leave her yet. I lay my cheek on the mattress and close my eyes.

Someone pats my shoulder, and I blink, disoriented.

The nurse smiles at me. "You fell asleep. I hate to disturb you, but we have to do a procedure. We'll let you come back in about an hour."

I stand and leave the room, emotionally and physically drained. I just need to rest my head somewhere and pull myself together. When I open the doors to the waiting room, I'm not prepared for the person I find on the other side.

Reed.

# Chapter Twenty-Six

My heart leaps into my throat.

Reed sits next to my father, and when he sees me, he stands, stuffing his hands in his pockets as he waits for me to make the first move.

I run my hand through my tangled hair. "What … how did you know where I was?"

"Scarlett." He steps forward, and I see his bruised and swollen left eye.

"What happened to your face?"

He gives me a wry smirk. "Tucker."

I smile, despite myself.

"I need to talk to you, Caroline. I need to explain."

I want to tell him that I don't want an explanation, but my mother's secret has taught me that things aren't always what they seem. I need to hear him out. I owe him that. And if I don't like what I hear, I can tell him goodbye. "Okay."

He releases a breath. "Thank you."

"My mother's having a procedure, and they say it will take an hour. That's all you get."

He nods.

"Dad, I'll be back."

"I like this guy," my dad says, pointing his thumb at Reed. "Give him a chance."

I shake my head as I start to walk down the hall, not waiting for Reed. I keep going until I spot a coffee vending machine. Reed steps in front of me and gets two cups.

When he hands me mine, I refuse to look into his face, and continue down the hall, looking for somewhere private to talk. We come to the cafeteria, and I find a table in the dimly lit room. It's three in the morning and the food line is closed. We'll be alone.

I sit in a chair and take a sip of what has to be the world's worst coffee while I wait for him to start talking.

"How are you doing?" he asks.

I snort. "I'm doing great, Reed. Best night of my life."

He inhales and scrubs his face with his hands, but pulls them away when he rubs his eye.

"Did Tucker really punch you?"

He nods, looking down at his cup. "He knew that I'd upset you."

"How in the world did you even see him to get punched?"

"I needed to find you, and you wouldn't answer your cell phone. So I called Scarlett and begged her to tell me where you were. I said if she wouldn't tell me on the phone, that I'd come over. Tucker got on the phone and told me if I came over he'd punch me."

"And you went anyway?" I ask, incredulous.

"I needed to find you, Caroline." He rubs his forehead then looks at me. "I'd ask you why you didn't ask me to come with you, but I know why. What I want to know is, if we hadn't had our argument tonight, would you have told me? Would you have asked me to come?"

"Yes."

He nods, and turns his cup in his hand. "I fucked up, Caroline."

I don't say anything.

He leans his forearms on the table. Taking a deep breath, his eyes fill with pain. "I told you that this isn't my story to tell, but Lexi gave me permission." Reed swallows. "Last year, Lexi was a freshman at a small private college out east. Very private. Very expensive. But it turns out that expensive tuition doesn't mean that it's safe."

He takes a sip of his coffee, then puts the cup down. His face contorts with disgust. "A guy at her school became infatuated with her."

My chest tightens with dread.

"It started off with little things. Notes, small gifts, secret-admirer kind of things always left anonymously outside her dorm room door or on her usual seat in classes. It was obvious the bastard knew her schedule." His voice breaks. "Lexi never told us. She said she didn't want to overreact. But then things started showing up in her dorm room. Campus security changed the locks and assured Lexi she was safe."

He swallows and blinks back his tears. "Her roommate was out one night, and the guy showed up." Reed looks into my eyes. "He raped her, Caroline. My baby sister was raped."

"Oh, God, Reed, I'm so sorry." No wonder he's so overprotective of her. I feel like an ass.

"The worst part is he got away with it. His family is prestigious and has deep pockets. It was his word against Lexi's."

I reach across the table and loop my fingers over his. He takes a deep breath and clings to my hand.

"Needless to say, Lexi was a mess. It was the middle of the spring semester so my parents forced her to go home. The fact the guy was still there, and the fact she's the daughter of John Monroe, made going back to school a security issue. They were also worried about a scandal, that it would somehow come back that Lexi had brought it on herself." His mouth presses into a line and anger hardens his face. "My parents wanted her to give up college for a year or two and wait for everything to die down, but that devastated her even more. Her entire life had been derailed because of one psycho. I couldn't let that happen."

I'm not surprised he refused to stand back and let his sister suffer.

"I convinced my parents to let Lexi go back to school if I went with her. She could live with me in an apartment off campus. They refused until we agreed to change our last names. They didn't want the press to find out where we were. Pendergraft is my maternal grandmother's maiden name. And Southern is a respected university, but it's hidden in the middle of Tennessee. I thought we could get lost here."

"But by the end of last spring, you surely had been accepted into a postgrad program. Where were you going to go?"

"Stanford."

"Where Dr. Knuth's at. You gave up your dream for your sister?"

He looks incredulous. "Lexi is far more important than a degree from Stanford."

I sit back in my seat and close my eyes. "I'm an idiot."

He leans across the table, and lifts my hand to his mouth. "No, Caroline. No. You had every right to be upset. I'm sorry I didn't trust you sooner."

I look at my hand cradled in his. This is still Reed. My Reed. His last name shouldn't matter. If I let his family affect how I feel about him, how is that any different than if my background influenced Reed? He didn't keep his identity from me because he was ashamed of where he came from. He did it to protect his sister. But if he went to those lengths to protect her, what else would he do?

"You knew about Brandon's criminal record and his father."

He stiffens slightly but looks unapologetic. "I saw him talking to Lexi after you left that night at the bar. I had him investigated."

"That's how you knew about the rapes on campus. You checked into it before you came here."

"And when I found out you were walking across campus in the middle of the night, I flipped out."

I grin. "I noticed."

His grip on my hand tightens. "God, Caroline. It was hard enough watching Lexi go through that. I can't stomach the idea of it happening to you."

"Even back then? We'd only reached our agreement that day."

"I was attached to you already. Besides, I told you, I knew you were *the one*. The more I'm with you, the more I know I was right."

"And what about the woman you went out with in those photos?"

"Amelia and I broke up last year. There's nothing there. What we had was more about convenience. I never felt a fraction of what I feel with you with her."

One part doesn't make sense. "What about the fashion show? If you two were trying to stay hidden, why would you do something so public?"

"Lexi." He grimaces. "The night at Scarlett's party, she saw us together and quizzed me about you. You'd mentioned the fashion show, and I told her about it." He closes his eyes and shakes his head. "She sensed the chemistry between us and called the chancellor and told him she was a representative of the Monroe Foundation and wanted the foundation to partner with the apparel department for the fashion show. She was trying to get closer to you so she could convince you what a great guy I was. When our parents found out, they were livid, but they couldn't back out and disgrace the foundation. So they agreed, as long as I was the committee chair so I could keep an eye on Lexi."

"So you were cranky because you didn't want to be there."

"That and I was frustrated after our near-kiss in the club."

"And you were at the club because of Lexi?"

"She likes to have fun. I endured it for her. The only reason I went to Scarlett's party was because Lexi had been cooped up with no social life. That was her first outing since her attack, so I wanted to be with her and make sure she handled it okay. I figured Scarlett's party would be a good first step. And then I met you." His mouth twists into an ironic smile. "So the next week, she said she wanted to meet some friends at a club. I told her she could go, but I went kind of as her bodyguard and sat at a table close by, there if she needed me. I know it sounds paranoid—"

I shake my head. "No, Reed. It sounds totally understandable. And very sweet. She's lucky to have you."

"I hated going at the time, but now I'm grateful. I'm not sure we'd be together if I hadn't almost kissed you that night."

"And what about us?" I ask. "What now?"

His fingers stroke the back of my hand. "That's your call, Caroline. I'm yours, no matter what my last name is. But I'm going to be a college professor, and I'd like to live on my own salary when I get out of school. I'd prefer not to use my parents' money and deal with the strings that come along with it." He looks into my eyes. "Can you live with that?"

"Reed, when I thought you were going to be a college professor with hundreds of thousands of dollars in student loans, I told you I wanted to be with you. Why would that change?"

"Because now you know about the money."

"It was never about the money. It was about the security. I don't want my future children to go to bed hungry or have to endure the ridicule I faced."

"I think you know me well enough to know I'd never let that happen. You told me so earlier tonight. I'd work three jobs if I had to, to provide for my family."

"I know."

He laces his fingers with mine and looks into my eyes. "I've told you everything, Caroline. I love you, and I don't want to live without you. Tell me what I need to do to make this right."

I shake my head. "Nothing."

Panic floods his face. "Caroline, please."

"Reed, there's nothing to be done because I forgive you. I understand why you did what you did. I just wish you had trusted me sooner."

Relief washes over his face. "I had to make sure Lexi was okay with me telling you. That's why I wanted to wait for her. I wanted her to tell you herself. I'm sorry." He pauses. "So are we good?"

"No more secrets?"

"None."

"Then we're good."

He stands and walks around the table, lifting me from my seat. His mouth lowers to mine and I expect his kiss to have some urgency. Instead, it tastes of contentment and peace.

And it's exactly what I need.

"You look exhausted, Caroline. Let's go back to the waiting room and you can stretch out on the loveseat there."

I laugh. "I believe *stretch out* and *loveseat* are an oxymoron."

"You need to try to get some rest, Caroline." I understand his bossiness now. It's his need to protect me. He couldn't protect Lexi, so he's even more determined to do everything he can to protect the people he loves.

On the way back to the waiting room, I tell him about my talk with my mother. He stops and looks into my eyes. "That had to be healing. To find out not only did she love you, but she did everything in her power to make sure you succeeded."

I smile softly. "Yeah."

When we get back to the waiting room, my father is dozing in his chair. Reed sits on the loveseat and pulls me down next to him. He drapes my legs over his and he wraps his arm around my back, resting my head on his chest. It doesn't take me long to doze off, because I know I'm exactly where I belong.

# Chapter
# Twenty-Seven

My mother dies late in the afternoon. My father grips her hand while Reed and I stand on the other side of the bed. Reed holds me close as I cry into his chest, and I can tell that it kills him that I'm upset, and there's nothing he can do to make me better.

The hospital asks about arrangements for my mother's body, but Dad looks lost. Reed shoots me a glance, seeking permission to intervene and when I nod, he takes control, making arrangements and phone calls. This is something he can take control of.

After all the arrangements that can be taken care of on a Saturday are made, Reed offers to take Dad home.

My father scowls. "I drove here on my own, and I damn well can drive home on my own."

Our parting is awkward. Despite our hug when I first showed up, my father has never been demonstrative. He pats me on the arm.

"We'll be by the house tomorrow afternoon," I say.

He nods, then turns and walks away.

As we watch him go, Reed wraps me in an embrace. "What do you want to do? Do you want to stay here in a hotel tonight or go home and come back tomorrow to make the funeral arrangements?"

I rest my head on his arm. "I want to go home."

When we get back to campus, it's too late to go to the fashion show, and I'm too exhausted to face it anyway. I can only hope that Scarlett and Lexi—who volunteered to help her—got everything organized. As long as the kids were happy, that's all that matters. It's not even about the grade anymore.

When we're almost to Reed's apartment, Scarlett calls.

"Caroline, it went wonderfully! The kids were great and they loved their clothes. The entire show was a huge success."

I sigh with relief. "Thanks for helping."

"You sound exhausted. How are you?"

"Tired. Sad. But Reed is with me and has been a huge help."

"I'm glad you didn't kill me for telling him where you were. But any guy who willingly let Tucker punch him just so he could find you deserved to know."

"I'll call you tomorrow."

Reed's cell phone rings, and he glances at me with a grin. "Lexi."

Reed puts her on speakerphone, and she gives him a similar report, as well as a report on the show overall, only with much more detail and excitement.

"We've come back for the night, so we'll see you at home," he says before he hangs up.

When we get to Reed's apartment, I take a shower then climb into bed with him, grateful I haven't lost him. Grateful this hotheaded, overprotective, loyal, and incredibly sexy, self-proclaimed math nerd is mine.

I kiss him gently on the lips. "Thank you for believing in me."

"Thank you for not giving up on me."

I'm about to fall asleep when my phone rings, and I roll away to reach for it.

Reed pulls me back down. "Let it go, Caroline."

"What if it's my dad?"

He releases his hold, and I sit up, checking the caller ID, surprised to see it's my advisor.

"Hi, Ms. Carter. Thanks again for understanding about the show."

"Caroline, I'm so sorry about your mother. Of course, your place was with her."

"Thank you."

"I know this isn't an ideal time, but my friend from New York was very impressed with your collection. I wanted to give you a heads-up that she's going to call you sometime next week to offer you the job."

The job in New York. It was my initial goal, but it was never my dream. I'd only decided to go after it for lack of a better purpose. But designing the clothes for these children, and making them happy, has given me more joy than I imagined. It's helped me find my real purpose.

"I'm very honored and flattered. Please tell her thank you, but I'm not interested in moving to New York."

Reed sits upright.

"Are you sure you want to make such a big decision without thinking about it?" Ms. Carter asks. "Your mother just died and you're under stress. I know that Mimi will wait a week or so for your answer."

"I don't need another week to decide. I've been offered another job, and honestly, it's a much better fit."

I hang up. Reed watches me with a wary expression. "Caroline, don't turn that job down for me. We'll make it work. I promise."

I shake my head. "I don't want the job in New York, Reed. I never really did. I've decided to take the job as a liaison between the Middle Tennessee Children's Charity and the Monroe Foundation, even if it feels skeevy taking a job you set up. The good I can do outweighs the guilt."

His eyes narrow. "What job as a liaison?"

"The day Evelyn talked to me alone, she told me that the Monroe Foundation was impressed with my work and wanted to create a position to provide new clothing to the children." I lower my gaze. "Are you telling me you didn't set it up?"

He looks perplexed. "I didn't have anything to do with that."

"You're kidding?"

"No, I swear. And I didn't tell anyone that we were dating either."

"Maybe Lexi?" I ask.

"I don't think so. They weren't very happy with her so they sure wouldn't have listened to her suggestion." He pulls me back down into his arms. "I think you got this one all on your own. Evelyn must have gushed about you. I know she sang your praises to me."

"Will that be too weird if I work for the foundation? I know you don't want your parents' money."

"Caroline, there's a difference between a handout and a paycheck. You'll be perfect for it."

"Thanks."

I settle into him, and he's soon asleep, the rise and fall of his chest soothing my raw nerves. When I met Reed, I had no idea my life would change in every conceivable way. Reed instigated a redesign of every expectation I ever had.

And I wouldn't have it any other way.

# Epilogue

I wake to Reed's kisses. They cover my face then move down to my neck as I drift from the haze of sleep to consciousness. I pull his mouth to mine and kiss him leisurely, sighing my contentment into his mouth.

His hands are under the covers, finding the hem of the T-shirt I'm wearing and lifting it up and over my head. Now I'm completely naked since Reed dispatched with my panties last night before we even made it into bed. The only reason I'm wearing a shirt now was because he gave me his as I drifted off to sleep.

He has no clothes to remove. He likes to sleep naked next to me, not that I ever complain.

We've been together a little over two months and it's as though we've always been together, yet every day is new and full of possibilities.

His mouth resumes its descent, his head disappearing under the covers and finding my breast. I arch up to him, the familiar heat spreading throughout my body, and I tangle my hands in his hair. His hands skim my body, down my waist to my thighs, before one hand finds the aching spot between my legs. He soon has me breathless and needing more.

I'll never have my fill of this man.

We make love without words this morning. We've become so attuned to one another that we read our signs—the little sighs and grunts that signal what we want and need.

Reed knows I'm more than ready, but tortures me a little longer. He chuckles as his mouth finds mine again, his tongue joining with mine. And finally, he gives me what I want—every part of him, body and soul.

Afterward, we lie together in each other's arms. We still haven't spoken a word. Sometimes we make love like this, slow and gentle as though we have all the time in the world. Other times it's hot and passionate and full of dirty talk. Like last night.

Reed kisses my temple and whispers, "Merry Christmas."

I look into his loving eyes. "Merry Christmas. Thank you for the best Christmas ever."

"And I haven't even given you your present yet," he teases.

"You're all I ever wanted, Reed. You're my present."

He pushes up on an elbow and gives me an ornery look. "Well, if you don't want what I got you...."

I bolt upright. "Oh, no you don't."

He sits up and pulls me into his arms as I giggle. "Why don't you put something on and I'll give you an early present?"

I lift an eyebrow. "Usually those kinds of presents involve the removal of clothing."

"This isn't one of those kinds of presents, although I'm *very* fond of those kind."

I grab Reed's T-shirt and slip it on, then pull a pair of panties out of the drawer.

Reed steps into a pair of sweatpants and a T-shirt. His eyes linger on my bare legs.

"Focus," I say, pointing two fingers at my eyes.

"Your legs are very distracting."

"I can put on some pants if you like."

He grabs my wrist and drags me out the bedroom door. "I'm focusing."

The living room has been transported into a Christmas Wonderland. Reed's intention was to give me the Christmas I always wanted but never had. The result looks like someone threw up every kind of Christmas decoration imaginable.

I love it.

He leads me next to the tree, a seven-foot, Douglas fir with a start on top that nearly touches the ceiling. The branches are full of so many clear Christmas lights that I'm sure it can be seen from space.

Reed sits in front of the tree, pulling me down next to him.

"Are you sorry you're not with your parents?" I ask.

He frowns. "No. I want to be home for Christmas, that's with you and Lexi. Not in a ski lodge in Aspen. Plus, Scarlett and Tucker are coming over later."

"And don't forget, Brandon is coming for New Year's."

Reed scowls. "I don't know why he can't stay in Nashville for all of winter break."

"Because he and Lexi are crazy about each other. And you agreed to try to be nice."

"Hmm." He still worries over Lexi, and I think he always will. Even when she's the grandmother of half a dozen kids. It makes me love him even more.

I lift my fingertips to his face, smoothing his worry lines. "I want to give you your present first."

A smile fills his eyes. "Okay."

I pull a rectangular box out from under the tree and hand it to him, suddenly anxious. What if he doesn't like it?

He takes it and grins, carefully slips off the bow, then rips the paper. When he opens the box, he stares at the book inside, expressionless.

Oh, God. He hates it. "I know how much you admire Donald Knuth…." He's still not reacting and now I'm talking non-stop in my nervousness. "It's a first edition copy of *Surreal Numbers*. I wrote Dr. Knuth, practically begging him to sign it, but first I had to track down his address—"

Reed lifts the book out of the box.

"—I was pretty persistent, which I think explains his signature—"

Reed looks up, incredulous. "*He signed it?*"

I nod.

He reads out loud, his voice tight, "*Reed, With Caroline behind you, nothing will stand in your way, Donald Knuth.*"

"Do you like it?"

His mouth drops open, and he looks up at me. "Do you know who this is?"

"Well, yeah … I tracked him down…."

His eyes bug out and he leans forward. "Do you know what this is?"

"Does that mean you like it?"

"Oh, my God, Caroline! This is the best present I've ever gotten in my life. Ever." He wraps his arm around my back and pulls me to him, kissing me senseless. Then he drops his hold and examines his book.

"I'm glad you like it."

He shakes his head. "Not like. Love." His smile falls. "My present for you pales in comparison."

"Reed, I don't care. *You're* what I want." And I really mean it. It makes me happy that I came up with something he loves so much.

He puts his book back in the box and closes the lid, before reaching behind the tree and pulling out a ring box with a bow.

My heart slams into my ribcage.

Reed takes a deep breath. "Caroline." He smiles and caresses my cheek. "I love you, and I want to spend the rest of my life with you."

Tears fill my eyes as he opens the box and shows me a solitaire princess-cut diamond ring.

"Caroline, will you marry me?"

I start crying, big ugly tears flowing down my face.

"You're freaking me out. Is that a yes?"

I jerk my head into a nod.

Reed grabs my hand and slips the ring on my finger, as though he's worried I'll change my mind.

I hold my hand closer to my face. "It's beautiful, but it has to be at least three-quarter carats, Reed. We can't afford this."

"It was my grandmother's. And it's a little over one carat."

I throw my arms around his neck. "Thank you."

"I had this amazing speech prepared, and I forgot every bit of it after you gave me that book."

Lexi comes down the hall, rubbing her eyes. "What's all the commotion about?" She stops at the end of the hall and she jolts awake, her eyes focused on the ring. "Is that what I think it is?"

I wave my hand at her.

She runs to us and squats on the floor, squealing with excitement as she hugs us both. "When are you getting married?"

"I ... uh...." I look at Reed.

"I just asked her, Lexi. We haven't had a chance to figure that out yet."

"What about this summer? After Caroline graduates?"

Reed grins at me, his eyebrows rising. "Well ... what do you think?"

I'm so full of happiness I can hardly think straight. "Yeah."

Lexi squeals again. "I want to help plan it! Are you going to make your dress? What colors do you think you want? What's your favorite flower?"

I laugh and glance at Reed. "I think you're going to have your hands full for the next six months or so."

He leans over and gives me a kiss. "I wouldn't have it any other way."

# Acknowledgments

They say that writing is a lonely profession, but I seem to find myself surrounded by people. There's no way I could write and publish a book on my own.

Thank you to Trisha Leigh, my critique partner and biggest supporter. I couldn't do this without her support.

Thank you to my beta readers: Rhonda Cowsert, Anne Childon, and Becky Podjenski—your insight and support was invaluable.

Thank you to two readers who won a contest and named characters: Lysa Lessieur who named Lexi, and Claire Taylor who named Brandon. I love when I have readers name characters, dork that I am.

A huge, huge thanks to the real mathematician Dr. Donald Knuth, who not only gave me permission to use his name in conjunction with Caroline's gift to Reed, but also conversed with me via mail. I am not a math person (understatement of the year) but became a total Donald Knuth fangirl.

And as always, thank you to my children for loving and supporting me with this crazy life. I've never been happier.

# About the Author

Denise Grover Swank was born in Kansas City, Missouri, and lived in the area until she was nineteen. Then she became a nomadic gypsy, living in five cities, four states and ten houses over the course of ten years before she moved back to her roots. She speaks English and smattering of Spanish and Chinese which she learned through an intensive Nick Jr. immersion period. Her hobbies include witty Facebook comments (in own her mind) and dancing in her kitchen with her children. (Quite badly if you believe her offspring.) Hidden talents include the gift of justification and the ability to drink massive amounts of caffeine and still fall asleep within two minutes. Her lack of the sense of smell allows her to perform many unspeakable tasks. She has six children and hasn't lost her sanity. Or so she leads you to believe.

You can find out more about Denise and her other books at:

www.denisegroverswank.com
or email her at denisegroverswank@gmail.com

Made in the USA
San Bernardino, CA
11 June 2018